DEAD WATER CREEK

DEAD WATER CREEK

A Morgan O'Brien Mystery

Alex Brett

A Castle Street Mystery

THE DUNDURN GROUP
TORONTO · OXFORD

Copy-editor: Andrea Pruss
Design: Jennifer Scott
Printer: Webcom

Canadian Cataloguing in Publication Data

Brett, Alex
   Dead Water Creek / Alex Brett.

(Castle Street mysteries)
ISBN 1-55002-452-3

   I. Title. II. Series: Castle Street mystery.

PS8553.R3869D42 2003   C813'.6   C2003-902207-2   PR9199.4.B72D42 2003

1   2   3   4   5   06   05   04   03   02

The Canada Council | Le Conseil des Arts
FOR THE ARTS | du Canada
SINCE 1957 | DEPUIS 1957

ONTARIO ARTS COUNCIL
CONSEIL DES ARTS DE L'ONTARIO

We acknowledge the support of the **Canada Council for the Arts** and the
Ontario Arts Council for our publishing program. We also acknowledge the
financial support of the **Government of Canada** through the **Book Publishing
Industry Development Program** and **The Association for the Export of Canadian
Books**, and the **Government of Ontario** through the **Ontario Book Publishers
Tax Credit** program.

Care has been taken to trace the ownership of copyright material used in this book.
The author and the publisher welcome any information enabling them to rectify
any references or credit in subsequent editions.

J. Kirk Howard, President

Printed and bound in Canada.⊛
Printed on recycled paper.
www.dundurn.com

Dundurn Press
8 Market Street
Suite 200
Toronto, Ontario, Canada
M5E 1M6

Dundurn Press
73 Lime Walk
Headington, Oxford,
England
OX3 7AD

Dundurn Press
2250 Military Road
Tonawanda NY
U.S.A. 14150

DEAD WATER CREEK

In the summer of 1992, about 482,000 sockeye salmon seemed to disappear on their way to the spawning grounds in the Fraser River system ... sockeye yield high returns to commercial fishermen — some $250 million annually, half the total value of British Columbia's commercial salmon fishery.

Peter H. Pearse, *Managing Salmon on the Fraser: Report to the Minister of Fisheries and Oceans on the Fraser River Salmon Investigation*, November 1992

chapter one

Monday, October 21
Weaver Creek, British Columbia, Canada

Cindy parked in the clearing, shut off the engine, and waited. Around her, the forest was alive with sound, but all of it soft, subdued: the wind caressing Douglas fir, the murmur of water spilling across a rocky bed. Then a shriek cut the air — an omen — and she smiled. If eagles were circling, death was nearby.

She grabbed her field notes and slid from the van.

At the water's edge she did a quick visual survey, counting the number of sockeye females defending their redds. Then she stepped back and scanned the shore. Just as she'd hoped. Rotting corpses of spawned-out fish crowded the banks of the creek. She willed her shoulders to relax, flipped open her yellow Rite-in-the-Rain notebook, and wrote the date on the first empty page. She noted the percentage of cloud cover just below the *date and, notebook still in hand, began to walk slowly along the bank, counting redds, surveying numbers, and checking her downstream sites.*

When she saw her enclosures she smiled again. For once they were intact. Most mornings she arrived to find the posts upended and the wire mesh flattened against the stream bed, evidence of the scavenging bears that prowled the stream at night.

She continued down the creek to the gate, the barrier that controlled fish entry into the spawning channel. She edged her way out to the middle. From there she could see that the holding tanks below were full, salmon thrashing and squeezing their way through the narrow slit that gave them access to the spawning stream. There was an audible click every time one shot through, as the Fisheries counters kept track of this year's return.

Thank God the numbers were up. At least today she could work.

Back at the van she pulled on chest waders, made several more notations in her field book, then picked up her dip net and transect chain and headed for the stream. She was fully absorbed until half an hour later, when she heard a vehicle turn onto the spawning channel road. Annoyed, she stood up and watched the entrance. Cindy preferred to work alone or, if necessary, with her technician, Dinah, but to have to stop work and make small talk with some Fish and Wildlife officer, or worse, one of the locals, was a waste of precious time. And with the bizarre returns on the stream this year, she had already lost so much time that her research was in jeopardy.

She listened, thinking she would ignore whoever it was, and she heard pebbles spray as the truck suddenly reversed and accelerated back down the road. Poachers *who had seen her van? Could be. She'd have to ask Eddie. She shrugged and got back to measuring the size of gravel along her second transect.*

She didn't think of the vehicle again until after four o'clock. With hands and feet numb from the frigid water, she dragged herself out of the stream for a hot cup of tea. Sitting high above on the bank, her hands wrapped around the thermos cup, she looked across the stream and felt her stomach contract. There were distinctly fewer salmon churning the waters. She was sure of it.

She hurried back to the van and peeled off her waders, replacing them with sturdy hiking boots. The sun was just disappearing behind Sumas mountain, and in the next few minutes the fragile autumn warmth would vanish as the damp and cold of the water rose up to permeate the air.

Down at the gate the counters were silent, the holding tanks empty, and the pool beneath them deserted. There were no sockeye coming up Weaver Creek. In an odd sort of way it was a blessing: whatever was causing the periodic disappearance of the fish was occurring at this very minute, somewhere on the river. She debated the sense in following the stream down through dense forest so late in the day, just when the bears were beginning their evening rounds, but her research was at stake. The spawning season on this stream was nearly over, and it might be her only chance to discover what was causing the problem.

Then she remembered the truck, and that clinched her decision.

She left the road and descended into the forest.

Monday, October 21
National Council for Science and Technology,
Ottawa, Canada

It was an accident, the salmon investigation landing in my hands: unexpected fallout from a particularly explosive weekly meeting. Or should I say weekly *roundup*. That's what Bob — my boss and Chief of Investigations — calls the Monday morning staff meetings that he was forced to establish by management's latest business guru. Of course, according to Bob, he developed the idea on his own.

"To improve two-way communication," he told us at the first meeting. "Make sure you're in the loop. That your fingers are on the pulse. Empowerment. That's the key word."

That particular Monday, I had arrived at the roundup five minutes early so I could have my choice of seating. Our conference room is small, bland, and windowless, with a large Formica-covered table taking up virtually all the available space. I edged my way toward the head of the table: Bob's unchallenged domain. Once there, I neatly arranged my files in front of his usual spot, placed a precisely ordered list of my current projects conspicuously on top of the stack of files, and slid into Bob's chair. I sipped my coffee and smiled.

Through the door I could see my colleagues begin to wander out of their offices, stroll to the coffee machine, and congregate in small pre-meeting discussion groups. Nobody was in a hurry. Bob is always late.

Duncan was the first to drift in, and he gave me a sly smile as he noted my position in the room. Both Duncan and I have been labelled as resistant and uncooperative, with a big dose of bad attitude, in the face of our "renewal process." That's because we made the same error early on. During the staff input stage — the one-on-one consultations with management — we both provided candid and honest answers to the questions we were asked. Rather than tell management what they wanted to hear — that everything was fine and they were doing a great job and a little tinkering and some new jargon should basically do the trick — we told the truth. That fundamental change was needed, and change started at the top. Oops. We came out of those meetings pegged as employees with an unhealthy attitude who were afraid of change.

Since then, Bob had used the Monday meetings to load up his two most undesirable employees with impossible projects on ridiculous deadlines, believing that we'd soon become discouraged enough to seek employment elsewhere. He'd obviously missed the course on "Employee Evaluation: Harnessing the Hidden Power." I had no intention of quitting. I was ready to fight.

I gave Duncan my most charming smile and patted the chair to my left. "Why don't you sit here?" A common front could be useful as the meeting unravelled.

He took in the neatly arranged files, the detailed project list, and my charcoal grey pinstriped suit. "No thanks. I'd rather live through the meeting."

Wimp. Oh well. Not everyone was up to constant battle and confrontation. I could understand that. Then I looked more closely. His hands were empty: no files, no notebook, not even a pencil. Something was going down.

"Duncan ...?" But just then several of our junior colleagues arrived, and I didn't want to ask too much.

Bob finally made his entrance at 9:17 A.M. I bent over my files, watching the movie unfold from the corner of my eye. Like a sleepwalker, he blundered toward the head of the table. Then he saw me and stopped abruptly, creating a mini *tsunami* that swept over the rim of his coffee cup and came close to producing third-degree burns on Conrad, one of our young engineers. Conrad lunged forward just in time. That seemed to wake Bob up, and he looked down at his hand, then at the floor, then up at me, trying to take it all in.

Bob looks surprisingly like a Cabbage Patch doll, and is often referred to as Mr. CP, or simply CP, by the secretaries and clerks. The effect was exaggerated this morning. His cheeks were rosy, and his wispy, fair hair stood out in tufts around his head. The fact that he was standing stock-still with a befuddled expression on his face didn't help. One of his bulging files had become dislodged by the sudden stop and was sliding, in slow motion, to the floor. I looked up as if I'd just noticed his arrival and turned on my thousand-watt greeting smile.

"Hi, Bob. Have a good weekend?"

"I ..." he stammered. "I ..."

You could see the indecision do battle on his face. Should he ask me to move? It *was* the power position in the room, and he *was* the boss. On the other hand, the new management style was horizontal and non-hierarchical. Asking me to move might be interpreted as a lack of commitment to the new principles. His eyes darted around the room, looking for safe haven, and finally fixed on the empty chair at the other end of the table. I was hoping that one of my colleagues would have demonstrated their commitment to a non-hierarchical structure by taking the other end-chair, but everyone was afraid for their jobs. Conrad collected up the stray papers and handed the file folder, now damp with coffee, back to Bob. Bob glared at me, then edged his way to the chair at the other end of the table. Once settled, he struggled to recoup his authority.

"So," he said heartily, "everyone have a good weekend?"

There was a murmur of affirmation around the table.

"Good. Great," he said. "Well ... umm ..." he shuffled the papers in front of him. "I guess we can get on with it then. I went over a few files this weekend ..." (that meant that he culled the files that had been sitting on his desk for at least a month and were now facing critical deadlines) "... and there are some interesting biotechnology grant requests that require background checks." He glanced around the room. "Anyone up to that?"

"What's the deadline?" That was Douglas. Young. Keen. And with chronic ulcers at the age of twenty-four.

"The deadline?" He spoke as if it was the first time he'd ever heard the word. "Oh. Let's see ..." He flipped open the file, making a show of running his finger down the margin of the first page. "Ahh ... that would be Wednesday." Then he snapped the file shut. "It's a simple review really. Nothing complicated."

I tried, really I did, not to roll my eyes. No science investigation is simple. It doesn't matter if you're looking at financial irregularities or outright research fraud, you still have to search the literature, sometimes you need to do site visits, and you often have to review the material with experts in that field. Not surprisingly, no one leapt forward to take on a boring project with an impossible deadline. In the silence, Bob's face suddenly lit up, and his eyes rested on me.

"Morgan. Maybe you could handle this."

But I was ready. "No problem. I'll just add it to my current projects. However, as you can see," I held up my carefully prepared list, "Wednesday is not a possibility. Unless you'd like it as my first priority. Then I could get it done by Friday, that's if I can get a hold of reviewers. Of course, it will mean bumping the deadlines of all the other projects you assigned me last week." I smiled sweetly. "But whatever you'd like, Bob."

"Let me see that list."

I passed it to Conrad, who shot it down the table. Bob looked it over, his lips moving as he passed from one item to the next. Then he nodded.

"I don't see a problem here. We'll reassign your current projects to junior officers. They need the experience anyway." His smile was vanilla pudding. "And I have several other files of a similar nature, and with similar deadlines, that I'd like you to get started on right away."

I had the sensation of reeling backward, gasping for air, as if I'd been punched in the solar plexus. So this was it. This was how he was going to get rid of me. Pass me projects one week, get me to do the legwork on every single one, then pull them out from under me in the final stages, so that the report would be written by (and the investigation attributed to) either himself or one of his loyal lieutenants. Even though I hate the guy I had to admit it was a brilliant scheme. And effective. I was a senior investigator. My career would be ruined. I took a deep breath and forced myself to centre and focus. He was no different from an opponent in karate class, and I couldn't afford to show him that he had scored a hit. I kept my voice light and friendly. "Well, you're the boss, Bob. If that's how you want to handle investigations —"

"It is."

"Of course, it's very inefficient. And we're likely to really screw something up when the reports are being done by someone not involved in the investigation —"

"I think the level of competence among the rest of the staff," he paused, then swept his hand dramatically around the room, "is at least as high as your own. Or wouldn't you agree, Morgan?"

Duncan saved me from that one, bless him. "Is this change in procedure permanent?"

Bob hardly bothered looking at Duncan. "In Morgan's case? Probably. She's so efficient at the investigations stage, why waste that talent compiling the final report?" He shoved four bulging folders toward me. "Friday for preliminary results."

A wave of depression almost swept me out into the vast sea of despair that sits just beyond my consciousness. I'd been outmanoeuvred by an overgrown Cabbage Patch doll. Maybe it really was time to leave. Just as the undertow was about to drag me into open water I reached out, flipped open one of the files, and scanned the contents. It was a mess, with the most recent correspondence dated over two months ago. I flipped quickly through the other files. Same thing. It was nice to know that I could still depend on Bob for at least some things. By now, he had moved on to other pressing items, specifically, the merits of mocha java over Colombian for our staff coffee machine.

"Oh, Bob," I interrupted, raising my index finger. "Did you receive these files recently?"

Bob looked up, annoyed. He fixed me with a stern look, then dismissed me with a wave of his hand. "I can't remember the exact date. Not long ago."

Why didn't I believe him. He tried to get back to the agenda — clarification of the new rules governing sugar and milk privileges — but I didn't let him.

"Gosh," I said, loud enough to draw attention to myself. I had one of the files open in front of me, and as I slowly turned the pages, I punctuated each new page with a surprised murmur of disappointment. "Oh, my! Goodness, how did that happen? That's just not possible. And how will we deal with this?" All eyes were on me. When I was good and ready I shook my head sadly and looked up at Bob. "Somebody really screwed up in the director general's office. These files have been sitting on someone's desk for at least six weeks. That's why they have impossible deadlines." I looked meaningfully around the room. "Well, I don't think we should take this, do you?"

"No way."

"Not again"

"Bloody DG. We always take the blame."

I could see the sweat beading on Bob's upper lip. "Just get them done. ASAP!"

"Oh, I will." I paused for effect. "But I'll also send an e-mail to you, with a cc to the director general, confirming the date that I received the files. Just so that our group isn't blamed for any delays."

People around the table nodded in agreement. Bob's face had gone an unbecoming shade of red, and his lips were a tense and quivering line in what passed for his chin.

"We'll discuss it after the meeting. My office."

"Excellent," I said, and closed the files in front of me. I was going to skewer the bastard.

The meeting droned on. I tuned out, not really caring about the latest memo from the DG or a circular from Treasury Board. I did perk up when Bob finally turned to Duncan.

"So, Duncan, it doesn't look like you have a lot on your plate these days." Bob was almost snickering as he took in the empty table in front of Duncan.

Duncan is tall and thin with an Alan Alda sort of natty look: simple wool sweaters with matching wool or corduroy pants. Today it looked like he, too, was playing cat and mouse, with Mr. Cabbage Patch definitely cast as the rodent. However, like many rodents, Bob seemed blissfully unaware of his place in the food chain.

Duncan smiled. "Sort of looks that way, doesn't it."

"Why, that's wonderful, just dandy, because I have an urgent file here, international involvement, politically sensitive, high security clearance required, big money — and it involves a trip to scenic Vancouver. It's yours!" He could hardly contain his glee. "Everything's booked. You leave for Vancouver tonight."

If there had been an eighth dwarf named Nasty he would have looked just like Bob at that moment. Duncan is a single father with two kids under the age of six. Travel for him is a logistical and emotional nightmare, and damn near impossible on such short notice. But Duncan was unflappable.

"I don't think so, Bob." He paused, as if seriously considering the proposal, then shook his head. "Nope: definitely not in my stars this week."

Bob shot to his feet. "Are you refusing a project? You'll be disciplined. Possibly suspended. It'll go on your record."

"I'm not refusing a project, Bob. I'm refusing to work for you."

"What do you mean by that? You can't refuse to work for me."

Duncan rose unhurriedly from his chair. "I have another job, and I'm afraid you'll have to excuse me because I have a lot of loose ends to pull together by the end of the day."

Bob's first reaction was delight, but an instant later reality set in, that being that he would have to cover for Duncan on such short notice. "You can't just walk out of here. You need to give two weeks notice."

Duncan looked innocent. "But I start two weeks' vacation tomorrow. You approved it last month."

Bob is administratively challenged, and the idea that he might remember signing a vacation request a month ago was farcical. Bob glared at Duncan, who shrugged slightly and headed for the door. I, of course, couldn't hold myself back.

"Congratulations, Duncan. What's the new job?"

He stopped, turned, and made an obvious effort — unsuccessful — to keep a straight face. "Special Science Advisor to the Minister of Industry."

Everyone in the conference room gasped. Except me. It must have been the tension because, try as I might to stop it, a grin spread across my face. We all knew that Bob had applied for that job.

I didn't miss a beat. "I'll take the job in Vancouver," I said, plucking the file from where it lay in front of Duncan's recently vacated spot. This job was a plum: a successful outcome might even catapult me out from under Bob. I pushed the biotechnology files back into the centre of the table, gathered up my things, and stood.

"I'm sure your other highly competent staff members can handle these ... how did you describe them? Simple and straightforward investigations." I glanced down at the new file and read the label: *International Network for Pacific Salmon Population Dynamics.* I almost laughed out loud.

"Perfect," I said in Bob's direction.

chapter two

Back in my office I took a few minutes to gloat. I imagined myself returning triumphant from Vancouver to a new fifth-floor corner office with a teak desk and credenza. I was just about to sink into my imaginary leatherette chair when my mind, unbidden, flew back to Vancouver and began to make its way down 12th Avenue toward the dismal east end. I could feel my stomach twitch as we hovered past the elementary school, the derelict yard, the swings dangling askew.

The house was down a side street, white clapboard and looking abandoned. As my mind pulled me toward it, willing me to open the door, to step inside, I felt myself numb. I hadn't thought about my mother in months, and her intrusion into my life was unwelcome.

I jerked my chair forward and caught sight of the file sitting innocently on my desk. I grabbed for it, flipped it open, and focused all my attention on it, forcing the past to recede. Work, I have always found, is the most potent antidote to memory.

The first thing that caught my attention was the appearance of the file. It was way too trim and neat for a project with high security clearance, especially one involving Pacific salmon. Since these animals migrate across international borders, the Network had to involve research partners from Japan, Russia, and the United States. With that amount of bureaucracy the file should have been bloated with back-and-forth correspondence, directives, and memos, the foreplay of an investigation, but the only thing inside was a single, neatly bound sheaf of paper that was maybe a hundred pages long.

I picked it up and fanned through it. There were letters, some newspaper clippings, grant applications, curriculum vitae, and the printout of a very inadequate reference search, but no external correspondence with any other funding bodies, foreign governments, or research institutes. That meant that none of the other research partners had been notified of the investigation.

I flipped to the front of the file, hoping to find something to explain the lack of background material. Normally, the first page in any file is NCST Internal Form 16-52-C, which covers financial codes and any special instructions or concerns related to a project. But instead of the usual form, there was a post-it note with a scrawled message attached to the first page. It was from our director general, Ms. Patricia Middlemass. Bob had scratched out his name and jotted in "Duncan." The note from Patsy (she would behead me if that nickname ever slipped out in conversation) was surprisingly informal. Usually her missives arrive on official letterhead in triplicate and are written in a language that only a lawyer can understand. They are known around here as CYA (cover your ass) memos, and Patsy is gifted in her ability to produce them. Her instructions for this project, however, were terse.

> ~~Bob~~, Duncan
> Investigate financial impropriety <u>only</u>.
> Some documentation available here
> (see file) but onsite records needed.
> Extreme discretion. Security clearance
> required. Three days' travel, more by
> my approval only.
> P.

Typical Patsy, to restrict travel time. She was in a fury of cost-cutting these days — a vital part of renewal, we'd been told — and travel must be the newest front for deficit reduction. I shook my head, pulled off the post-it note, crumpled it, and aimed for the garbage can; then I stopped. I flattened it out and read it again.

Patsy's note really issued two distinct orders. The most obvious one was to investigate financial impropriety only, but by default, that implied a second directive: Keep your nose out of the science. Don't touch the research. Now why, I wondered, would our busy director general be involving herself in the details of an inquiry? And why would she be giving her orders on untraceable scraps of paper? I carefully folded up the crumpled post-it note and tucked it between two pages near the front of my day book. I made a mental note to return to it when I was more familiar with the file.

With the note removed I could now read the top document; the last thing we had received relating to this project. It was a letter dated August 28, almost two months ago, written by a Dr. Jonathan Edwards at the University of Southern British Columbia. And he wasn't happy.

Dear Sirs

I am sending this letter via registered mail to obtain proof that it has indeed been received by the Grants and Funding Branch of the National Council for Science and Technology (NCST). This is the third letter I have sent regarding an intolerable situation occurring in the International Network for Pacific Salmon Population Dynamics (INPSPD) project: I refer, of course, to the mismanagement and misuse of grant funding by the Canadian project leader, Dr. Madden Riesler.

I have provided you on two occasions with the background evidence required to launch an investigation and have heard nothing in reply. For this reason I have decided to take the only route open to me. If I do not receive a reply from you forthwith, indicating that an investigation is in progress, I will take my complaint to the media.

I find your behaviour reprehensible and incompetent, and I will be discussing these concerns with my Member of Parliament.

Yours truly,

Dr. Jonathan Edwards
Assistant Professor,
Department of Zoology,
University of Southern British Columbia,
Vancouver, BC, V6T 1D6

So much for client service. I briefly wondered how much time "forthwith" gave us, and decided that it was probably considerably less than the time that had already elapsed since his final letter. I reached for the telephone and was halfway through dialing his number when I realized that it was only 7:15 A.M. in Vancouver. Normally, I would have sworn loudly and banged down the phone, but for once the three-hour time lag was welcome. It gave me enough time to do a quick study of the file and at least have my excuses lined up when I finally managed to reach Edwards.

I worked methodically forward from the initial letter of complaint through to the final threat of going to the media, and I began to see why Edwards was so annoyed. As far as I could figure out from the dates of letters and submissions, the file had sat dormant for a period of ten months. His first letter of complaint, at the very bottom of the sheaf of papers, was received by us a little over a year ago. The letter had been stamped "Received: 6 Sept" and noted in the log of the file. A very cursory reference search was attached to the letter, but not mentioned in the log. Following this, there was nothing. No notes. No action. No follow-up.

Dr. Edwards had sent a second letter in June of the following year, almost ten months later. The request for an investigation was again made, and supporting documentation was supplied. This time there was a more substantive follow-up: past grant applications were acquired, some internal financial records were appended, and confidential documents relating to the Canada/US Pacific Salmon Treaty were attached, but no action was taken. In fact, it looked as though nothing was really done until the last registered letter was sent. Then, with the threat of media involvement, the file was sent on to Bob. Who of course didn't read it, because he works on the government's thirty-day rule: don't even lay your fingers on a file until it has sat in your in-box for at least thirty days. Then, from his in-box, the file would have gone to the bottom of his *tô-do* pile, accounting for the two-month lag before it fell into my hands.

I swivelled around in my chair to face the window. It was a spectacular northeastern autumn day with the sun bright and hot, the sky an expanse of cloudless blue. The "happy workers," dressed in shirtsleeves, strolled along the sidewalk underneath my window, puffing on cigarettes and chatting in pairs. Only the maples aflame in orange and red were telling the truth: winter was almost upon us.

I've always held to the theory that it's best to have friends in low places, since they're the ones who do the work and actually know what's going on. On impulse, I picked up the phone and called Lydia.

"Office of the Director General, Grants and Funding."

I know Lydia well, and preliminaries aren't required. "It's me. I'm looking for the scuttlebutt on a file."

"I see." Her voice was polite but cold: professional. That meant that Patsy's office was occupied *and* the adjoining door was open. You'd think a busy director general would have more to do with her time than eavesdrop on her executive assistant, but Patsy considered it part of her job description. Lydia continued in the same tone. "How may I help you?"

"International Network for Pacific Salmon Population Dynamics. Does that ring a bell?"

"Yes, I understand. But Ms. Middlemass is booked at that time. Would another time be possible?"

Well, well. Pay dirt. "Could you meet me on the path in fifteen?"

"That would be fine. I'll book you in for then."

I hung up the phone and smiled to myself. Lydia manages Patsy's office like the captain of a well-run frigate. She knows every nuance of every file that enters or leaves the office, and she issues orders to her subordinates with an assurance based on infallible knowledge. Despite her command of Patsy's dominion, she finds the whole thing — the work, the politics, the fretting, the constant jockeying for position — both tedious and silly. In short, Lydia has a life, something the Council tries hard to discourage.

With fifteen minutes to kill I did a rapid accounting of what I already knew, even after my brief look at the documents. The good news? Elaine was not involved. If she had been — if she'd been named as one of the researchers on the original grant request — then I'd have had a serious conflict of interest. Elaine was my secret weapon. She was not only my best friend from graduate school, but she had just recently escaped the post-doctoral mill for a professorship at Southern (as the University of Southern B.C. is known). She was honest, clear-headed, and would know most of the players. While she disapproved of the government interfering with science, we went back a long way, and I knew she could be convinced to help. Insider information could cut weeks off an investigation.

Now for the bad news. Dr. Madden Riesler was a big man on campus, and not just in Vancouver. He sat on funding committees, editorial boards, and government panels, which meant that he had *connections* — both political and scientific. That made investigating him problematic. It also made Dr. Edwards either very brave or very stupid, but it was too early in the game to know which.

I could hear Duncan moving things around on the other side of the wall, so I picked up the salmon file and

scooted down the corridor to his office. Duncan and I
had always worked as a team, helping each other follow
up leads, covering home base when the other was in the
field. I didn't like to think about life around here without him. When I arrived at the door I stood for a
minute, watching him load books into a cardboard box.
Then I sighed.

"You bum," I said, and walked through the door.
He looked up from the box and smiled. Duncan is
warm, gentle, and thoughtful. Exactly the kind of man I
could never fall in love with. He moved the box off the
chair and motioned for me to sit down.

"Hey," I said, "I wouldn't want to disrupt your
packing."

"Actually, I've been cleaning up all week, surreptitiously of course. This isn't quite as sudden as it seems."

Now that I thought of it, his office had looked
awfully orderly this past week. I felt a little jab of hurt
that Duncan hadn't let me in on the secret, but I
assumed he had his reasons. Duncan had perched himself on the edge of his desk and was looking casual, yet
professional. Receptive, yet in control. Damn. He was
perfect for the minister's office. I took the file and slid it
onto the desk beside him. He picked it up and fanned
through the pages.

"I should thank you for that," I said, nodding to the
file. "But I think I'll withhold judgment until the investigation is complete."

He raised his eyebrows. "What's up?"

"The investigation has been restricted by the fifth
floor and I haven't even started."

I could see him scanning a few pages. "Salmon.
That makes it hot politically. We start a new round of
negotiations next week, and if there's no headway we're
going to have war on the Fraser."

"I've thought of that. Keep everything under cover for political reasons. But there are other possibilities."

"Like?"

"Ever heard of Riesler?"

"Big cheese. Does good work as far as I know."

"But nothing juicy?"

He turned to stare out the window for a couple seconds, the wheels furiously grinding in his head. The guy has total recall for any investigation he has ever come in contact with, as well as an encyclopedic knowledge of who knows whom in the research community. When he turned back to me it was with an answer. He spoke by rote.

"Overly ambitious. Best work behind him. Reputation built on graduate students' work. That kind of thing. The usual researcher jealousy, but nothing seamy."

"Jonathan Edwards?"

"Never heard of him."

"And that's not surprising. He's a junior prof at Southern. He's accused Riesler of embezzling Network funds."

"I hope the good Dr. Edwards doesn't have a mortgage."

"An uplifting thought." But, of course, Duncan was right. If word got out that Edwards had started an investigation against a guy like Riesler, funding would dry up faster than a prairie slough in August. Even worse, Edwards would be shunned by his colleagues, and despite the stereotype of the scientist toiling alone in the lab, modern science is a cooperative venture impossible to carry out in isolation. And all this would happen even if Riesler was guilty, unless we were talking big-time crime: murder or grand larceny. It was a bit depressing really, and it meant that I had to tread lightly in my investigation, keeping the nature of my business confidential. We both pondered Edwards's fate for a minute, then I continued. "What's your take on the Network?"

"Big money, big science, big politics. In short, a hornets' nest. I'm glad it's you and not me."

"Any connections with the Council?"

"You mean other than brokering and funding? Something more personal?"

I nodded.

He straightened and his eyes brightened. It was as though a little jolt of electricity had zinged up his spine. "Now why would a nice girl like you ask a question like that?"

"Because the file seems to have disappeared from September to June. No records, no chronology."

What had begun as a slight smile morphed into a grin. "No kidding." Then he switched off his external functions and went back into think mode, staring at the corner of the room. When he was ready he focused his attention back on me. "Hard to say. It's a megaproject. I know there's government and industry money involved, so there are a lot of players, but I don't see any obvious connections. What's your guess?"

I shrugged. "Somebody on the fifth lost the file? When it resurfaced nine months later they freaked and slipped it back into circulation without a word. That's what I'd do if I lost it."

Duncan was examining me, his clear hazel eyes unblinking. "But you're not convinced."

"A total budget of twelve million dollars over five years. That's a tempting jackpot."

"And certainly enough to cover incidentals, like making an annoying file disappear."

"My thoughts exactly."

Duncan paused for a minute before continuing. "Then there's politics. Who's got what at stake?"

"What do you mean?"

"Whose career, whose reputation, is on the line here?"

I thought about that for a second. "It would have to be someone who could influence Patsy. The restrictions are in her writing."

I could see that the neurons were already firing again, running through a databank of connections that were well beyond my comprehension. Duncan loves a good internal scandal. And as far as I could see, the Network put a whole lot of butts — some of them very big — on the line. Because the data could have a major impact on fishing quotas throughout the Pacific Rim, even a hint of impropriety could lead to accusations of data manipulation for political gain, the "you get more fish than we get because you cheated" sort of accusation that would discredit the whole project. Given that the Pacific salmon fisheries were an international flash-point, the Network had to appear squeaky clean.

I shifted in my chair. Duncan had had enough time, and I didn't want him doing all the work right now. "So," I interrupted his thoughts, "when do you start the new job?"

He started slightly. "Tomorrow. Nine o'clock. There's no vacation for the committed."

"If you don't take a vacation you will be committed, but it's your life." I stood up and reached for the file. "As you're wandering through the corridors of power, can you keep your ears open for me? If you hear anything about either the salmon project or anyone connected with it, even if it's whispered behind closed doors, could you give me a call? I'm going to need all the help I can get."

He laughed. "Hey, I'm not an investigator anymore."

I tweaked his cheek, which was as soft as I imagined a baby's bum would be. "Once an investigator, always an investigator." When I was almost out the door, I shot him a smile over my shoulder. "Good luck in your new position."

Good. That hook was baited. Now I'd have to wait and see what it pulled in.

chapter three

When I got back to my office I changed into sneakers and was out the door. Our section is on the ground level of the building in a little cul-de-sac that runs off the main corridor. When I arrived at the corridor I turned left and headed out toward the loading dock and mail room. That way I avoided passing Bob's office. Once outside, I jogged across the small expanse of grass behind the building that buffers the woods from the parking lot. Lydia was already seated at our regular spot: a bench along the main trail just out of sight of the building. As usual, she looked like a raven-haired version of Catherine Deneuve ready for a perfume photo shoot.

As I approached she stood and formally extended her hand. I smiled and extended mine in return: not my usual style of greeting, but with Lydia it comes with the territory. Then, with no words spoken, we turned and began to walk down the path. We'd been here, and done this, before.

About forty metres from the bench we hit a side trail that was rarely used by Council employees. We turned onto it and walked quietly, enjoying the silence. The woods smelled of autumn, the soft earthy odour of leaf mould mixed with slow, organic decomposition. Every few metres a golden leaf, poplar or birch, floated to the ground and settled with a whisper. In summer the under-story was in shade, but now sunlight dappled the ground, dancing on the tapestry of leaves that had already fallen.

We came up over a rise and hit a curtain of cool, damp air. The path then dipped and made an abrupt left, meeting a brook that it escorted downstream for two hundred metres before looping back to the main path. There was a bench overlooking the brook and we sat down. It gave us an excellent view of uninvited guests, and the burble of the water masked our conver-sation to anyone not within visual range. We were silent for a moment more, absorbed in the peace of the forest — an island of sanity in an otherwise idiotic world — then I took a breath and broke the spell.

"Tell me about the file."

She turned slowly, as if pulling herself away from the stream. Her voice was cool. "What exactly concerns you?"

I was taken aback. Usually Lydia was more forth-coming. "Gee, Lyd. For starters, according to the chronology of the documents, the file seems to have van-ished between September and June. Any idea where it might have been?"

She hesitated, then turned back to the stream. Her back was ramrod straight: the bearing of a queen. She took her time, enunciated each word clearly, but in a flat, expressionless voice. Quite a performance. "I lost it."

I had to stop myself from laughing. I would have at least chuckled, except for the sensation of a very serious subtext underlying the little game.

"No, you didn't." I let a few seconds pass, then I said gently, "I do need to know where it was. If someone was sitting on it, I have to know who and why before I dive in head first. Otherwise I'll be eaten alive. You didn't lose it, so either someone told you to make it disappear or you're being used as a scapegoat. Which is it?"

She turned back to me. Did I see a hint of amusement in her eyes? "Of course, your expertise in interrogation puts me under significant duress to be as truthful as possible."

"That, and the moral and legal imperative to tell the truth in the course of a federal investigation; don't forget that," I said. I like to be helpful.

"Quite right." She nodded and sighed dramatically. "Well, I really have no choice, do I?"

"None whatsoever."

"In that case ..." then she went back to deadly serious, "... let me say first that I am reassured by the fact that you think I did not lose the file. That is precisely why I have been waiting to see who the investigating officer would be. If you should decide to call Patricia for an explanation, she will tell you that I *did* lose it."

"But you didn't." She shook her head. "Someone on your staff then?"

"One of my girls? Absolutely not."

I waited, and she paused as if gathering her thoughts. Her hands were settled in her lap, her legs crossed at the ankle and tucked under the bench. I had one leg crossed over the other, at the knee not the ankle, and an arm flung over the back of the bench. I felt like a bohunk sitting with a duchess. She continued. "I'll tell you what happened from my perspective. It will not answer your primary question, mainly, the location of the file from September through to June, but it may give you some avenues of inquiry."

She spoke, then, as if reading from a script; as though she'd run over the story so many times in her mind that it was now memorized and distanced from emotion. "When the first letter arrived I logged it. That means I opened a file for the project, gave it a code number, and entered it in my master database. Once in the master database, every time a file moves across my desk its destination is tracked. That way I know where all the files are at any given moment in time. I followed this procedure for the salmon file. However, I did not send the file directly to Bob, as I would have for a more minor investigation. Given the nature of the complaint and the political implications I stapled an urgent tag to the folder and placed it directly on Patricia's desk. I didn't see it again, which was unusual, but I assumed that it had gone to the president and was being handled at a higher level. Then the second letter came. That was ten months later. I was alarmed and took it personally into Patricia. When I asked her where the file was in the process, so that I could add the letter, she said, 'How should I know? I gave it back to you three days after I received it.' I was shocked, but I said nothing, and I went to check my log. If I had received the file and forgotten, it would appear there."

At this point Lydia turned to look me in the eye, as if defying me to believe her. "When I called up that entry, it was no longer there. The complete log of that file had disappeared. Patricia was furious."

"Was it just that entry and nothing else?"

She nodded. "Needless to say, I was very concerned, so I decided to investigate further. In addition to the system backups, I personally back up all our files on disk every three months: at the beginning of January, April, July, and October." She reached into the pocket of her suit jacket and pulled out a computer disk. "This backup was done in April, eight months after we received the initial letter from Dr. Edwards. The file exists on this backup, and there is no record of it ever coming back to me."

"Does Patsy know about this?" I nodded to the disk.

"Actually, no. When I tried to discuss it with her she made it very clear that, as far as she was concerned, she had her answer and the subject was closed."

I reached out and took the disk. "Mind if I keep this for you?"

"Thank you. I would be most grateful if you would."

I slipped it into my jacket pocket. "But somewhere along the line the file was obviously recovered."

"Yes. Another curious event. I was not happy at being accused of losing the file. I have never, in my life, misplaced so much as a sheet of paper. However, I am eight months away from early retirement. I cannot afford to make any significant waves."

That was the understatement of the year. Patsy is a card-carrying member of the "off with her head" school of personnel management. Insubordination is not tolerated, and that includes defending yourself against false accusations, particularly if she's the one accusing. In Lydia's position she was better to eat the crap and retire happy eight months from now with a plump little buy-out package. If she so much as squeaked about this file she risked being fired and out on the streets with no bucks and no job. The Red Queen had done it before.

She continued. "The best I could do was suggest that we mount an all-out search of the files the following day. The girls and I would put everything else aside and comb the filing cabinets, since some sort of misfiling was the most likely explanation. It took us two days to locate the folder. It had been placed under optoelectronics."

I must admit, I felt a stab of regret. P for Pacific and O for optoelectronics. That sounded to me like an honest mistake. "So it was misfiled."

"That would be the obvious conclusion, yes. However, engineering and life sciences are filed in different cabinets. In fact, they are filed in different rooms. No one on my staff would make such an error."

At this point my intellect piped up and chirped *principle of parsimony, principle of parsimony* like some hormone-crazed male warbler. It was true: good scientific practice demanded that I accept the simplest and most likely explanation to fit the existing facts, and, although the idea of a conspiracy was tempting, the most plausible explanation was that someone, somewhere, had simply forgotten that they had the file. When they realized that they were holding a hot potato they panicked and tried to cover their tracks. Personally, I hoped that unfortunate someone was Bob. I smiled. It certainly merited further investigation.

Lydia continued. "You know, Morgan, I would prefer to have this removed from my permanent record before I leave the Council."

"She put a reprimand on file?"

Lydia nodded slightly. "And suggested that I not discuss the situation with any of my colleagues."

I let that sink in for a minute. "Could Patsy herself access your master database? Could she get in there and erase a log?"

She smiled vaguely. "I'm afraid the answer to that question is no. Ms. Middlemass is not what you would term computer literate. I'm not sure she could even find the power switch."

"Who else then?"

"I don't know, really. The file is password protected, but all the girls in the office know the password."

I took a moment to organize the information in my head and plan out a strategy that kept Lydia at arm's length from my inquiries, then I touched her sleeve. "I will need your help. Names and information mainly."

She gave an almost imperceptible nod, both of us knowing that she'd lose her job if she, or I, were caught looking into this.

"But, Morgan, if you wish to keep the project, may I suggest that you leave work early today, preferably before one o'clock, when Ms. Middlemass will be returning from a lunchtime meeting. The file was not to land in your hands."

On our stroll back to the trailhead we chatted, mainly about Lydia's New Age daughter who spent inordinate amounts of time mumbling over little piles of crystals. It was supposed to help her find a job. Lydia had suggested reading the want ads of the local newspaper, but apparently this was not how jobs "come to us." When we reached the end of the path I agreed to wait five minutes before leaving the woods and returning to the office, mainly to protect Lydia from Patsy's spies. Just as she was walking away I thought of something.

"Lydia?" She turned back. "Are you sure Patsy said *three days* later. Not three or four, or several, or a week. Something less defined?"

Lydia shook her head. "She said it quite distinctly. 'I gave it back to you three days after I received it.' That's exactly what she said."

As Lydia disappeared around the building I thought back to Patsy's post-it note directive. Keep my nose out of the science? I don't think so. After all, my first responsibility was to discover the truth, not toady up to the needs and desires of a fifth-floor megalomaniac who had never conducted an investigation. And if I managed in the process to hang Patsy out to dry, all the better. She'd hurt too many innocent people in her fifteen-year reign.

Anyway, what post-it note?

In the office I changed back into my working shoes and made my way to the ladies'. As I passed Bob's office his secretary, Michelle, called me from within. "O'Brien," she yelled. I stuck my head in the door. She jerked her head toward Bob's office door. "CP called from his meeting. He wants to see you in his office when he gets back."

"When's that?"

She looked at her watch: one of those domed jobs with Mickey Mouse floating around inside. I was surprised she could read the time. "Half an hour or so."

"Okay. Tell him to give me a call when he gets in. If I'm not sitting right at my desk I'm around the building somewhere. Tell him to keep trying."

She gave me the thumbs up. "Ace," she said.

I made two phone calls before leaving. The first was to Air Canada. The agent cheerfully bumped up Duncan's reservation from 6:00 P.M. to 1:45, although she was surprised at my insistence on having a connecting rather than a direct flight.

"I can put you through Toronto. You'd only wait half an hour for a connecting flight." I could hear her ticking away on her keyboard.

"How about Winnipeg?"

"There will be a two-hour stopover, and you'll have to change planes."

"Perfect. And please change the booking to A. O'Brien." My middle name is Albertine. To this day I wonder how much rye my mother had drunk before she signed the papers for Vital Statistics. At least she didn't forget the last three letters.

Following the airline, I called Sylvia in Vancouver, outlined briefly what I needed, and made a date to meet her at the Thai Kitchen for dinner. The instant I hung up I stuffed my laptop into my briefcase, shoved the salmon file in beside it, and headed out the door, making for the loading dock. I was just about to cross the platform when Bob drove into the lot. I stepped back into the darkened bay and watched him climb out of his car, slam the door, and stalk across the parking lot to the official back door of the building. Bob was definitely not a happy camper.

When I was sure he was well inside the building, I crossed quickly to my car, got in, and was out of there before he even reached his office.

chapter four

The plane trip from Ottawa to Winnipeg was uneventful, except for a juicy little filet mignon and a passable French cabernet: better than I'd get at home. With time to kill in the Winnipeg airport I called Duncan and updated him on my interview with Lydia.

"Oh, by the way," he said. "Bob was down. He stomped around your office, opened desk drawers, and rifled your files. He also used inappropriate language."

"Did he find what he was looking for?"

"Nope. Because she'd already left. As an employee of the Crown I have been instructed to inform you, immediately on contact, that you must report directly to your supervisor on receipt of this message. There. I've fulfilled my obligation."

"Registered. Oops. The line is busy. So, are you going up to say a formal goodbye to Patsy?"

"I could be convinced."

"Mention the salmon network. How pleased you are that it's gone to me. See what kind of reaction you get."

"And what do I get for this?"

I hesitated for a moment, as if summoning up the courage to make a great sacrifice. "I'll babysit."

"You're on."

Actually, I adore Duncan's kids. Whenever I go over we consume popcorn, coke, and trashy kids' TV, all the programs that their dad doesn't let them watch. Still, I try to retain some dignity in the negotiations and pretend that my compliance is worth significant payment in kind.

"I'm meeting Sylvia for dinner — "

"God, how's she doing?"

"Not great." I veered away from details, mainly because I didn't want to confront them earlier than I had to. "I've got her doing a search on this, so I'll have a lot more background by tonight."

"Keep me posted."

"I will. And Duncan, keep your nose clean, but not that clean."

The Winnipeg-Vancouver leg of the voyage was more exciting, with an inflight movie and Angela. I watched her manoeuvre her bags down the aisle, feeling dread, then resignation, as she stopped at my row, smiled, and said, "Hi there. Jeez. They don't give you much room, do they?"

She had more carry-on luggage than a hockey team, mainly shopping bags from Eaton's, The Bay, and Holt Renfrew. She dumped all her bags on the seat and stood in the aisle, surveying the situation and blocking all the traffic behind her. She looked a bit like a middle-aged cherub, or how one would imagine cherubim would look if they ever aged to forty. But instead of fair hair, hers was jet black and cut in short, stylish waves that framed her face. She was dressed casually, but the jeans were designer, the neon yellow sweatshirt was new, and the cowboy boots looked like they came from an endangered species. Someone in the queue behind finally got annoyed and gave a firm shove, which travelled down the line to her.

"Oh, sorry," she said, looking back, and wedged herself into that tiny space in front of the seat to let the others pass.

Having adjusted to my fate, I tried to be kind. "I can fit a bag in front of my seat. All I have down here is a briefcase."

"Gee, thanks a bunch," and she swung two bags in my direction. I arranged them as best I could, then sat up and took a good look at her. She had pulled out a compact and was patting her hair into place. I couldn't help asking, "You go to Winnipeg to shop? It seems a bit bizarre, coming from Vancouver."

"Oh, I don't live in Vancouver. Ellesworth." She snapped the compact shut and took in my blank stare. "Above Nanaimo, on Vancouver Island. And I got to tell you anyway, Vancouver's not so hot. I'd rather shop in Winnipeg any day. Sorry if that offends you." She didn't sound sorry.

"I'm not from Vancouver. Ottawa, actually."

A shadow of loathing crossed her face, and she shifted to the other side of her seat. "Really."

"But I used to live in Vancouver when I was a kid," I said quickly. "And I went to university in Winnipeg." She relaxed a bit and moved back toward the centre of her seat. Apparently, with that pedigree whatever I had wasn't contagious. I finished up lamely, "So I'm not really an Ottawa person, if you know what I mean."

"Where I come from we don't have much good to say about Ottawa, if you know what *I* mean."

I did, so I let a second pass before changing the topic. "So, what brought you to Winnipeg?"

"Oh, my mum. Jeez, I wish she'd move west where I could keep an eye on her, but you know how old people are. 'Winnipeg's been good to me my whole life,' she says. 'I'm not going to abandon it now.' Like Winnipeg cares. Well, that's fine for her, but my George has to work, and he can't do that in Winnipeg."

"But he can in Ellesworth?"

"Logging. He runs a feller operation on the blocks above Campbell River. On a good day on flat terrain he can take down four hundred trees. Makes a good living." She reflexively held out her hand and examined the two chunks of diamond-encrusted gold on her fingers. Together they must have weighed more than a fork. The funny thing was, she wasn't doing it to impress me. It was as though she was trying to remind herself that these were the benefits of all their hard work.

"You must worry about him. It's a dangerous job."

She shrugged and switched on a smile. "What can you do? It's not so bad really."

"And with the way things are going —" I was stopped by her frank, appraising, and not very friendly look.

"You people in Ottawa think we're all stupid, don't you? Well for your information, there isn't a man working out in that forest who doesn't know what's going on. What do you think they talk about over beer? They know we can't keep cutting like that and still have a forest for my son to work in, but what are you supposed to do? Get out? So somebody else can make the money instead of you? We worked hard to set ourselves up, and every year we got to upgrade equipment and cut more trees to make ends meet. The forest will be gone no matter what we do, so we might as well make the money out of it. Anyway, you know whose fault it really is?"

At this point she directed her index finger at me and gave me a good, sharp poke in the arm. It hurt, particularly with those acrylic nails. "The government. That's who. They let in those foreign companies who strip the land, don't reforest, then send the logs to their own countries for processing. Those are our jobs. If the government would keep their nose out of it," she poked me again, "we'd run the industry like it should be run."

I was tempted to remind her that forestry was within the provincial jurisdiction so she was poking the wrong person, but it probably wouldn't have mattered to her. Government is government and they're all bad. I rubbed my arm and mumbled something about getting the point, then the lights dimmed and the movie started: *Free Willy 3*. I wondered how she felt about that.

As we approached Vancouver, the sun was sitting low over Vancouver Island across the Strait of Georgia. Vancouver's airport spreads across a marshy island in the Fraser River delta, and as we neared the city the plane came in low over the river, following it out to its mouth. Beneath us, tug boats, seiners, and log booms moved sluggishly along the channel while yachts and pleasure craft darted between them. From above, the Fraser looked like nothing more than a vast aquatic highway.

Then suddenly the land dropped away and we shot out over open water, banking sharply to make our final descent. As the plane tilted, the clean line of demarcation — where the muddy Fraser hits the clear, cold waters of the Strait of Georgia — was visible below. The mass of flowing water created a solid, murky wall that ran several miles out, and fishing boats dotted either side of the line.

As we taxied into the airport I wished Angela luck with her mother, grabbed my briefcase and my carry-on bag, and slipped out of the seat before we'd come to a stop. It was going to take her at least half an hour to gather up the fruits of her labour.

For me, Vancouver equals pain, but even so I can't help but be seduced by the overpowering beauty: the city cradled by snowy mountains against a shimmering sea. I stood for a moment, breathing in the damp, salty air, remembering, and not remembering. When I was ready to move, I crossed to the rental lot, where I picked up my government-rate car: basically, a tin can powered by a blender engine, set on wheels the size of Oreo cookies. If this case involved a high-speed chase I was already dead. I consulted the map, just to refresh my memory, and headed into the city.

As I crossed the north arm of the river, I caught the scent of fresh-cut cedar, pungent and aromatic, escaping from a sawmill below. For a moment I was displaced, no longer in a car speeding toward the city but standing in a moist, dark glade dwarfed by towering trees. Then the car cleared the rise of the bridge and my eyes were assaulted by straight lines and concrete grey. I sighed, jammed my foot on the gas, and descended into the urban sprawl.

For once, someone in Travel had done their job. Instead of booking me into a downtown hotel, which would be more expensive and mired in traffic, they had put me in a high-rise hotel at the corner of 12th and Cambie. While it was slightly off the beaten path, it gave me straight-line access to Southern without having to go downtown. I made a mental note to send an e-mail to the travel clerk and thank her.

When I'd settled in my room, I pulled the salmon file from my briefcase and flipped through it until I found Edwards's number. It was late, but from his CV he looked like a keener. He answered on the second ring.

"Edwards." His voice was a resonant low bass, distinctive and beautiful.

I gave him my name, but when I got to the part about why I was here — to investigate Madden Riesler — he cut me off. Explosively.

"Bullshit! After a year and half? Come on."

"I understand your — "

"You're not here to investigate Madden. You couldn't get rid of me, so now you're going to conduct a nice little investigation that will clear him and screw me. Guess it pays to have friends in high places, huh? Well you know what? Sorry to say, you're too late. I've already gone to a reporter, and believe me, I used the word cover-up when referring to your department."

Bummer. That meant dealing with the press, my media-incompetent management, and the complaint itself. This was getting complicated, and I didn't like that. If I was going to tie it up fast I needed Edwards on my side, so I decided to go for the truth.

"Look Dr. Edwards, I'll level with you. I don't know why it took so long for us to investigate your complaint, but I intend to find out, and the best place for me to start is with the complaint itself."

"If you really believe that, then you're a patsy. Madden Riesler is not going to be investigated."

A patsy? I didn't like that word usage one little bit. "I'm not afraid of Riesler or anybody else. If there's a cover-up I'll find it *and* expose it, but first I need information. If we could just — "

"Get your own bloody information. That's what we pay you for, isn't it?" And the phone went dead.

His lack of cooperation was understandable, but annoying. I'd have to find out from Sylvia who covered the science beat for the local paper. That was probably his contact. Maybe I could cut a deal.

Having jotted a note to that effect I took a deep breath, picked up the phone, and dialed a number I knew by heart. I'd hoped to leave a message on voice mail — after all, it was 9:00 P.M. in Ottawa — but Bob picked up on the first ring. I had the impression he'd been waiting for my call.

"Robert Gregory, Chief of Investigations."

Really. Give me a break. The guy has call display and would know it was me. "Hi, Bob. I got your message from Duncan. What can I do for you?"

I heard some shuffling in the background, a chair moving. So he wasn't alone in his office.

"Morgan. You left earlier than expected."

"It seemed more cost-effective. Get me onsite and working sooner."

There was a slight pause, then: "I see. You wanted to get onsite and working sooner." He spoke at an unnaturally slow pace, enunciating clearly. I thought of suggesting the speakerphone so he wouldn't have to repeat everything I said but realized it was to my advantage to play the game his way. There was some more shuffling in the background, the sound of paper moving across his desk. After another brief pause he continued. "There is some concern here about the instructions in that file." I waited and said nothing. The silence stretched to fill a room, forcing Bob to continue. "What instructions did you receive?"

"The cover page was missing."

"The cover page was missing," he repeated ponderously. "I see, but did you receive ..." he hesitated. "Was there anything else?"

"Special instructions? No. I just assumed normal procedure. Really, Bob, I am a senior officer."

"There was nothing in the file?"

"Should there have been?"

His voice relaxed a bit. "No, of course not. Other than the cover sheet, which was missing. An oversight on someone's part, no doubt. Well then." More paper was shuffled. "I want this investigation tied up as quickly as possible with a minimum of disruption. Understood? Stick to the financial and stay out of the researchers' way. We don't want the Network disturbed. There are too many sensitivities involved here. That should get you in and out of there in what, a day? Maybe two?"

Again I didn't answer. I wanted him to sweat. When he finally spoke it was with forced joviality. "Because with Duncan gone those high-profile projects are just piling up, and really, you're the only with the clearance to handle them."

"You mean the investigation and the report, or just the investigation?"

"I'm sure we can reach an understanding on that."

I continued as though I hadn't heard the last part of the conversation. "You know, Bob, I have my own concerns about this Network file, and I may need your help sorting it all out."

"That's why I'm here."

Oh? Since when? But I kept that to myself. "I need to know where the file was when it disappeared from September to June."

There was dead silence.

"Bob? Are you still there?"

I heard a little hiccup, then a muffled sound at the other end. I hoped he wasn't having a coronary. With a guy like Bob, who smoked, was out of shape, and turned such a livid colour under stress, it could happen in the blink of an eye. Still, I thought it best to continue while I had the advantage. "You see, the reason I need to know is that a reporter may now be involved, and that makes things messy. So any help you can give me from your end would really be appreciated. Oh, and should I refer the press to you, or would Patsy prefer to take it?" Then I added pointedly, "Maybe you should ask her."

Another minute of silence passed, and by the time Bob gathered himself up to reply the jovial tone was gone. "No one speaks to the press," he barked. "That's number one. Number two: you use authorized channels to view the financial records. *Authorized.* When that's done I want you out of there. Number three: you report all findings directly to me. And I want you back here and standing in my office Wednesday nine A.M. Got that? Any shenanigans, O'Brien, and you're up for suspension."

I let a few seconds pass then asked politely, "And when should I expect the information on those missing months?"

He banged the phone down in my ear.

Two out of two. Not bad.

With the worst of my evening over, I wandered to the balcony door, slid it open, and stepped outside. I was on the twenty-second floor of a narrow tower in a mixed commercial and residential neighbourhood. Beneath me I could see café diners through the glass roof of a trendy little mall across the street, but at eye level I had a panoramic view of downtown Vancouver. It was a spectacular sight, the high-rises jutting over the black water of English Bay, patches of brilliant neon flashing like beacons in the fading light, and behind this, a backdrop of mountains: massive dark forms, ghostlike with the faint glow of snow.

I sighed. It was too much beauty all at once. Overpowering and almost painful. I checked my watch, briefly debated a jog, then decided to go for it. I knew the area well enough to know a reasonable route that would take me through well-lit, safe streets. Not that I can't take care of myself, but why push your luck.

I pulled on my jogging clothes and headed out the door. The hotel opens onto 12th Avenue, and even though it was 6:45 P.M., rush hour showed no sign of abating. There was a bumper-to-bumper stream of traffic flowing in both directions, and Cambie, just to my right, was gridlock.

I turned west on 12th Avenue and headed for the next major artery — Oak Street. I knew I could jog up Oak to 33rd, then loop back around and jog downhill for the last bit of my run. Given the traffic, the damage to my lungs from pollution would far outweigh any benefits derived from the exercise, but that damage wouldn't show up for years, and I tend to be a short-term girl.

The first couple blocks were tough, but then my body and brain began to loosen up and move into that altered state caused by lactic acid overload. By the time I reached Oak and had started the uphill climb, I was absorbed in the details of the case, moving through them in a process akin to free association. I started with Edwards. What did I know about him, other than he was a bit of a jerk with a tendency to interrupt? For one thing he was an American. That had interesting possibilities. Americans studying salmon in Canada would be, to some degree, *persona non grata*, given the volatility of the issue on the international stage. Maybe somebody wanted him to go back to where he came from.

Or maybe he was part of an American plot to discredit the Network. Someone in Washington was upset by the direction things were taking and Edwards was promised tenure and a big fat grant south of the border to cause a little trouble. We'd do it if our interests were at stake, so why not them? But whose interests were at stake? I'd have to find out.

Or maybe Edwards was just jealous. It wouldn't be the first time that a junior researcher had accused an established scientist of fraud: a sort of sour grapes approach to career advancement.

But how did any of these possibilities tie in with the file disappearing? I couldn't see the connection, which raised again the possibility that the disappearance was a random event, unrelated to the investigation itself. The problem was, every time I settled into that conclusion something didn't feel right, as if I was overlooking an important fact that was sitting right before my eyes.

I had a brief stint with the RCMP, which is to say that I completed my training and was honourably discharged to spare certain people certain embarrassment if they tried to jerk me around. It didn't matter. I'd realized long before the end of training that it wasn't the life for me. While I had balked at the militaristic training, I did manage to come away with some critical skills that have saved my butt on more than one occasion. The most important, beaten into me by a brilliant and marginally sadistic crime-scene investigator, was to trust my intuition, so when this niggling uneasiness about the missing file kept reoccurring I paid close attention.

I had begun mentally prodding the little doubt, seeing if I could crack it open, when I was momentarily distracted by the aroma of quality cappuccino escaping from a little café. I filed the location away under caffeine then returned to my uneasiness, trying another tack. Why, for example, was I focused on Edwards? Nationalistic prejudice? I consider myself above that, especially since I know from experience that fraud, dishonesty, and deceit are pan-national characteristics. The unifying force is greed, and that is neither cultural nor hereditary.

So what had led me, perhaps unconsciously, to Edwards?

Maybe it was Riesler's credentials. It was hard to believe that a gold-medallist from the University of Toronto, a Rhodes scholar in biochemistry, and a tenured professor two years after his dissertation would embezzle money. It's not like he lacked research grants, and he had a good salary, so unless he was supporting an expensive mistress or had an ugly addiction it wasn't about money.

By this time I was winded from the uphill climb, and starting to feel a stitch in my side. When I get to thinking and running at the same time, as the thinking speeds up so do the legs, but they don't have the stamina of my neural tissue. I hit 25th and made a bad decision, because, God knows, I needed the exercise after all those hours on the plane. But, instead of continuing to 33rd, I turned left, cutting my run short a few blocks. I could always blame it on the pollution.

As I jogged along, rhythmically panting in time with my legs, my brain fell into a meditative chant of "Why Edwards, why Edwards, why Edwards," timed with the intake and exhalation of my breath. After several blocks I wanted to change the channel, but as usual my brain resisted. Finally, in desperation, my unconscious cut in. *Because of the reference search, you idiot.*

Huh? What reference search? And then I remembered. Attached to the initial letter of complaint was, as I had noted at the time, a very inadequate reference search. It was inadequate because whoever had done the search had only focused on Edwards, calling up his publications for the last two years, and that was very fifth-floor. A poorly done search focusing on the researcher who had the least political sway.

When I hit the corner of 25th and Cambie I remembered something else. The search results had been clipped to Edwards's first letter of complaint, but the date of the search hadn't been entered in the action log attached to the file. So when exactly had the search been done? I picked up speed and headed downhill.

Back in the hotel room I didn't bother with stretching, another bad decision, but went directly to my briefcase. I pulled out the evidence kit and grabbed the magnifying glass, one of the small, high-powered jobs used by geologists. Then I opened the salmon file and flipped to the back. I looked up at the ceiling, said a brief prayer to the goddess of forensic evidence, then looked down at the reference search. It had been printed on a laser printer rather than on the large-format dot-matrix that the National Science Library used. That meant that someone had logged into the library from a remote location and had searched the database from there. And whoever it was had decided that Edwards was the guy to investigate rather than the infinitely more prestigious Dr. Riesler.

On the top of the page was a header, but the type was so tiny it was unreadable. I pulled the magnifying glass from its case, held my breath, and positioned it over the header: *Aquatic Sciences Citation Index search time 7 min 32 sec 1342 h Saturday 13 Oct 2001. Thank you for using Canada's National Science Library*.

I let out a long breath. That's what I had hoped for. Proof that the file was still active well after Patsy claimed she had returned it to Lydia. Active enough, in fact, for somebody to come in on a Saturday afternoon and conduct the search. To do that, the user had to have a special account with the library — they were charged by the minute for search time — as well as a reasonable knowledge of how the database worked. In my job, it is a comfort to know that nothing in the modern world is free of paperwork.

I smiled. Where there's paperwork, there's a paper trail, and no one is better than Sylvia at tracing a paper trail.

chapter five

The Thai Kitchen was up Cambie within walking distance of the hotel. I showered, put on a clean pair of jeans, and pulled on my all-purpose leather jacket. I left the laptop hidden under my shirts but took the file and my briefcase with me. The traffic was still imposing, but it had eased up enough for the cars and trucks to move along at a steady, if slow, pace. I took my time walking up Cambie, checking out the wood-oven pizzerias, upscale Chinese take-outs, and clothing boutiques.

The interior of the restaurant was dark, lit mainly by flickering candle lamps, so it took me a moment to locate Sylvia. She was sitting by the window sipping an amber liquid from a tiny glass. She looked like an exotic gypsy who at any moment might pull out a deck of tarot cards and lay them across the table. I'd expected her to be wan and pale, but from where I stood she looked vibrant, almost excited. I crossed the room and wrapped my arms around her, kissing her Montrealstyle, once on each cheek, then I slipped into the chair on the other side of the table.

"I thought you weren't allowed," I said, nodding to the glass.

"What's it going to do, kill me? Actually, it's sherry. Vile drink, but it stimulates the appetite. Not as effective as a joint, but cheaper and more accessible. You look well for a woman still working in the vipers' nest, although you could use a little blush. I like the hair, though. Very nice." She reached out and lifted a lock at the side. When Sylvia had left Ottawa my dark, wavy hair had been shoulder length, but I'd recently had it cut short in a layered style that was fashionable, easy to care for, and stayed out of my eyes.

"Yours looks spectacular."

"Well, thanks sweetie. Then I'll leave it on. I think it goes well with my bone structure, don't you?" She patted her hair, looking coy, then she caught my expression. I hadn't realized it was a wig. "Get used to it, babe. If you can't take the heat get out of the kitchen. Anyway, I'm in remission, sort of. On my last CAT scan the little bugger'd stopped growing."

"Just like that?"

"Apparently they do that sometimes. Might be the radiation, but I'm also off estrogen. Which is a drag, so to speak, because I'll start to grow a beard. Won't the undertaker get a surprise."

I hated these conversations. When I had first met Sylvia, she had been David: brilliant, sensitive, and doing a Ph.D. in the macho world of physics. Over the years, as he gradually went through the process of changing sex, I was witness to the taunts, the threats, and the intolerance of our learned colleagues. It sickened me. A year ago, when she was diagnosed with a tumour embedded deep in the cerebellum, the surgeon had been blithe.

"Probably the hormones," he'd said. "Guess you shouldn't have tinkered with God's work." And he'd turned and walked out of the examining room. So, while she still had the strength for humour, I couldn't say the same.

"So what's that mean ... in the long term?"

"Who knows. Who cares. Anyway, lighten up. Order a beer. I've got lots to tell you, and we have to get through it fast before Elaine the drain gets here."

"Sylvia — "

"She's such a downer. She was better for a while — I swear she was bonking someone but she wouldn't tell me who — but now she's back to her usual obsessive-compulsive self. Boring. And around me? Too depressing. I don't need that."

I smiled. "So things haven't improved."

"I tried. Asked her out for lunch a few times. But honestly? Mutual avoidance works for me. I invited her here for you, for old times' sake, but if she slips and calls me David she's dead. Of course, being Elaine, she couldn't make it for dinner. She's much too busy. But she said she'd come for dessert."

When the waiter came over he gave his full attention to Sylvia. She was remarkably beautiful as either a man or a woman: fine boned with curly black hair, pale skin, and an eye for dramatic detail. Tonight, she was wearing a red scarf in her hair, a snow white cotton peasant shirt that almost glowed in the dim lights, and, although I hadn't checked under the table, I assumed she had on her signature tight black jeans with elegant black boots. Like any self-respecting woman she avoided panty hose unless driven to it by some social necessity. I resigned myself to being invisible for the remainder of the evening and passed on my order to her. In record time the squid salad had appeared.

"They know you here?"

She glanced at the waiter disappearing into the kitchen and smiled. "Him? He's not my type. I like a little bit more on the feminine side."

That was a change, but I wasn't sure I wanted the gory details so I busied myself with the salad. After finishing her Ph.D. in physics, Sylvia left the labs to get a second doctorate in Library Science, where the level of tolerance for sexual diversity was higher than in the sciences. She quickly became an expert in large scientific databases and is known for her ability to pluck a single molecule from a sea of information. While officially there is no such thing as a forensic librarian there should be, because Sylvia's online searches could expose scientific fraud like an x-ray reveals bone. So, while I ate the squid salad Sylvia picked at her food and talked.

"I started with three searches, comprehensive. Riesler, Edwards, and the third guy you named: Jacobson. Edwards looks clean. Only publishes in first-tier juried journals. Doesn't publish a lot, but he's consistent. No duplication. The progression of articles looks reasonable, one experiment leading logically to the next. No surprises here."

"Is he a team player?"

"Guarded team player, I'd have to say. He publishes alone, or sometimes with two or three other people, all well regarded. One is his ex-advisor in California. He doesn't go in for group gropes with a hundred names on the publication, if that's what you mean."

"Graduate students?"

"He hasn't been out that long. Probably has a couple now, but they haven't published yet."

"What about the work?"

"Hey babe, I only do titles and abstracts. Read the fine print." Then she bent down, rummaged in her briefcase, and came up with a small pile of journal articles neatly bound with an elastic band and labelled *Edwards*. "But I do pull articles. Your bedtime reading. It beats a cold shower."

I took the bundle and slipped it in my briefcase. "How would you know?"

"Ooh. Nasty. But I'll take that as a compliment." She looked like she was about to say more, then stopped, gave a small shake of her head, and got back to the topic.

"I *can* give you a snapshot, but don't sue me if some error creeps in." I nodded. "Edwards works on salmon — all these boys do — and Edwards's schtick is stock identification. He's developing some kind of technique to determine the stock of a salmon by removing a scale and zapping it with a laser. If it turns out that it works, you could tell, for instance, whether a particular salmon came from Canada, Washington, Oregon, or Alaska. Russia or Japan for that matter. Just by zapping its scale. In fact, if his recent stuff proves out, you could even go so far as to say what stream the fish hatched out in and when, which in salmon, tells you very precisely what stock it's from. I gather Fisheries needs this kind of information to monitor endangered stocks."

"But you could also use it to enforce quotas on particular stocks."

"That's an interesting interpretation." She thought for a moment, then continued. "I'd say it's too preliminary for that, but if it works ... " she let her voice trail off and leaned back in her chair.

I'd finished the squid salad, which was seriously spicy and wonderfully divine, when the waiter arrived with the noodles and curry. I ordered another beer. I motioned to Sylvia's plate with the curry spoon, but she waved it away. "You eat, I talk. We're on billable hours here."

When I was about to protest, the eating, not the billable hours, she averted her gaze, so I let it go.

"What about Riesler?"

"He was fun. Must publish twenty papers a year, and he's first author on every one. What a guy."

I smiled. Both Sylvia and I knew that a man in Madden Riesler's position spent about as much time in the lab as I did at the dentist, and I have good teeth. As the head of a large university research lab his time would be fully booked with teaching, committees, grant applications, and the endless paperwork generated by any large bureaucracy. So the science was coming from his students: a legion of post-docs and graduate students toiling away at lab benches in an almost medieval system of apprenticeship. The fact that Riesler's name appeared first on all the publications told me a lot about the man. A more enlightened supervisor would have given the privilege of first authorship to the student who designed and carried out the work. It wasn't as though Riesler needed the recognition. So he was either greedy, despotic, or insecure, none of which were particularly appealing characteristics.

"Anything else?"

"Not really, except he's a splitter." I looked confused. It was her turn to laugh. "He divides up his work into the smallest publishable increments. Say you run three experiments that all attack the same question but from slightly different angles. Normally you'd publish the results in a single paper. A splitter divides it up into three different papers. Three publications. It pads the publishing record, and publishing, as you know, is the name of the game."

"But it's acceptable?"

"Acceptable? Sure. Most people would never notice, unless they do a comprehensive search over several years. Let's just say Riesler understands the game, and he's damn good at playing it."

"So our man is ambitious."

She leaned over the table and lightly brushed my cheek with her fingers. "Ambition isn't a crime, Morgan. Some of my best friends are ambitious."

I knew what she was saying, and I didn't like it.

"But it's another piece of the puzzle. What else?"

She leaned back in her chair, examined me for a moment, then signalled to the waiter, who brought over another sherry. I could see a flush working its way up her cheeks. She took a sip then continued, in no hurry.

"He works on salmon migration and stock identification."

I perked up. "The same area as Edwards."

"Yes ..." There was a noticeable pause. "And no." I stopped in midbite and looked up. There was a glint of mischief in her eyes. She'd found something. "Same goal, to identify stocks, but totally different technique. Riesler pioneered the use of genetic fingerprints for stock identification. The theory is that all fish from a stock will share certain genetic characteristics. In other words, if you look at their DNA then you'll be able to tell what stock they're from. Sort of like the DNA fingerprinting they do in criminal cases. It's turgid stuff, lots of blurry photos of DNA sequence data and endless descriptions of procedures and protocols. More your ballpark than mine ..."

At this point Sylvia bent down and extracted another bundle of papers from her briefcase, this one at least four inches thick. On top were the search results, listing all of Riesler's publications for the past twenty years. That alone was a tome. Underneath were journal articles. She handed the sheaf to me.

"... and they're all yours. Thank you for using Canada's National Science Library. By the way, I've just given you the review papers. Drop by tomorrow and I'll pull whatever else you want. We can do lunch."

I nodded to the pile. "So what's your take on this?"

"On the surface, and that's all I can give you, it looks to me like you got two guys in direct competition, and if these are commercially viable projects — if we're talking patents and technology transfer — it's more than just academic. You could be talking big money. Oh, you also asked about Jacobson." I nodded. "They're all in there." She motioned to Riesler's pile. "Must be Riesler's Man Friday ... or whatever. Everything he's ever published is as second author to Riesler. The boy's obviously got no life of his own."

I packed Riesler's stack of papers in my briefcase. That at least gave me somewhere to start. Sylvia and I chatted about her new life in Vancouver until the waiter came to clear the plates, then I checked my watch. Two beers, a jog, and a three-hour time change — I wasn't going to last much longer. I also had one more item on my agenda that I couldn't discuss in front of Elaine. I held off until the waiter was out of earshot, then I leaned forward.

"I have a favour to ask. A big one."

"And you need my permission? Since when?"

"Can you trace a reference search?"

There was a pause. "What do you mean?"

"If I know the date and time that a remote search took place, and the number of minutes it took, could you tell me whose account it was charged to?"

"Legally or technically?"

"Technically."

"I was afraid that's what you meant." She paused for a minute, analyzing the problem, then continued. "It could be done. I'd have to hack my way into the financial system, and that would be break and enter or trespass, as if you care."

"But it is possible."

"No guarantees, but I think so. I assume this isn't a formal request."

"It's an informal request between two very good friends who always help each other out."

"Ah. The very good friends angle. If I get caught you support me to the end of my natural life. You can't pop me off because I become inconvenient."

Since the prognosis on Sylvia's life could be calculated in months I thought it was a deal I could live with. I gave her the information from the header, which she scribbled in a notebook.

"But if you can't pick it up fast, get the hell out. I've got some other avenues I can try."

She looked up from beneath her lashes and smiled wickedly. "I'm not worried. It's challenge that keeps me young. But I still have to account for the time."

Since there had been no cover sheet, and hence no charge-code, in the Network file, I had given her Bob's personal charge-code to cover the time for the searches. I smiled. "Just bill it to the code I gave you. Triple time and a half if you have to."

Just then the waiter approached the table.

"Is there a Morgan O'Brien at this table?"

I looked up at him. "That would be me."

"You have a call. You can take it at the cashier."

Sylvia shook her head and muttered, "Figures."

I picked up the phone. "Hi, Elaine." I heard a sharp intake of breath on the other end. Guilt is such an overpowering emotion. "Give it a break. Nobody else knew I was here, so it had to be you."

She let out her breath slowly. "Sorry, Mo ..." She was the only person in the world, other than my mother, who ever got to call me that, "... but I can't make it. I'm still waiting for Cindy — she's my graduate student

— and she's supposed to be bringing in live fish from Weaver Creek that should have been here an hour ago. I don't know where the hell she's got to, but if she doesn't turn up soon screw her, she can unpack them on her own. Could we meet tomorrow morning instead?"

"You name the time. I'll take you out for breakfast."

We arranged to meet at eight in a café just outside the university gates. I can't say I was upset. Watching two of my closest friends go at each other wasn't my idea of a relaxing way to end the evening. As I sat back down in my chair Sylvia raised her eyebrows in a question. I nodded.

"Asshole." I winced. She looked up at me sharply. "I can't help it if it still hurts." I reached across the table and took her hand. She didn't pull away, but turned to look out the window so I couldn't see her face. I felt a flash of anger at Elaine so intense it hurt. Why couldn't she just accept Sylvia for who and what she was?

By unspoken agreement we made light conversation over a *crème brûlée* and finished up the evening early. Sylvia looked tired, and it was one in the morning for me. When I got back to the hotel I fell into bed and was asleep in minutes.

The phone rang at 5:00 A.M. I was on Albion Street and I had my mother by the scruff of her soiled nightgown, yelling at her, shaking her and yelling, angry at something she'd said or done or maybe not done. It didn't seem to matter. She flopped about like a rag doll, and it slowly entered my head that she was a rag doll, and I shook harder, watching with detachment as the head flopped from side to side. Then I heard the phone ringing far away. I held onto my mother with one hand and with the other groped behind me, slowly changing dimensions from the dreamworld to a high-rise hotel on 12th and Cambie.

"I thought you'd be up by now." It was Duncan. He was sounding pert and jolly, designed, no doubt, to annoy me. When I didn't answer, he continued. "She wasn't amused."

"It's five in the morning."

"No, it's not. It's eight. Anyway, I've got meetings booked all day and I wanted to get back to you on the Patsy thing."

I pushed myself up to a sitting position and cleared my throat. "Shoot." It sounded more like a croak than human language.

"She went all wooden and stared at me, didn't say a thing for a minute, then said something warm and caring like 'Good luck in your new position. Now you'll have to excuse me.' Then she reached for the phone and glared at me until I was out of the office. A real people person."

I was slowly resurfacing. "That's it?"

"Not quite." I waited. Duncan was going to play this for all it was worth. "Well, of course I wanted to say goodbye to Lydia, who, by the way, wasn't at her desk. So I waited a few minutes to see if she'd come back — "

"Out of Patsy's line of vision."

"Possibly. Anyway, I did happen to overhear Patsy asking for Bob. Lucky for him he wasn't there, because she wasn't very nice. Michelle was told to find him and get him up to the fifth ASAP."

Good old Bob. Never in the right place at the right time. So Patsy knew I had the file by the end of yesterday's workday, making her the most likely candidate for Bob's office visitor when I called later that evening. My head had finally cleared enough for me to remember what I'd wanted to ask Duncan. I scrabbled for my briefcase, which was lying on the other bed.

"Duncan, can you do something else for me?" He didn't reply, so I assumed he was calculating the extra hours he could tag on to his babysitting bill. I found the Network file and pulled out the remote reference search. "Could you find out who was in the building last year on October thirteenth between one-thirty and two in the afternoon?"

"You mean you want me to say goodbye to the commissionaire as well?"

"It would be a nice gesture."

It was a bit of long shot, but sometimes long shots paid off. The NCST building is locked on the weekend. If someone had done that search from their office computer they would have to stop off at the commissionaires' kiosk and sign out a key to get into the building. I was pretty sure that the commissionaires' office would keep those records for several years back.

When I had hung up the phone I briefly considered pulling the covers up over my head and refusing to face the day, but instead I braced myself, rolled out of bed, and headed for the shower. I had lots of reading to do and I needed to get my alias in order. Bottom line, Elaine could be the key to this whole damn thing, and if I was going to get her onside I needed to be prepared and have all my wits about me.

chapter six

At 6:30 A.M. I packed up my briefcase and checked the inside pockets of my leather jacket. I had had the lining especially tailored to suit my job, and right now the hidden pockets held an evidence kit, a small flashlight, a set of lock picks, and a pepper spray, none of it exactly government issue. Between a light breakfast and heading out the door I had managed to scan Riesler's latest review article on the state of genetic techniques for stock identification. It was impressive stuff, beautifully written and logically tight, and it gave me enough of the terminology to fake my way through a conversation if I was forced into an unexpected situation. After all, I was now Dr. Morgan O'Brien, a visiting post-doc from the Canadian Genomics Institute in Ottawa. I should at least know the lexicon.

Southern BCU sits on one of the most expensive pieces of real estate in North America: the tip of Point Grey. It made driving into the university a bit like entering the magic kingdom. Water surrounded the campus on the north, south, and west, and a wide belt of parkland — old-growth forest of cedar and Douglas fir — buffered it from the city on the east. Because of the parkland and the access to beaches and water, there wasn't a house on the point that would sell for less than $400,000.

As I moved west on 12th Avenue the houses went from the palatial estates of Shaughnessy to the funky, brightly painted wooden houses of Kitsilano, back to the upscale abodes of the Point. The peninsula narrowed, 12th Avenue fed into 10th, and I knew that if I went straight up the hill it would lead me to the main gates of Southern, but as I approached Alma Street I slowed. I could continue straight ahead or I could turn right, head down toward Spanish Banks, and take the beach road in through the back entrance. I felt my stomach contract. I would have to go down there sometime. It might as well be now.

I took a right, then a left further down at 4th Avenue. Ahead of me a steep hill rose up to the plateau of Point Grey, but just before it I turned on to a small road that dipped off to the right, almost hidden in an ancient stand of cedar. The road wove downward in a dark tunnel, then abruptly the trees thinned, the terrain flattened out, and the road made a ninety-degree turn. The dark tunnel burst open to reveal a wide ribbon of sand, a vast expanse of black water, and the fairy lights of North Vancouver sprinkled across the distant backdrop of mountains. I slowed the car. Despite the breathtaking beauty of the shore, I focused my attention on the other side of the road, the compact neighbourhood that climbed up the bluff. I'd forgotten how it looked: glass-fronted box houses that seemed to be piled willy-nilly, one on top of the other. No style and no taste, but million-dollar views and two-million-dollar price tags. I used to live along here.

I slowed as I approached our house and pulled into the parking lane. I left the engine running with the heater warming the car and stared. It was still the perfect house — a landscaped garden fronting a wall of glass that overlooked the mountains and English Bay. Once upon a time the perfect family had lived there: Daddy the doctor, Mommy the hostess, and the two beautiful, well-behaved children. Unfortunately, Daddy worked terribly hard and was hardly ever home, but that was just like all the other neighbourhood dads. And Mommy drank a bit too much, but then entertaining for Daddy was her *raison d'être* and she was just a social drinker. But as the two well-behaved children grew, the drinking went from social to solo, then became a full-time occupation, and the Daddy's absences became more and more prolonged, until one day he simply never came home. Then the money dried up, the perfect house was marred by flaking paint and an overgrown lawn, and the well-behaved children were no longer so welcome at the other neighbourhood homes.

I hadn't been down here since I was eleven. That's when my mother came out of her alcoholic daze long enough to realize that my father *wasn't* coming home. She sold the house for a fraction of its value and moved us to a rented house on Albion Street in the derelict, tough east end, and with the remaining money from the sale of the house she began the slow, painful process of committing suicide with drink.

I looked at the old house now, standing firm and solid despite our neglect, and tried to remember. I did know happiness in that house. I *must* have known happiness there in those early years, but all memories of that time seemed to have vanished in the turmoil of events that followed. Even confronted with the tangible evidence of an earlier era, that part of my past remained firmly locked away.

I turned and looked across the bay to the North Shore. Grey mist hung in the air, and the soft smudge of dawn was just appearing behind the mountains. The pale light draped the landscape, reducing all colour, all contour, to a monochromatic scale of greys. I took one last glance at the house, felt nothing, then put the car in gear and headed toward Southern.

Five minutes later I drove into the back of C-lot, the vast student parking area cut out of several acres of virgin old-growth forest. At this time of the morning it was almost empty, but I pitied the poor students who had to park in the outer reaches. It would be a forty-five minute walk to the nearest building.

I made for the first row of cars and spotted a tight space between a vintage red Mustang and a new blue Miata. I pulled in with room to spare. I still had some time before my meeting with Elaine so I got out my Southern map and tried to orient myself. From the car, dead ahead, was a covered parkade. If I followed the street that ran just to the left of the parkade, that should take me to the Life Sciences complex with its Zoology wing.

I zipped the map back into my briefcase and locked up the little beater. As I crossed in front of the row of cars I smiled. In addition to the Mustang, there was a neon-yellow Rabbit in perfect condition, and further down the line an old two-door Acadian that looked new. I'm a bit of a car nut, and coastal B.C. is the only place in Canada where you can see mint-condition older cars parked casually along the streets. Everywhere else in Canada they have long been devoured by road salt and slush.

Life Sciences was easy to find. It looked like a huge concrete bunker sitting at the corner of the biggest intersection on campus. Instead of going to the front I fol-

lowed the service road around behind, where, according
to my map, I would find a separate entrance for the
Zoology wing.

The doors were unlocked, but the lights inside were
still off, the corridor dark. Some light filtered in through
the windows that ran up the stairwells at either end of
the hall, but it wasn't enough to read by. I unzipped my
jacket and pulled out the flashlight. Since Zoology rated
a separate department I reasoned that it should have a
separate office, which in turn should have a listing of the
professors' office numbers posted somewhere nearby. I
wasn't disappointed. Halfway down the hall there was
an expanse of plate glass. Through it, I could see a high
counter that ran the length of a large room, blocking off
an open office in behind. At this hour the whole area
was black, but by 9:00 A.M. it would be as active as an
overstocked aquarium.

On a bulletin board next to the door I found what
I wanted: a listing of the profs with office and lab numbers. Edwards wasn't on it, which I thought was bizarre,
but I found Riesler's office and lab number and scribbled it in my notebook. I did the same for Jacobson,
then slipped the notebook back into my pocket. Riesler
had a lab and an office on the top floor, as well as a lab
in the basement. I didn't have time to see everything, so
I decided to check out his office and lab upstairs. The
rest could wait for later.

On the fourth floor there was just enough light for
me to read the numbers and names on the doors. I
walked slowly, listening for any activity, but the corridor
and surrounding labs were silent. Riesler's lab was near
the end of the hall. I was expecting a huge space jammed
with benches and equipment, but when I peered in the
narrow window I saw a small room, no more than three
metres by four metres. Windows ran along the outside

wall, with a lab bench tucked in beneath them. Another bench bisected the room. Both were covered with micropipettes, tiny Eppendorf vials, Nalgene squirt bottles half-filled with liquid. There was a fume hood in the corner, and I could see the dark brown bottles of reagents and stock chemicals crowded in behind.

In addition to the small pieces of equipment, there were two chest freezers, what looked like a heating or drying oven, and a small table-top centrifuge. In other words, the place had the look of barely contained chaos typical of most labs. I noticed a door in the left back corner of the room and, like a light switching on, the size of the room suddenly made sense. This must be a tiny private lab attached to Riesler's office. The bulk of his research, or should I say his students' research, would be done in the basement lab. I tried the doorknob. Too bad. Locked. I looked both ways to make sure nobody was coming, then I knelt down to examine the lock. It was a shame, really. When I had the time the door would be frightfully easy to open.

From there I headed for the stairs, but just before them I noticed a small corridor off to the right. Another entrance to Riesler's office? I shone my flashlight down the hall, and sure enough, there was a door with a brass plate on it: Dr. Madden Riesler, Assistant Dean of Science. Bloody hell. Assistant Dean? Why hadn't that been in the file? Since the halls were so quiet, and I was in the neighbourhood, I thought I might as well give his office door a try as well. Not surprisingly, it was locked, but I was happy to see that the mechanism was no different from the one on the lab door. Really, the university should do something about that. I'd have to mention it in my report.

On my way down the stairs I decided to do a quick scan of the floors below, just to see if I could find either

Edwards's office or Elaine's. I crossed the third floor quickly. No Edwards and no Elaine, although there were several doors without nameplates.

I was halfway across the second floor when I saw a large poster on salmon migration next to one of the lab doors. I had just started to read it — looking for a few quick tips — when I heard a door open down near the end of the hall. It was a cautious sound, so furtive that I instinctively switched off my flashlight and moved into the shadow of a door well. Across from me, near the end of the hall, a door slowly opened, exposing a wedge of black interior. For a minute there was nothing, as if maybe the door had opened on its own, then a young man, as graceful as a cat, stepped out. He was wearing a lab coat and latex gloves. He glanced up and down the hall. I held my breath. Satisfied, he pulled the door shut behind him, bracing it from the outside so it made no noise. Then in one fluid movement he was through the doors and had disappeared down the stairs.

When I was sure he'd gone, I stepped out of the shadows and strolled to the door. There was a number but no name.

What, I wondered, was that all about?

chapter seven

I was ten minutes late for my meeting with Elaine. The café was up the main boulevard in a little strip mall. I pushed open the door and was hit by the yeasty aroma of warm croissants and steaming bowls of *café au lait*, the essence of Vancouver. Elaine was sitting at a corner table facing the door, absorbed in what looked like a reprint from some lofty biology journal. I moved forward a step and let the door swing shut behind me.

Her hair had changed since I'd last seen her. It had always been long and thick, held back in a simple braid. Now it was cut short in a fashionable straight-edged bob that fell like a curtain across her profile. I had expected an upgrade in clothing with her new position in the academic rat race, but she was dressed no differently from the way she had dressed on the field trips of our youth: a hand-knit Icelandic sweater, button-down cotton shirt, jeans, and sensible shoes. In fact, her clothes were almost the same as mine, but I was simulating a visiting post-doctoral fellow. She was now Dr. Okada, Assistant Professor.

I shook my head, halfway between amusement and disgust. Elaine willfully chose the hardest possible route to get from point A to B, as if even a touch of compromise might sully those pure ideals that drove her in her work. Well, I had bad news from the other side; those pure ideals — like the pursuit of truth, objective and free of ego — were as dead in science as they were in government. It's a career like any other, and if you want the career you better play by the rules.

I felt the door open behind me, forcing me forward, so I crossed to the table and slid into the chair facing her. She looked up from her paper as if being drawn back from another world. A smile spread across her face, and she leaned over, cupped my chin in both her hands, and looked into my eyes. I reached up, closed my eyes, and pressed her hands to my face. I felt a surge of energy flow through them that coursed through my body like a living current.

Ten years ago we both would have been uncomfortable with such strong emotion, but somewhere along the line we seemed to have come to terms with a relationship that ebbed and flowed with the power of the tide. One moment I could be overwhelmed with love for her, and the next totally enraged by her pig-headed, simplistic view of the world. We had actually talked at one time of having an affair, just to see if all this emotion was really about sex. In the end we'd decided not to. It would probably have ended in a death by shotgun at close range, the only question being who would be at which end of the gun.

The waiter approached the table uncertainly. I gently placed Elaine's hands back on the table and turned to him. I loved Elaine, but I needed coffee and food. When he had disappeared, I turned back to examine her closely. She had fine lines around her eyes and tension in the muscles around her mouth. She looked tired and depressed, not what I expected from a woman entering the second year of her dream job.

"What's up?"

"End of field season exhaustion." She smiled slightly. "Remember that?"

I did, only too well. Which is one of the reasons I left. But Elaine had lived through field seasons before.

"There's something else."

She frowned. "I left before Cindy got back last night. When I got in this morning the fish weren't there, and Cindy had left me an e-mail to say that her mother's in the hospital and she's gone home to New Zealand ... *indefinitely*." Then she looked up and glared at me as if I were in some way responsible. "What the hell does that mean, indefinitely! It's two weeks before the end of the sockeye run, for Christ's sake!"

Like all new professors, Elaine was on a short-term contract, and job competition was brutal. If you didn't cut it, and cut it fast, you were out. For someone in her position, losing a graduate student — and a source of publications for the lab — could mean no contract renewal and no prospects of another job. Still, I didn't want to get dragged into her hysteria.

I shrugged. "Maybe she'll be back by the end of the week."

Her voice was fierce. "When we were students, we would have let our mothers die alone rather than lose a field season."

I looked down at the table, giving her time to absorb her own words, then said quietly, "Unfortunately, I didn't have that choice to make." She cringed. Good. "And where the hell did all that devotion get you? Your first real job at the age of thirty-four."

She didn't bother to reply; just skewered me with her eyes and picked up her coffee. Fortunately the waiter arrived with my order, giving us both a break. I'd only been with her for five minutes and she'd already ticked me off. It was an old argument that always came down to the same thing: Elaine's limited and simplistic view of life. It went like this: if you were brilliant (which she was), worked hard (which she did), and relentlessly pushed back the frontiers of knowledge (which she also did), then you would rise to the top. That meant you would get tenure, become a full professor, and be a respected and sought-after member of the research establishment. The notion that her progress might be hindered by some of life's little *isms* — in this case to do with sex and race — was heresy against the party line that defines science as objective, impartial, and bias-free. While Elaine might be silly enough to still believe that crap, I was no longer so naive.

I took a sip of coffee and debated launching into a tirade on science and corruption, then caught myself. I needed Elaine's cooperation — both her insider information and her astute assessment of people — to get to the bottom of this case as quickly as possible. And Elaine is as stubborn as they come. If I got her in a snit it could take days to effect a thaw. I decided I'd better be helpful.

"Can someone else run the experiments?"

"I'm tied up in classes and committee meetings for the next three days. There's Dinah, my technician, but I'm not sure how much she knows."

"I could help out for a day or so." She gave me a curt nod, still annoyed. "Come on, Elaine, I haven't lost my touch."

That got a slight smile. Not exactly a vote of confidence, I thought wryly, but there was at least a shade of relief on her face.

"I appreciate that." She saw my skeptical look and warmed a bit. "No, I do, really. It just seems like the worst possible timing. I'm so damn close to writing up."

I figured this was a good time to work my way over to my own agenda. "I gather you're not still working on toads."

She shook her head. "Salmon. The ultimate in olfaction."

I kept my voice low and conversational. I didn't want to tip her off to anything until I was ready. "That's a big change."

Her eyes lit up. "Not really. I'm still doing basically the same thing, trying to understand how the olfactory system works, but because it's salmon, and the olfactory system plays a role in their homing migration ... well, let's just say funding isn't a problem."

She picked up her coffee and sipped it, looking almost smug.

"So," I said, "you must know Madden Riesler."

I was watching her reaction, but carefully so she wouldn't notice. At the sound of the name she literally beamed. She opened her mouth to say something then caught me observing. Damn. She pulled back like a startled snake. I tried to divert.

"I hear he's brilliant."

Now she was observing me and her defences were up. She continued warily. "He's why I'm here."

Before I could catch myself I blurted out, "But you're not involved in the Network."

At that she sat bolt upright, all her senses attuned. I could almost see her swaying back and forth, trying to determine the nature of the threat. She knew something was up, she just didn't know what.

She spoke carefully. "I met Madden at my last post-doc in California. He was doing a sabbatical there. I liked him, he liked my work. When this position came up he recommended me, and that's what got me the interview. End of story."

Damn. That complicated Elaine's impartiality, not that she'd ever admit it. Since I was already in so deep, I figured I might as well continue.

"So I guess you know Jonathan Edwards as well?"

Her eyes narrowed. "I know Jonathan."

"I thought he was in your department?"

She paused before answering, keeping her eyes locked on mine. "He moved." Then she picked up her coffee bowl and took a sip, but didn't release her gaze.

It was becoming increasingly difficult to sound nonchalant. "Was there a problem?"

"The problem was — " then she paused, and struck. "You're a shit." She banged her coffee down on the table. The bowl arrived several seconds before the contents and splash-down was not a success. Most of the liquid ended up on the table or on her reprint, but Elaine didn't seem to care. "You're investigating Madden, aren't you?"

"I'm investigating the Network, not Riesler or Edwards *per se*."

"Because of Jonathan, that leech." I didn't answer. Her voice was deadly and low. "Did you plan to tell me? Or were you just going to pump me for information?"

I shifted uncomfortably. "Of course I was going to tell you."

"Just not yet."

I sort of shrugged and nodded. Let's face it. I'd been caught in the act. It was definitely a tactical error not coming clean with Elaine right off the bat, so I let a few seconds pass. "Okay, I'm sorry. But I wanted your untainted opinion first."

"You know my opinion. The government has no business interfering with research."

"You can have the research. I'm interested in the money."

A look of disgust crossed her face. "Money? That's all you people care about is money."

"You'd care too if someone was spending *your* research grant on vacations in Hawaii."

"Madden wouldn't do that."

"Which is why I'm investigating the Network: all of it. Anyone who might have access to the funds. And the more you help me, the faster I'm out of here."

I sipped my coffee and let her work that one out. I could see the neurons firing. Finally she said, "If you're interested in Network money, then you better talk to JJ."

"JJ? Is that Jacobson?"

She nodded. "Madden's lab manager. He oversees the research program. That includes all the Network finances." Then she grimaced. "He's a jerk, but apparently he does a good job."

"Isn't it always the way," I said, shaking my head. Finally, thank God, she loosened up a bit and smiled. I do hate arguing with Elaine, so I reached out and put my hand on hers. "Truce? I'll pay for breakfast."

I could see her soften. "Oh yeah, sure. On your expense account."

The humour was dry, but at this point any humour was a positive sign. Elaine looked at her watch. "Christ. I've got a nine-thirty to prepare for." She grabbed her coat. "Four hundred hormone-pumped first-year biology students packed like sardines into a tiny lecture hall. Imagine. Actually, don't even try."

I left money on the table and hurried out behind her. It was just after nine o'clock, and the day was typical Vancouver. Moist and overcast. Gentle and warm. A world of intense green foliage against layers of soft blues and grey. I looked at the sky. By midmorning the mist would be burned off by a brilliant autumn sun.

I had to trot to keep up with Elaine. "You know your missing graduate student?"

"Cindy?"

I nodded. "Could I use her office while she's gone? I need a base of operations, preferably in the department."

Elaine gave a dramatic sigh. "Will it get you out of here sooner?"

I nodded again. "And by the way, I'm *Dr.* Morgan O'Brien now, a visiting post-doc from Ottawa." I held out my hand. "How do you do."

She didn't take it, just threw me a withering look. Impersonating a Ph.D. was really over the edge.

Elaine, like me, takes all stairs two at a time. On the second floor she pushed through the fire doors. I was right behind her. She stopped in front of an unmarked door and pulled out a set of keys. I could hear her fumbling through them. I leaned against the wall and waited. I heard the door unlatch, and I pushed myself off the wall. Elaine started forward, then stopped abruptly. She was standing absolutely still.

My voice was conversational. "Aren't you going in?"

I'm not even sure she heard me. When she finally turned around her face was clouded and uneasy. Then she seemed to focus, see me, and like a blind being snapped shut, the expression returned to normal.

"Sorry. I'll get you those keys."

Then she turned and walked into her office.

The same office that I had seen the early-morning intruder leave less than two hours ago.

chapter eight

As Elaine moved into her office, I followed, curious to see what I would find. From her reaction I knew she'd noticed something, but not something she felt compelled to share. That meant she was assuming I wouldn't see it.

It was a small office, with bookshelves lining one wall, filing cabinets along another, a desk on the back wall, and a work table just inside the door. Nothing seemed out of place. The surface of the work table was covered with neat stacks of files, journals, and papers to mark, and the desk top was clear. I glanced at the desk chair, hoping to see a report or book with a friendly little *thank you* post-it note attached, but the seat was empty. I wandered over to the bookshelf and made like I was examining her books, always a popular pastime with academics, and immediately noticed the bottom shelves, a section devoted to old files and theses.

Elaine is a registered neatnik, with books and papers precisely arranged, pens consolidated in a single holder, everything in its place. Dust and dirt, however, don't faze her, and I'd seen plants and grungy coffee cups neglected for years on end. Given the healthy layer of dust on the shelf, these papers hadn't been disturbed, at least not by Elaine, for several months. Someone, however, had been looking at them, and had tried to conceal it. I knelt down to get a better look. A coffee cup, which even the mould had died in, had been moved off the edge of the shelf then carefully replaced, but not carefully enough. A hairline displacement was evident in the dust. Also, papers in some of the files had been pulled out of alignment, something Elaine would have tidied up before she replaced the file. Why would anyone be interested in old files and theses?

I heard the metallic jingle of keys behind me and stood up. "Cleaning staff come in here much, Elaine?"

She slid the filing drawer closed and shook her head. "Cutbacks. They empty the garbage, that's all." She crossed the room to me. "Here." She dropped the keys in my hand, then took my elbow in a firm grip and propelled me toward the door. "It's 105 in the basement. The offices are on the right, behind the chamber. Cindy's is in the back, Dinah's is the one in front. They both should be open. Log in on the lab account if you need network access. Dinah can help you. Oh, and if you see her down there tell her to wait. We need to touch base before class. Still on for dinner?" I nodded. By this time we'd reached the threshold, and she gave me a solid nudge that sent me into the hall. She wanted me out of the office. "Good," she said. She had the edge of the door in her hand and was closing it as she spoke. "Call me here. Not before eight."

I managed to twist around and get my foot wedged in the door just before she slammed it. All I could see was a narrow strip of her face through the slit in the door. Her eye glared at me.

"O'Brien!"

"What's your problem? I haven't finished."

She made no move to open the door. "I told you, I'm in a hurry."

"Then I suggest you open the door, because I've got all day." She opened it a bit, at least releasing the pressure on my shoe, but I knew enough to keep my foot firmly in place. Now I could see most of her face. "I cut through here this morning and saw a guy who looked familiar, but I can't place him." I gave her a rough description of the man who'd been in her office. "Ring a bell?"

"It sounds like Graham Connell, Madden's student. I'm sure you'll meet him later. Is that all?"

"Where would I find him?"

"Christ, Morgan. The fish museum, okay? Near my lab. But don't tell him I told you. Anything else?"

I took my time answering, as if pondering the question. "I think that's it." Then I smiled and said, "Have a nice day," and pulled out my foot. She slammed the door in my face.

Elaine and *abrupt* are synonymous terms, so for her this kind of behaviour was normal, just more dramatic than usual. I wondered if she actually knew someone had been in her office or she just suspected. It was an intriguing question, but not one I would know the answer to until she was good and ready to talk. In the meantime I'd do a little investigating on my own.

Going down the stairs I focused my thoughts on the real investigation, and what I had learned from Elaine. So far, I knew she liked Riesler, hated Edwards, and had implied that Jacobson might be involved. Edwards was associated with some sort of scandal but she wasn't going to tell me what, Jacobson was a jerk, and a person — maybe Riesler's graduate student — had broken into her office. Nice department, but it got me no further ahead than I had been when I left Ottawa yesterday afternoon. Things were not going as planned.

As I neared the basement I could feel moist, cold air seeping up the stairwell to forewarn me of the wet labs below: damp rooms crowded with tanks that teemed with aquatic life, everything from sturgeon to sea slugs. By the bottom landing the odour of mildew and rotting fish had mixed with the clammy air, and when I swung open the vestibule doors I got it full force, along with the sound of cascading water.

In another place — the northern rainforest or the Canadian shield — the sound would have been reassuring, even sublime, a perfect complement to the smell of moss and pine; here in the stark light of the basement corridors it was ominous and unfriendly.

I walked slowly down the hall, reading the names of professors posted beside lab doors. In the labs I caught glimpses of white-coated people moving between the tanks. When I saw Riesler's name I slowed and glanced through the door. His lab was double the size of the others and alive with students and helpers. The central area housed tanks, but I could see offices along the back and a large glassed-in area to the left. It looked like a fully equipped high-end genetics lab. I moved on before I was noticed.

By the end of the hall I still hadn't found Elaine's lab, but I had found a door labelled Fish Museum. Someone was moving around inside. The door was ajar, so I pushed it open. It was like walking into the Coliseum when you're the entertainment. A thousand malevolent eyes stared down from the shelves: preserved fish packed so tightly in jars that they strained against the glass. The place reeked, a combination of formaldehyde, lab alcohol, and fish. I decided against tuna for lunch.

The guy in the lab coat hadn't heard my entrance. He had his back to me and was moving down a counter lined with dissecting trays. I stood quietly and watched. Jeans, high-top sneakers, about the right size and colouring. Under his arm he held a large, wide-mouth bottle: one of those mega-jars that holds bulk ketchup and mayonnaise for the restaurant trade. But instead of mayo, this jar was half filled with an aquatic version of E.T., a hideous little fish with bulging eyes, a misshapen head, and limb-like fins. The specimens were suspended in a greasy yellow liquid. The technician stopped, wiped his nose on his sleeve, then continued, dipping his gloved hand into the jar, pulling out a fish, and flopping it into a dissecting tray. As I watched his hand disappear into the liquid and pull out another fish, I decided against lunch altogether.

"What is it?" I said pointing to the bottle.

He swung around, surprised. I smiled. My mystery intruder. At first glance he was handsome, with blonde hair and luminous blue eyes framed by long, dark lashes, but he was older than I had thought, definitely not an undergraduate, and the first impression of him being handsome was due solely to his eyes. His face was, in fact, sharp and angular, giving him a hungry look verging on cunning. He made no attempt to hide his scrutiny of me. When he was satisfied with the examination, he pulled another fish from the jar, this one about forty centimetres long, and held it up by the tail. "A chimaera. Also known as a ratfish. Pretty wild, eh?"

I grimaced. "I wouldn't want to see one staring up from my dinner plate, that's for sure." I looked him in the eye. "I'm looking for Dr. Okada's lab. Is it around here?"

I saw a spark of interest in his eye. "Sure. See that little hall?" He waved the poor pickled chimaera in a vague over-to-the-left direction. I looked out the door. At the end of the hall there was a little corridor almost hidden by the wall. I nodded. "Down at the end. It's sort of out of the way. You a new graduate student?" He threw the fish into an empty dissecting tray, but kept his eyes on me.

"Visiting post-doc. Just checking out the possibilities."

"Really." For some reason he wasn't thrilled with the answer, but he put down his jar of fish and moved toward me. "Graham Connell. I'm a Ph.D. student with Dr. Riesler. I'm also the curator of this." He swept his hand around the room and gave me a charming, lopsided, little-boy grin. "It pays the bills."

Then he held out his hand, the same one that had been in the jar. I felt a cool, oily liquid on my palm.

"Morgan O'Brien, from the Canadian Genomics Institute. I've been working on *E. coli*, but I'm interested in moving over to fish, something a little more applied."

When he released my hand I had to resist the urge to smell it or wipe it on my pants. I was sure I detected a smirk around his eyes, but his face remained serious and his tone was friendly. He must have decided that I'd be more useful as a friend than an enemy.

He produced another charm-the-pants-off-women smile. "Well, if you need a tour guide I'd be happy to oblige."

I smiled back. Two could play at this game, and I had the advantage. I knew we were playing a game. "Really? Gosh. I'd love to find out more about Dr. Riesler's lab. I've read some of his papers and they're very impressive." Then, just to make sure I didn't threaten him, I said, "Of course, it's not quite my area of interest, but it's fascinating stuff. How about this. You take me for a tour, I'll take you for a beer."

"You're on. I'm teaching a lab this morning, but I'm free after. How about twelve-thirty?"

"Great. We'll have ..." I tried to sound enthusiastic, "... lunch."

"And you can tell me all about your research."

"Love to." Then I lowered my voice and leaned forward. "And I'd value your honest opinion on the department. I mean, not just the propaganda. You know ... problems, tensions, egos ... I'd kind of like to know before I ..." I let my voice trail off and shrugged.

He laughed. "You want to know it now, not later."

"Right. Like after I've committed myself. And it's hard to get that kind of information."

He pulled his lips back in something between a smile and a sneer. "I think I may be able to help out. If I'm not out here," he jerked his head toward a door in the back corner of the museum, "check my office."

"Perfect," I said, and meant it. With that, I turned and started down the hall.

I could feel him move to the doorway behind me. "There is one thing ..." he said. I stopped and turned. He was leaning against the door frame watching me. "You better learn to identify a chimaera before you switch to fish."

It wasn't until I was out of sight down the dead-end corridor that I heard the door to the museum close.

Elaine's name was embossed on a metal plate just to the side of her lab door. That must give her a thrill, I thought, after all those years of graduate school and post docs. I tried the door, but it was locked. I banged on it, but there was no answer, so I let myself in with the keys Elaine had given me. Inside the lights were on.

"Dinah? Hello?" Still no answer.

The lab was a big open space, but so crowded with equipment that it looked like a rummage sale for used aquarium supplies. In the middle there were four huge tanks, the size of above-ground pools, swirling with water. To the left there was a glassed-in room with a large apparatus sitting in the middle. It had a dissecting microscope mounted on a mobile arm at one end, a delicate measuring device at the other end, and a bank of electronic equipment attached, including a computer and several oscilloscopes. Elaine's single-cell recording equipment, probably.

The environmental chamber sat like a parked airstream trailer near the wall to my right. As an undergraduate I'd worked in one of those chambers over a frigid Winnipeg winter. We'd been raising jumping wabeens, a bizarre little unisex fish from the Florida everglades, so the temperature and humidity were set to tropical. The light inside was a soft blue, filtered through the water and glass. I would spend my days wrapped in the silent warmth of the chamber, cleaning aquariums, hovering over sick fish, preparing and doling out brine shrimp. Then every afternoon I would exit to the brilliant white of the prairie at twenty below. It made me wonder why people live in Canada.

Elaine had said that the offices were behind the chamber, and that took me by the big tanks. The first two were empty, just swirling water. I moved to the tanks behind, curious to see what might be in them. The one to my left was empty, but on my right, a dark, motionless form sat at the bottom of the tank. With the frothing water it was hard to make out what it was, and I leaned over. It looked like a seal. Without warning, the thing turned and shot straight up at me. I leapt back. There was a flash of scarlet, and something large broke the surface where my face had been, spraying water. Then the form split in two, half going around one side, half going around the other, to reconverge again at the bottom of the tank. I clutched my chest. What had looked like a single body was in fact an undulating school of large sockeye salmon, maybe ten to fifteen housed in the vat. I let out my breath and dropped my hand. Really. For a bunch of fish. I *had* been in Ottawa too long.

Just then, the door of the chamber opened and a man, with his back to me, lifted two buckets of gravel and started to walk out, holding the door open with his hip. I cleared my throat, but the noise of the water covered it.

I tried again. "Hello."

The person at the door looked back, still holding the buckets, and registered my surprise. What's more, she knew exactly why. She turned slowly and, looking mildly amused, said, "Can I help you?"

I scrambled to reorganize my response. The woman was an Amazon. I'm not wimpy. At five-eight and with years of karate behind me I have exceptional physical strength for a woman, but those buckets of gravel must have weighed sixty pounds each. I could lift one, but I certainly couldn't heft one in each hand and stand there casually carrying on a conversation.

When I had recovered my composure I said, "I'm looking for Dinah."

She lowered the buckets, taking her time, showing me she wasn't in any hurry, then she straightened up and crossed her arms, shifting her weight to one foot. She must have been over six feet, and the attitude made her look taller.

"What can I do for you?" she said cooly.

"You're Dinah?"

"Mmm."

While she might be mistaken for a man from the back, nobody would ever make that error head on. Her auburn hair was cut short, but gently feathered around her face. With her pale, lightly freckled skin and delicately sculpted features she could have been strutting the fashion runways of Paris and Milan. Her eyes, though, were her most startling feature: large, clear, and a dark topaz, and right now they were trained on me. It was like being assessed by a timber wolf.

"Elaine said you'd direct me to Cindy's office."

She cocked her head slightly. "Cindy isn't here. She doesn't usually come in until around ten, but you can leave a message on her desk."

"I could, but I don't think she'd get it. She's gone to New Zealand. I'll be using her office while she's away." I started to move forward.

At the news, Dinah's eyes widened, then her cool shifted into surprise and something else I couldn't read. She put her hand on my shoulder to stop me.

"What did you say?"

"Cindy's gone to New Zealand. Her mother's in the hospital."

Dinah's eyes narrowed. "When?"

Oh. Now I could identify that emotion. Raw and burning anger. "When what?"

"When did Cindy leave?"

I shrugged. "Last night? This morning? I'm not sure. You'll have to check with Elaine." I looked pointedly at her hand on my shoulder and said, "Do you mind?"

Dinah sucked in her breath then exhaled the word "Fuck." She glared at one of the buckets, pulled back, and kicked it so hard that it skittered across the cement, tottering precariously before finally coming to a halt ... fortunately upright. When I turned back to look at her she'd covered her face with her hands, but not quickly enough to hide the tears welling in her eyes. Her final statement was halfway between a curse and a sob.

"The bitch," she said, and she took off out the door.

chapter nine

I managed to find Cindy's office on my own, although it looked more like a recycling depot than a place of learned thought. It also stank of formalin.

When I pulled out the desk chair, the cushion was greasy and wet. I wiped my finger across it and sniffed. At least that explained the odour. Cindy must have dropped a sample before leaving the lab the night before. Formalin is a diluted form of formaldehyde and equally as toxic. Short-term exposure in an enclosed space, like this office, could cause brutal headaches, nausea, and blurred vision. With long-term exposure you were headed for the cancer ward.

On the side wall, running just below the ceiling, were three blacked-out windows. I pushed aside the papers and empty coke cans, climbed up on the desk, and managed to pry one open. Clean, cool air spilled into the office like a sacred, healing force, and I surveyed the scene from above. I read in a book once that a messy office is the sign of a brilliant mind; someone who does-n't require external order to keep all their thoughts lined up and in focus. If it was true then Cindy was a genius.

As soon as I had wheeled the chair out into the lab, I began to gather up all the papers on her desk. Most of it looked like scrap paper, but there were several unmarked file folders buried at the bottom. Out of curiosity I flipped one open. Inside were raw data sheets, "massaged" data, where the raw data had been run through several statistical tests, and some computer-generated tables and graphs. It looked like the results of an experiment on gravel composition and survival, although survival of what I wasn't sure.

I flipped open another file. Same sort of thing: the component parts of single experiments being prepared for analysis and publication; definitely not for the garbage heap. I rooted around, separating the files from the scrap paper. As I pulled the last file toward me, a tattered Rite-in-the-Rain data book slipped from between the covers.

There was no label on the cover, no name and no dates, so I fanned through the pages. It contained field notes from this year's season. The date, time, and weath-er conditions were noted at the top of each page, followed by an observation on the density of something per square metre. Following this there were five columns of num-bers, each column headed by a code of some sort. The book was full, with the entry on the last page dated "14 October 1038 h." A week ago Monday. It didn't mean much to me, but with Cindy's sudden absence Elaine might be needing this record to continue her experiments. I opened up my briefcase and popped it in.

Once the desk was clear enough to work on, the next order of business was calls: Sylvia, the hotel, and maybe Dr. Edwards, but I needed a phone book. There was nothing on the shelves, so that left the desk draw-

ers. I braced myself and opened up the top right-hand
drawer. It was even scarier than the surface of the desk.
In addition to random pieces of paper — old data
sheets, computer printouts, course notes — my hand
came in contact with sticky, lint-covered cough candies,
frayed Kleenex (looked used, but I didn't investigate further), and an unhealthy supply of long, black hairs. I
found a photo of, presumably, Cindy and her mother,
with Cindy looking as disorganized as her office. Her
hair needed a good trim, and although she was pleasant
looking she would never be described as pretty, in part
due to her teeth, which were crooked and overlapping in
front. She wore a tatty South American poncho and was
squinting at the camera, her arm around a matronly-
looking blonde. Both women were smiling. I put the picture back where I found it: next to the half-eaten bagel.

I finally located the phone book buried in the bottom
left-hand drawer. I excavated around it and managed to get
enough of a hold to pull it out. As I did so, I heard a set of
keys slide from between the pages. I put the book on the
desk and rooted around in the drawer until I found them.
The key chain was in the form of a salmon with *You're my
Chum* enamelled on the side. Cute. On the back it was
stamped *Campbell River, BC*. There were Volkswagen
keys, lots of official university keys stamped *Dept. of
Zoology, Do Not Duplicate*, and several other keys that I
couldn't identify. These must be Cindy's extra keys.

After a brief moral skirmish I shrugged and dropped
the keys into my jacket pocket. As a graduate student,
Cindy would have access to all sorts of interesting places,
and I prefer legal access to break and enter. Anyway, it was
the least she could do after making me clean up her office.

There was an urgent message from Bob waiting for
me at the hotel. I was to call him ASAP. I ignored the
message. Instead I called Sylvia to cancel lunch.

"Any more on who did that search?" I asked.

"I don't sleep here, you know." She sounded a bit cranky this morning.

"So when will you know?"

"Tomorrow, maybe. I'll give it a shot when Ottawa closes tonight, but it may take me a day or two to figure out how to hack my way in.

"Okay. Just keep me informed. Can you do another search in the meantime? This one's urgent."

Sylvia grunted, a vestigial response from her days as a man. "As usual."

I ignored the comment. "Graham Connell." I spelled it out. "And if you find anything —"

Just then I caught a movement out of the corner of my eye. I looked up to see Dinah lounging in the doorway.

She gave me a wry smile. "Stinks in here."

I kicked myself for not being more careful, then continued in a normal voice, " — leave a message at the hotel, or send me an e-mail. I'll check in later." And I hung up the phone.

If someone had told me that less than twenty minutes ago this woman had run from the room distraught, I wouldn't have believed them. She was clear-eyed, confident, and in firm control of her emotions. She looked down at the floor, toed the cement, then looked back up at me. "Sorry about what happened back there. It was dumb. It affects my work, is all. She could have told me herself."

"I get the impression she left in a hurry."

"Maybe." She paused for a second and looked away. "And maybe not. Anyway ..."

I waited, but she didn't seem inclined to continue.

"Maybe you and I should start over." I extended my hand. "Morgan O'Brien. A post-doc from Ottawa, but

I'm also an old friend of Elaine's. I'll try to stay out of your way down here."

After a moment's hesitation she pushed herself off the door frame and took my hand. Her grip was firm, no damp dishrag here. "Dinah, Elaine's technician. But you already know that."

I smiled. As a technician, Dinah would be a font of valuable departmental gossip. "Elaine said you'd show me how to access the network, and she wants you to stick around. She'll be down to see you before class." I got out of my chair and came around behind it. "Maybe you could show me now."

Dinah looked at the chair, then at me. "I'll grab a chair." And she disappeared down the hall. A minute later she was back, and she pulled a chair in next to mine. As she sat down, all I could think of was king crab: ninety percent legs. I knew I shouldn't, but I had to ask.

"How tall are you, anyway?"

"Just over two metres. I used to hate it, but now I don't mind." She settled into her chair then turned and gave me the once-over with her eyes. "So," she said after a minute, "how do you know Elaine?" I could see her watching my reaction as if I were a subject in a study on primate behaviour.

"Graduate school. We shared an apartment and we used to do our fieldwork together. It was less complicated than with the men. You know. Their wives got jealous, you always had to rent two motel rooms instead of one, and they had special restaurants they had to stop at, usually because there was a waitress with big tits."

"And you weren't into that." Her voice was matter-of-fact.

I shrugged. "I tend to judge a restaurant by the cuisine."

She nodded a response, as if that told her something she needed to know, but kept watching me with that odd, wolfish stare: curious and calculating. It was unnerving.

"So," I finally continued, "have you been working for Elaine very long?"

"I came over with Cindy."

I must have looked surprised. "From New Zealand?"

She laughed. "From Madden's lab. Elaine sort of inherited us from Madden. Cindy was having ..." she hesitated.

I rearranged the expression on my face to one of warm concern. "Ah huh?" I said, with that upturned intonation at the end. I learned that in the RCMP too: Interrogation 101, another valuable skill. It works like a hot damn: you can keep even the most resistant interviewee disclosing for hours with the judicious use of a warm and inquiring smile and a carefully placed *Ah huh* followed by expectant silence. Like most people, Dinah felt compelled to fill the silence.

"She was having problems with someone in Madden's lab. She needed to get out, and Elaine offered to take her in. I was part of the package, which was okay 'cause a lot of my work was for Cindy anyway. So now I work for Elaine, but I'm still paid through Madden's grant."

Elaine. That dirty little liar. End of story, like hell. With her technician paid for by Riesler, if Elaine had any sense at all (which was open to debate) she would side with him in departmental disputes.

"Do you know Jonathan Edwards?"

She made a silent "Oh" with her lips and shook her head, as if I'd asked a naughty question.

"Ah huh?" I said, and waited.

There was a pause, then: "He's gone to Natural Resources. Around here that's considered a demotion. It's like the more applied the work the less important it must be. And nobody's really saying why he left." Then she leaned closer to me and lowered her voice. "But if you're going to see Dr. Edwards don't let the boss lady know. She'll have a fit."

That was hard to believe, even for Elaine. "You're kidding, right?"

She shook her head. "The way she acts, you'd think he broke up with her, when she's the one who called it off."

My eyes almost popped out of my head. "They were lovers?"

Dinah brought her hand up to her mouth. "Oh God, you didn't know. Don't tell her I —"

And just at that moment, the boss lady walked in the door.

The conversation stopped dead. Dinah busied herself examining the floor. I glared at Elaine, but being Elaine she was oblivious.

"Oh good, you've met," was all she said, then she came around behind me and perched herself on the far side of the desk. She had pinioned Dinah with her eyes.

"You know what's going on with Cindy's project?"

Dinah didn't look up, kept her eyes on the floor. "More or less," she mumbled.

"What the hell does that mean, *more or less*. Can you, or can't you, do the work on your own?"

Dinah had regained some of her composure and sat up straight, returning Elaine's gaze. She was almost as tall sitting as Elaine was standing up.

"I can figure it out by tomorrow, but I'll need a second person on the net."

"Tomorrow?" Elaine hopped off the desk and crossed the room. She examined a complicated-looking chart stuck to the wall, then she turned back to Dinah. "You don't have a field run tomorrow. You don't have another one until Thursday."

I heard Dinah take a deep breath, as if bracing herself, but when her voice came out it was firm and strong. "There've been a few problems."

Elaine didn't move a muscle, just bore into Dinah with her eyes. When she finally spoke her voice was flat and deadly. "What kind of problems?"

"Back off Elaine." That was me. "It's not her fault that Cindy left."

Elaine shot me a nasty look, but turned back to Dinah as she started to explain.

"The return to Weaver Creek is way down. The numbers seem to fluctuate wildly. For a couple of days they're okay, then nothing. No fish returning at all. Some days we can't even work. There aren't enough fish. Cindy scheduled some extra runs to make up the days we lost. It should be okay."

Elaine was now the picture of controlled rage: glassy eyes, tight jaw, and a mask-like expression. "Why wasn't I told?"

Dinah cleared her throat and allowed her glance to slide sideways. "Cindy wanted to be sure that it wasn't an artifact. That it was real."

I spoke up. "It's not part of the normal population cycle?"

Dinah shook her head. "We looked at the return rates for the past thirty years. There's nothing like this in the records."

"Terrific." Elaine pushed herself off the wall. "Just what I need right now. And what does Cindy think *is* going on?"

Dinah shrugged slightly. "Somebody dumping toxic waste at night? That's the most likely explanation, but there's no big fish kill downstream. It could be poaching, someone stringing a net across the stream and taking everything that's coming up. Cindy was going to take some samples yesterday, but I don't know where she got with it."

"So we're going to lose the field season," said Elaine.

"Not all of it." Dinah's voice was hopeful. "I can complete the runs if we can find someone to help me."

"I can help out," I said, looking at Elaine.

"What's the point," she snapped. "If something's disrupting the population and we don't know what it is any data we collect is absolutely useless. That goes for all the olfaction work too. Dinah, pull all the runs done on Weaver Creek fish."

I kept my voice low and non-confrontational. "One step at a time, Elaine. Let Dinah and me complete the runs and see if we can figure out what's going on. Worry about the big picture later."

Elaine's breathing was audible. She looked like a bull preparing to charge. Finally she said, "Damn it," and banged her fist against the wall. Then she looked at me. "It seems you've come on the perfect week. We might be needing an investigator after all." Then she addressed Dinah. "Notify the Department of Fisheries and Oceans and the Salmon Commission. See if anyone knows what's going on. And when you go up tomorrow bring me back samples on dry ice; brains, livers, and a couple of whole fish. We'll check for parasites and toxins. And let Madden know. It may affect his work too." She started to move toward the door. "And this time," she stopped at Dinah's chair and gave her a sharp poke in the shoulder, "keep me informed." Then she stormed out the door.

Neither Dinah nor I dared to breathe until we heard the lab door slam shut. When I was sure Elaine had gone I turned to Dinah. "She's under a lot of pressure right now. It's no excuse, but we've got to cut her a little slack."

"Yeah, well ..." Dinah didn't sound convinced. "Anyway, thanks for the defence back there."

She rose slowly from her chair as if she didn't quite know what to do next. Then she looked at me. "What did she mean by *investigator* anyway?"

"An in-joke. Not very funny in the circumstances."

She nodded absently, then picked up her chair. "Goddamned Cindy," she muttered, and left the office. A minute later I heard her leave the lab.

I waited a second, listening, then hit the redial button on the phone.

"Hi babe," came Sylvia's husky voice. "Changed your mind about lunch?"

"I need another search. And I need the printout and articles by four today. Comprehensive. The last five years."

I could hear her typing in the background. "Shoot."

I paused. "Dr. Elaine Okada."

The typing stopped, and there was silence on the other end of the line. I thought Sylvia might refuse, but then I heard the typing resume. Her only comment was, "She'll kill you," and that I already knew.

Graham wasn't in the lab when I arrived. The ratfish were. Or at least what remained. They lay sliced open, pinned back, and hacked apart in their dissecting trays, which someone had carefully lined up on the side counter. I passed them with hardly a glance, making my way to Graham's office.

The door was open, so I walked right in. I'd already started my greeting when it registered that the back of the head at the desk was not Graham's. At the sound of my voice, the man swivelled around and surveyed me with interest. Then he said, "Ah," and shut the file he'd been reading. He turned and came gracefully to his feet, extending his hand. "Dr. O'Brien I presume." His voice was smooth and gently self-mocking. It took me a moment to respond.

"Forgive me. I was expecting Graham. You are ..."

"Madden Riesler. Please, call me Madden. I'm afraid Graham is tied up elsewhere." He turned up his hands in a gesture of helplessness. "Research beckons. But I told him that I'd be delighted to conduct the tour myself. Elaine speaks very highly of you."

"Really?" I tried not to sound too surprised. Elaine must really want me off her turf.

"Absolutely. I think she hopes to see you here in a more permanent situation, and I'll do everything I can to help."

"That's very kind."

"My pleasure. I have the greatest respect for Elaine's work."

He had taken my elbow and was guiding me out of the office. In another man I would have found this offensive, but not in Madden Riesler. It had to do with his manner. Charming, understated, slightly self-effacing, and very respectful. In fact, he was beguiling, and I tried to maintain enough objectivity to analyze my reaction.

In the corridor he began telling me about his lab and his research. I tuned out, nodded and smiled at random intervals, and took a moment to examine him. He was certainly handsome: lithe and small, with a quiet confidence that was unmistakably masculine. His eyes were electric blue, and the colour was accentuated by a faded denim shirt and jeans that casually set off his trim frame. While his face was young, slightly narrow with well-defined cheekbones, a prominent nose, and clear, unlined skin, his hair and close-cropped beard were a dramatic grey blending to white. The effect was startling, and very attractive, as if the best features of several different people had been pulled together and moulded into one. When he grinned I could see tiny wrinkles frame his eyes, but other than that, I would never have guessed that he was nearing fifty.

I suddenly realized that he'd stopped speaking. "Finished the inspection?" he asked, then chuckled.

"Caught in the act."

"And did I pass?"

I thought about that for a minute. Would I give this guy hundreds of thousands of taxpayers' dollars to spend however he saw fit? You bet. Hand me the cheque and tell me where to sign.

It was a disturbing thought.

chapter ten

I was surprised to see that Riesler's lab was almost empty. When I went to university research technicians rated only slightly higher than laboratory rats, and most of the techs had little choice but to work through lunch. Now, with unionization, things had obviously changed.

As Riesler held the door open for me he asked, "Did you have a chance to talk with Graham at all?"

I shook my head.

"Now that is unfortunate. You must try to catch up with him later." He lowered his voice. "Don't say this to my other students, but Graham is by far the most brilliant and productive researcher I've ever had in my lab, and with no fish biology background whatsoever. Of course, he went to a great school — Johns Hopkins — but in terms of fish, and fish genetics, he knew absolutely nothing. But then," he leaned over, as if to whisper in my ear, "sometimes that helps. You approach problems differently, see things in entirely new ways." He straightened. "And Graham's publishing record is excellent. I don't know how he does it really."

That was curious. I didn't remember seeing Connell's name in the list of Madden's co-authors. Maybe he worked on another species. "Does he work on salmon?"

Riesler looked surprised. "So you're familiar with our work?"

"I'm interested in the Network. That's why I'm here." At least that wasn't a lie.

He banged his forehead with the heel of his hand in an exaggerated, comical gesture. "Not you too? Why is everyone so interested in that damn Network? Is it the money? Because money isn't everything, you know. Has Elaine mentioned the Asia project? It's not necessarily cutting-edge research, I grant you, but in terms of the potential benefit to starving people, well, what's more important after all." I started to say something, but he put his hand up to stop me. "We'll talk salmon if you insist, but not until you hear my Asia pitch. I could really use someone with your skills on that project. Just keep an open mind, that's all I ask."

He took my elbow and propelled me toward a steel door at the side of the lab. I had no choice but to move along with him. He pulled it open and we stepped into the hot, fetid air of the rainforest. The light was an eerie blue, filtered through the water of aquariums; rows of them, running floor to ceiling on shelves. Each one housed a single fish. They looked like goldfish but were bigger, the size of dinner plates. As the door clanged shut behind us they turned, in unison, to stare. It reminded me of a TV showroom with all the sets tuned to *The Nature of Things*.

"Impressive, isn't it." Madden was beaming, the lord of the manor. He moved slowly down the row, and I followed. As we moved, the fish, like synchronized swimmers, pivoted slowly, keeping track of our progress. Their aquariums were bare: no pebbles, no plants, just stark glass boxes with an air stone bubbling in the corner. There was barely enough space in each aquarium for the occupant to move.

"Very," I said, trying to sound truthful. In fact, I found the room unspeakably sad, but Madden continued proudly.

"A few years back I was approached by an overseas aid consortium to do some work on aquaculture, on these guys. Tilapia. They've been farmed over there for generations, but the approach has been hit and miss, no real understanding of why some grow faster than others, some are more resistant to disease, that sort of thing. It wasn't too challenging at first, I'll grant you that, but one thing led to another, and now we're on the verge of doing some very fine work. Within a year we'll be seeing dramatic improvements in growth, yield, survival, and that means increased production. Just to put this in perspective, a lot of these fish farms are mom-and-pop operations in countries that are desperately poor. A very small increase in productivity can make a huge difference to the lives these people lead."

He looked at me and his voice became soft and apologetic. "I hate to disappoint you, Ms. O'Brien ... may I call you Morgan? But most of my time these days is focused here. What goes on out there," he nodded to the lab beyond the door, "they don't need me. Between my lab manager and Graham it runs itself."

When we were back outside standing in the lab Riesler put his hand on my arm. "So, what do you think?" His enthusiasm was almost catching, but not quite. He caught my expression and sighed. "I can see it's salmon." I nodded. "Oh well." He gave a good-natured shrug. "I gave it my best shot. But if that's what you really want the person to talk to is JJ. He runs the day-to-day operation."

When I spoke I kept my voice neutral. "But you must choose the researchers. Manage the allocations."

With a look of satisfaction he shook his head. "Not anymore." I was surprised, and he registered it. His voice took on an edge of impatience. "Look, I manage the science. That means I keep a close watch on the directions and outcomes, and I do all the PR nonsense that the government demands of me, but I don't have time to track every penny and allocate every component for a project of this size. I'd never get anything else done. No. How the science gets done is up to JJ, and when he's home," he pointed to an office in the back corner of the lab, "he's usually hiding in there."

He turned and started to cross the lab to JJ's office, passing between several large tanks shimmering with salmon. In one, I caught the telltale crimson of sockeye. In another, huge fish shimmered an iridescent silver-blue. They were so spectacular I was momentarily transfixed. I felt Riesler come up beside me.

"Beautiful, aren't they," he said, leaning over.

"What are these?"

"Sockeye, but these ones are ocean phase, also know as sea run. Sockeye only turn red on their spawning migration. In fact, these fish are for Elaine. They came in yesterday. If you see her, tell her she can pick them up when she's ready. There's a tank open in the housing room."

I filed that information away in my growing *boy-is-Elaine-ever-in-deep-shit* file. Riesler started to move off again, but I wasn't quite ready to end the conversation.

"I'll be talking to Jonathan Edwards as well. I understand he's moved to Natural Resources."

Riesler stopped and turned casually toward me. He seemed perfectly relaxed, and I could see no sign of tension or discomfort in his demeanour. "Yes. It was a most unfortunate occurrence. I suppose Elaine has told you a bit about that. But by all means talk to him. He's a clever fellow."

"What do you think of his new technique for determining salmon stocks by analyzing the scales?"

"I can see you're well informed." Then he spoke carefully, the objective scientist. "I think it shows promise, but he needs to substantiate his claims. JJ would actually be a better person to ask. As I told you, my life's in there." He motioned to the tilapia door. "At this point, JJ's more up to date on the salmon work, but," he lowered his voice, "JJ and Edwards don't get along, so tread carefully."

"Ah huh?" I waited, silent, but with a look of expectation on my face. It took a moment, but the disclosure side won out.

He sighed. "Suzie, that's JJ's wife ... ex-wife, that is, at least, I think they're divorced now. She's a lecturer here. Anyway, she and Jonathan had a ..." He searched for a word. I could have helped him out with several, some more savoury than others, but he found what he was looking for. "... tryst, I guess you'd say, at a conference a few years back. It was brief, or so I understand, but JJ never forgave him. He blames Jonathan for the breakup of his marriage. I would hope it doesn't cloud his scientific judgment, but just so you know. He can't necessarily give you a fully objective view of Jonathan's work."

The front wall of JJ's office was a window from the waist up, and I saw someone stand and move from the desk to a filing cabinet. Riesler followed my eyes and his face lit up. He seemed relieved to change the subject.

"Oh good. JJ's in." Then he turned back to me quickly. "I hope this conversation remains confidential. I'm not sure who in the department knows," then he touched my arm lightly, "but I'm sure I can depend on you to be discreet."

Madden then moved off to JJ's office. I gave myself a minute to think, admiring the fluid movement of the fish. They swam as if they were part of the water itself, liquid rather than bone and muscle. Madden Riesler was not what I had expected, so what didn't fit?

When I was ready, I followed him into JJ's office.

Madden was standing beside JJ, who was seated at his desk holding a DNA radiograph up to the fluorescent lights. Madden was speaking.

"I would have expected the dark band to ... ah, here she is." He performed a brief introduction then looked at his watch. "I'm afraid you'll have to excuse me for the next fifteen, twenty minutes. I've got a call to make, but that should give you just enough time to talk." He gave JJ a solid clap on the back and smiled at me. "This gentleman is the answer to all your questions."

As Madden left the office JJ half stood and motioned to the wooden chair on the other side of his desk. Even with a lab coat covering his shorts and golf shirt I could see the broad shoulders and muscled thighs of a man who worked hard to keep his body buff, although the aesthetic was somewhat diminished by a ludicrous Prince Valiant haircut and large, beakish nose.

When he was reseated in his own chair he pushed it back on two legs and jammed his hands into his lab coat pockets.

"So what can I do for you?" His voice was unpleasant, high-pitched and slightly nasal, and the smile on his lips was forced. He was obviously going for a casual-yet-helpful demeanour, and it might have worked if not for his eyes. They were narrow and closely set, an abnormally pale grey-green, and they seemed to have a life of their own. While JJ's body language and tone of voice declared his willingness to help, his gaze skittered around the room as if being controlled by another mind. It was disconcerting, and I began to wonder if it was some sort of nervous tick or neurological disorder. I thought it best to pretend I didn't notice and forge ahead.

"What can you tell me about the Network?"

"What's your interest? Genetics? Population studies? Habitat renewal?"

"Finances, actually."

The skittering stopped and he fell forward in his chair with a thump. "The finances? Why?"

I shrugged. "I'm interested in applying for funds. I need to know how it works."

Pause. "And you've spoken with Madden?"

"Oh yes. He's enthusiastic, but I need more details. He said I should look over a typical project budget that involves field and lab work to get some idea of the scope of these projects. Of how the funding and allocations work."

"Madden suggested that?"

I nodded and smiled. We were getting somewhere. The eyes were on the move again and he'd laced the fingers of one hand so tightly through the fingers of the other that the knuckles were turning white.

There was a pause, then JJ hung his head dramatically over his hands, feigning deep thought. After almost a minute he took an audible breath, shook his head slowly, and dropped his voice half an octave to lend a certain gravity to the next statement.

"I'm sorry, but there are confidentiality issues at stake here. I can't just pull out files and let you see who has applied for money and how much they got, no matter what Madden says."

"It's all on the public record," I reminded him gently. "Remember? The taxpayers' dollars at work?

Anyway, I don't need to know who the application came from. I just need to see some numbers."

"I told you. I can't just —"

"I'd really hate to bother Madden with something like this."

He managed to glare at me for a second before his gaze lurched away, then he reluctantly stood up and moved to the bank of filing cabinets the filled the wall to my right. He slid a bottom drawer open, shuffled through the files, and withdrew a folder. He opened it and extracted a single piece of paper. Back at his desk he made a show of poring over the sheet and blacking out all references to the researchers and their home institutions. When he was ready he passed it across to me and pushed his chair back again. I could see a sheen of sweat on his brow.

I took the paper from him and made an equally good show of going over the information, running my finger down the columns of numbers and muttering to myself. Actually, I couldn't have cared less what was on the paper, but despite this, after a few minutes of seemingly intense concentration, I looked up and smiled. "This is great," I said. "Exactly what I need." Then I went back to reading. I could hear the squeak of his chair as he shifted uneasily. When I was finished my performance I pushed the paper back across the desk.

"Excellent. That helps a lot. Now what about procedures? Is there a lot of red tape? Ten signatures needed for every purchase?"

He shook his head. "Just me. I'm it. And I make sure things run smoothly. You can bet on that."

I looked surprised. "You have signing authority?"

He sat up straighter and nodded. "I'm the signing officer for Network funds."

"But Madden must oversee the expenditures. He must monitor their distribution."

That statement got under his skin. "Why the hell should he? I've got a Ph.D., for Christ's sake. I don't need Madden to tell me what to do and he knows it, so he leaves me alone. And why should a top researcher like him be wasting time on administration? If you come to the Network," he poked himself in the chest with his thumb, "I'm in charge."

This *was* getting interesting, and I suddenly wondered how Connell and JJ squared up together. "So what about Graham Connell? Does he have signing authority too?"

At the sound of Connell's name the chair banged to the floor again and JJ's face went sour. "Connell? I wouldn't let that little parasite sign for a test tube."

"I've heard he's brilliant."

"Who told you that? Graham? He's —" Just then someone appeared at the door, and JJ directed his erratic gaze to the new visitor. "What?" He barked.

The man at the door looked like a graduate student, maybe a post-doc. He didn't seem either surprised or put off by JJ's manners.

"Sorry. Didn't see you were with someone." He motioned to the computer. "Better check out GeneMed. It's taking a dive." Then he turned and walked away.

"Oh shit," said JJ. He whipped around to his computer monitor and rattled the mouse. The screen saver opened up to his internet browser sitting on the Stockwatch site. I could tell that he'd momentarily forgotten I was there. He typed in a symbol and when the graph came up I could see a nice sharp peak heading abruptly downhill. "God damn it," he said, and banged the table with his hand. "God *damn* it!"

I cleared my throat. He turned on me and quickly brought himself under control.

"Day trader?" I said.

"Just a hobby," he answered, but he looked pretty rattled. "Look, I've really got things to do."

Yeah, I thought, like unload some bad stock before it plummets even more. However, since our meeting had been so productive I thought I might as well try one more question.

"There is one last thing." I said, slowly getting out of the chair. "I heard a rumour a while ago about a guy who was promised Network money and never saw a penny. Is it true?"

JJ's face froze momentarily. Even his eyes stopped moving, then he quickly recovered. "Who told you that? That's crap. I'll tell you what that's all about. The Network has very high standards. This isn't some two-bit Canadian project run out of Ottawa. We're working with the best in the world: Americans, Japanese, Russians. If a researcher who applies isn't working to that kind of standard they don't get in and some of them get pissed off. I'd take a good hard look at who started that rumour and why. I bet you're going to find some second-class jerk who's whining because he ..." then he said with emphasis, "or *she*, didn't cut it."

"So you haven't received any formal complaints?"

He turned from me back to his computer screen, effectively ending the conversation. "You'd have to ask Madden," he mumbled. "He'd be in charge of that."

chapter eleven

I walked slowly up to Madden's office, running over what I'd discovered. For one thing, I now knew that the Network financial files were located in JJ's office. That gave me a goal for this evening. It was also clear that JJ was a glowing candidate for embezzler of the year. Day trading in biotechnology stocks was as risky as running the ponies. You could lose a lot of money in a very short time. With signing authority on Network funds JJ would have no problem investing —and losing — a few hundred thousand that didn't belong to him. I'd have to ask around, see what rumours were circulating on his private life and finances. Dinah would be a good source there, and JJ's ex-wife might also be very forthcoming on personal details, especially if the final divorce settlement was as acrimonious as I imagined it might be.

But, while it was tempting to slot JJ into the role of the villain, I still felt uneasy. For one thing, Riesler wasn't what I had expected, so was my preconceived picture of him completely wrong, or was he acting out an elaborate charade? And then there was Graham. How did he fit into this? Was he part of my case or the proverbial red herring? And then, of course, there was still Edwards, the disgruntled junior professor. Before I could make any real progress I'd have to interview him.

By this time I'd reached the top floor. I pulled open the vestibule door just as Riesler came barrelling through.

"Oh. Good," he said when he saw me. He was wearing a grey tweed sports jacket over his denim shirt and had car keys in his hand. He spoke with the urgency of someone in a big hurry. "I just called down to JJ. He said you were on your way here." He put his hand on my arm. "I'm terribly sorry, but something urgent has just come up and I can't make lunch today."

"Not a personal emergency, I hope," I said sympathetically.

He shook his head. He'd moved around me and had one foot already on the stairs. "Nothing like that, but urgent nonetheless. I'd still like to get together. How about dinner tomorrow?" He was backing down the stairs.

"Dinner would be fine."

"Good. Then I'll find you tomorrow. We can firm up details then, and again, terribly sorry." Then he turned and disappeared down the stairs.

The truth is I was just as happy to be on my own. I was beginning to feel both cranky and jet-lagged. I needed a burger, a nap, and a run — in that order — before I could process any more information. I headed back down the stairs, picked up my coat and briefcase in Elaine's lab, and left the building. I'd be back soon enough. I had a busy night ahead of me.

The day had broken into brilliant sunshine, and unlike the east, where the maples blazed in colour, the trees here were just beginning to show a hint of red on the tips of their outermost leaves. I trudged up the hill to my car, contemplating the case as I saw it so far. There were so many disparate threads it was hard to know which ones, if any, were connected. This was not what I had planned for my three-day, quick-and-dirty case in Vancouver.

The parking lot was packed, a sea of brightly coloured car roofs glistening in the afternoon sun. I threw my briefcase in the back seat and took the main gates out of Southern. I kept my eyes peeled for a burger place, but quickly realized that the area was too trendy for such vulgar commerce, and by the time I'd hit 12th Avenue I was back on automatic pilot, thinking about Riesler.

Why didn't he match his publication record? I ran that over in my mind. I tend to believe that people don't change no matter how hard they try to convince you they have. My mother, for example, gave up drinking at least once a month with a solemn promise to never touch another drop. She died a raging alcoholic when I was sixteen. On the other hand, building a character profile based on a publication record was far from exact, especially since publication records are always out of date. The articles I was seeing in journals today were based on experiments that were run at least a year ago, and probably two to three years ago. If Riesler's epiphany was recent it wouldn't be reflected in his publishing record for at least another year. I made a mental note to go over his publications one more time. Maybe I'd see something telling: a hint of a new direction or a citation to a paper "in press." What I really needed, though, was a contact; someone who had known Riesler over the years and seen the kind of change he must have undergone. It would have to be someone who could be trusted to keep the conversation secret. I filed that problem away. Finding the right person was a perfect job for Duncan.

Back at my hotel I zipped across the street, grabbed a take-out burger from the White Spot, and took it back to my room. The message light on the phone was flashing. It was probably Bob, so I ignored it. After finishing my burger I tried to read one of Edwards's journal articles, but within minutes my eyes glazed over and my eyelids began to fall shut. I put everything aside, lay down on the bed, and was unconscious in less than a minute.

My power nap was rudely interrupted by the phone. I didn't answer it, just let it ring, but when it stopped I called down to the desk. There were three messages from Bob, but the latest was from Sylvia. *Call immediately.* I looked at my watch. It was three-thirty, half an hour before our scheduled meeting. I dialed her office number and she picked up on the first ring.

"Hey babe, screening your calls?"

"Trying to keep Bobbins a continent away. What's up?"

"Your boy Connell didn't come up clean, and I suggest you get yourself over here before you waste your time on other things."

"Can you give me a snapshot?"

"Patience, my friend, is a virtue, and anticipation is everything. I wouldn't want to ruin your fun. Anyway, you have to see it. It's a visual thing. And it's good." She paused. "It's very good."

My run was short, fast, and brutal, but it woke me up. Forty minutes later I was back in my car heading west toward the university and the federal government lab complex that sits at the edge of the property. I showed my ID at the door. The guard scrutinized it, gave a curt nod, and handed it back. He buzzed Sylvia, and a minute later she was through the swinging doors and towing me back down the hall at a healthy clip. White coats were scuttling this way and that, and I could hear high-tech equipment clicking and whirring in the rooms on either side of the corridor. I seemed to remember that this section had something to do with engineering: friction and wear research, bearings, lubricants, that sort of thing.

Sylvia's office was reclaimed lab space. A bench ran across one wall and a government-issue couch — lacquered birch upholstered in tangerine — was pressed up against the other. A large desk faced the window, but the blinds were closed. The only light in the office came from the three computer monitors sitting on the desk, each with a different screen saver. Cockroaches skittered across one. The middle screen scrolled "Resistance is Futile" in royal blue. On the third, a black kitten leapt after mice that popped out of thin air and whizzed across the screen. I found all the movement disorienting, particularly since it was the only source of light.

Sylvia crossed to her desk. She picked up two file folders and chucked them onto the coffee table in front of the couch. "Have a seat." She nodded to the couch. "There's a light behind. You want coffee?"

I nodded and sat down. She turned to the lab bench, where a small drip coffee machine sat between the gas outlets and a sink. I switched on the light and busied myself with the files. When the coffee was gurgling and the office infused with that sublime aroma, Sylvia came over and sat down by me. She shook her head with a "tsk, tsk" and gathered up the papers I'd spread across the coffee table.

"You have to do this in a specific order. It's like a voyage of discovery; a story unravelling. First, take a look at this."

She pulled out a reference search and slid it across to me. It was Graham Connell's publication record. I read it over: six publications, all in reputable journals.

"It looks okay to me. He's bright, Riesler's wonder boy, so I'm not surprised."

She was smiling like the Cheshire cat. "A young man with a brilliant future, but nothing to raise suspicion. So take a look at this." She handed me another sheet.

The coffee had stopped brewing. Sylvia got up and crossed to the bench, giving me time to look at the second document. It was another reference search for Graham, but this one picked up Connell spelled with both one *L* and two. There were over twenty citations, way too many for a graduate student. I looked more closely. Sylvia had organized the list by date rather than by subject. Within a six-month period Connell had published in eight different journals, and none of the journal names were familiar. Not only that, he'd published in an astounding range of subjects, from salmon egg survival to bioinformatics. If I hadn't actually met him (and none of the journal editors would have) I would assume that he was a principle researcher in a lab the size of a Wal Mart. Out of curiosity I skipped ahead to the next page. Sure enough, a year later he'd returned to the same journals to publish follow-up articles, and that took serious commitment and organization. This guy was a professional.

Sylvia came back with the mugs and slid in beside me. I glanced up at her. "Holy shit."

She nodded. "He's good, isn't he. He's so good I almost missed it, but they all get cocky when they think they have the system beat." I could see a flush of excitement on Sylvia's pale skin. For her, it was the thrill of the chase. The kill, which was my job, was trivial. A necessary but inconsequential act. She leaned forward, cradling her coffee.

"I didn't like his record. It was too pristine, and that's not how real people work, so I pulled some of his papers and checked the citations. There it was. Reference to an article by G. Connel, published in some obscure journal, with a glowing review of the paper in his introduction. The little jerk, laughing up his nose at everyone. It took me an hour to find a database that carried the journal, but once I did it was like opening Pandora's box, the crap just spewed out. But you haven't seen the best part yet."

She pulled the other file from under the papers, and held it up. "The other search you requested."

She pulled the top paper and handed me a page with the header "Okada, Elaine: search query for 1/89 to 10/02." My stomach contracted. Elaine couldn't be involved in this. I took a deep breath and scanned the entries on Elaine's record, but nothing hopped off the page. I looked up at Sylvia.

"I don't get it."

"Maybe this will ring a bell." She pulled two reprints from the file. The top one was entitled *Odour-coding properties of Bufo boreas (western toad) olfactory cortical neurons*, and Elaine was first author, followed by several of her colleagues at Berkeley. The second reprint — *Olfactory neurons in Bufo cognatus (great plains toad): odour coding properties of cortical neurons* — had only one author: Graham Connel.

"Damn." I threw both reprints on the table. "So he's not fabricating the work. He's stealing it."

"He could be doing both. By tomorrow I'll be able to tell you the names of the people he's ripping off and we can eliminate the plagiarisms and see what we're left with, but it's going to take a bit of digging. He's altered things just enough to obscure his trail. This," she motioned to the two articles on the table, "was serendipity. It walked off the screen and hit me in the face when I was pulling Elaine's publications. I knew you'd be relieved."

I flipped to the end of Elaine's list and checked her latest publications. They were all from her time at Berkeley, and I needed something more recent. Maybe Elaine had told Sylvia more than she told me? I closed the file.

"Who's funding Elaine's work? Do you know?"

Sylvia paused, then exhaled dramatically. "Jesus, O'Brien, what are you on to? Elaine's clean. She's the victim, in case you missed that point."

"Elaine had an affair with Edwards, the guy who made the complaint." I watched Sylvia's reaction carefully. "Did you know that?"

"It's not the sort of thing she'd tell me, is it."

"Well, she didn't tell me either."

"Big deal. You're not her mother."

"Agreed. But guess who's funding the hired help?" She shrugged. "Riesler, the accused. She lied about that too, told me the relationship was arm's length. Why?"

Sylvia shook her head. "You two never change. You're still two big, stupid dinosaurs hellbent on collision. Well, get this straight, O'Brien. I am not going to be between you at the moment of impact. Been there; done that; never again thank you very much." She patted my arm. "My advice to you? Evolve, babe. Language works. Just *ask* her what the hell is going on."

"Oh, that's great advice from you. Too bad — "

I was interrupted by the phone. Just as well. It gave my brain time to catch up with my mouth and take the necessary steps to shut it down.

The conversation from Sylvia's end was rather dull. "Ah huh ... ah huh ... ah huh ... No kidding ... You're sure? ... Bingo. I owe you. Next time in Ottawa."

By the time she'd hung up I was feeling contrite. She turned from the phone but didn't come forward. Instead, she leaned back on the desk and crossed her arms in front of her chest. "Now, what were you saying, O'Brien?"

"Me? Nothing. Absolutely nothing. Except thanks for the good advice."

"You must be a psychic. That was the call on your seven-minute reference search."

"I thought you were going to hack your way in?"

"There are easier ways to get things done. I called in a favour: one of the clerks in the billing office. No big deal."

Then she said nothing, just watched me, expressionless. Finally I said, "What do I have to do, grovel?"

"That would be nice." Then she broke out into a big grin. "Patsy. The search was billed to your boss."

chapter twelve

A deep, visceral joy spread through my body, ending with a dumb grin on my face. Then: "Damn!" I kicked the table.

"I thought you'd be delighted."

"I would be, if Patsy knew how to boot up a computer." I thought for a minute. Either someone had stolen her charge code or, more likely, someone was doing the search for her. Either way, it must have been done by someone within the Council. Still, it was frustrating: so near and yet so far. I'd have to wait and see what Duncan turned up from the commissionaire. Not looking up, I started to gather all the reprints together. "Can I keep these papers?"

"They're yours."

I was stuffing the files in my briefcase when I heard her clear her throat. "I need a favour," she said. She didn't sound happy about asking.

"Shoot."

"I have a doctor's appointment tomorrow. I was wondering if you would ..." her voice trailed off.

I stopped my busy work, looked up, and mentally gave myself a good swift kick in the rear. Sometimes I get so tied up in my own world I forget that my friends have problems too. However, there was no point in getting maudlin. That would really piss her off. "Hold your hand? What time?"

"The appointment's at five, but we need to leave here about four-fifteen."

"No problem. Is there something going on?"

She shrugged, but her sardonic mask had slipped back into place. There was even an evil twinkle in her eye. "I'll take you out for dinner after, maybe to a bar."

"Don't get your hopes up." I zipped up my briefcase. "Thanks for this. It helps a lot. And I think I will take your advice and have a little heart-to-heart with Elaine."

"Oh boy," was Sylvia's only comment.

I drove back over to C-lot and made for the first row where I'd parked this morning. It was getting late, and I hoped that some of the early birds would have called it quits and gone home to study. In fact, the same spot that I'd left earlier in the afternoon was still open, and I nipped right in.

As I walked along the line of cars I noted that the Mustang was gone, but the Rabbit and Acadian were still parked where I'd seen them this morning. But now, parked next to the Rabbit, there was a pale blue Valiant in perfect condition. I peered in. The interior looked original, although some body work and a paint job lowered the value slightly. But if a Slant 6 was hidden underneath the hood the car was a collector's dream. Only in Vancouver.

Dinah had said that Natural Resources was just across the street from Life Sciences, so I headed toward the Zoology entrance, but instead of going in I continued straight, jay-walking across the street that bordered the Zoology wing. Directly across there was a low, white building. A receptionist was just packing up and reaching for her coat. She had blood red nails that would put a grizzly to shame.

"I'm looking for Dr. Edwards," I said. She looked blank. "He works on salmon."

She looked at me as if I were the incarnation of the bimbo queen and said, "This is Geophysics. Maybe you should try Zoology."

She was obviously in a hurry to get home so I took my time responding. "I'm looking for Natural Resources," I said slowly, enunciating each word as if speaking to a naughty child.

She caught the edge in my voice and became significantly more polite, pointing to the right with one of her claws. "The path at the side of the building? Just go down it. It's the temp at the end."

I went back outside and found the asphalt path leading between Geophysics and a large five-story building beside. By the time I'd reached the bottom I knew why Natural Resources was a demotion. For starters, it was almost impossible to find, and the "temp" the receptionist had mentioned was a temporary building, probably WWII vintage, that looked like it had originally been built as army barracks. Fortunately, when I got inside, I could see that it had all been renovated and was clean and bright. I could hear Bach's Mass in B Minor pumping out of one of the labs. As I got nearer to the music I could see the name on the door, and it was Dr. Jonathan Edwards.

Music was my escape as a kid. I'd played in orchestras, sang in choirs, and marched in military-style bands. I closed my eyes and almost let myself be transported by the purity and hope — the belief — in those crystal voices. *Credo in unum, Patrem omnipotentem.* I believe in one God, the Father Almighty. Not that different from science, really. I took a deep breath and banged on the door.

"It's open," came a voice from the other side. A gorilla of a man sat hunched over a binocular microscope. He didn't look up but continued to manipulate the dial on the microscope stage, and I could see the slide zinging back and forth in his field of view. He paused to jot something down in a notebook sitting open by the microscope, but didn't take his eyes off the oculars.

"Yes." His voice was abrupt, not really rude, but preoccupied.

"Morgan O'Brien from the National Council for Science and Technology. We spoke on the phone."

The slide stopped abruptly. Then it started to move again. He wrote something else in his notebook. It looked like he was hurrying to finish up a measurement, and that gave me a minute to scan the room. Dr. Edwards was obviously another highly organized mind. Papers and equipment were strewn everywhere, and, while the lab had all the requisite equipment — hood, freezers, water baths, drying ovens, centrifuge — all of it looked slightly out of date, like last year's model. The exception was the massive apparatus at the back of the lab: a gleaming stainless steel tube about two metres long that lay horizontal on a chest-high pedestal. With a viewing portal at each end, it looked like some kind of robotic submersible for deep-sea exploration, except that it was firmly anchored by a tangle of wires and tubes to a bank of monitoring equipment — digital counters, oscilloscopes, and a PC scrolling "Gone Fishing" in large crimson letters against a backdrop of aquamarine.

I heard Edwards push himself out from the bench, and when I turned back he had swivelled around and was examining me. I didn't avert my eyes, just stood there and waited, taking equal time in examining him. We were like two male dogs on their first encounter; suspicious and wary, but curious too.

I'd expected an urbane young professor in loafers and gold-rim glasses, but Edwards looked like a turn-of-the-century prospector just back from the Klondike. Even sitting I could tell he was huge: a solid six-foot-two or -three, blue-black hair and beard, and hazel-green eyes. The hair and beard were shaggy, but beneath the lab coat his jeans were clean and nicely fitted, his plaid shirt was tidy, and a pair of red suspenders complemented the colours of the shirt. I glanced back up at his face and was suddenly aware of what I hadn't picked up on the first take. Hidden beneath all that hair was an alarmingly handsome man: high cheekbones, a strong, definitive nose, and full lips. With a little trim and dressed in Armani, Dr. Jonathan Edwards could easily be on the cover of *GQ*, and I could see why Elaine had fallen for him. That, and his voice: a low, soft bass that resonated through my body as a pleasurable hum.

"Your mass spectrometer?" I said, nodding at the tube.

"My baby," he answered. "What do you want?"

I put my briefcase on the counter, opened it, and pulled out Connell's publishing record. "Take a look at this."

He was surprised, but pulled the papers toward him. As he read, his eyes became wide. He reached over, switched off the music, and glanced back at me. "Have a seat."

I pulled a lab stool over and sat down. Five minutes later he hadn't said anything direct, but I'd followed his index finger down the margin and knew he was studying the thing entry by entry. I heard him mutter in disbelief more than once. When he got to the bottom he tossed the list on the bench and stared at the wall for a full minute. He was obviously shaken. Finally he turned to me.

"Where'd you get that?"

"Doing my job. Remember? The one you told me to go and do?" He had the decency to look chagrined. Good. I continued. "Do you recognize any of the work?"

"Is it for real?"

"You mean did he really publish that stuff? He sure did. It's all out there."

He pulled the sheet onto his lap again and poked at one entry. "That's mine." He looked up. "It's 'in press,' part of a larger paper. Graham's never done any work like that. It has to be mine."

"Initial it. I'll get you the paper and you can check it out."

He pointed to another. "That's Elaine's. I'm sure of it. She's a prof in Zoology — "

"I know Elaine. Any others?"

"Hell yes. Hadley from Nanaimo. Westergarde from Dalhousie — he's a graduate student. This one could be Dickinson at the Freshwater Institute. Jesus, he's an eclectic little bastard. How'd he get hold of all this data?"

"I was hoping you'd tell me."

Instead of answering he stared at the wall behind me, processing. His foot tapped rhythmically on a leg of his stool. Since I had the distinct impression he was not going to make me party to his conclusions, I interrupted him.

"Why did you leave Zoology?"

He looked startled, then his eyes narrowed. "That's none of your business."

"It's not related to your complaint against Riesler?"

He hesitated, then came out with a definitive "No."

I let the silence fill the room until I could see Edwards squirm, then I fired another question.

"Could it be Connell who's embezzling Network funds?"

"Madden's in charge. I'm not going back on my accusation, if that's what you want."

"Fine. Then let's talk about Madden."

He looked at me for a second, then stood up abruptly. "I need a coffee. You want one?"

Good diversion, but it wasn't going to work. "Sure. With milk or creamer if you've got it."

He walked over to the side counter and poured two mugs of coffee from a carafe thermos that was sitting near the back, then he bent down and opened a little half-fridge beneath the bench. I tried not to look inside. I didn't want to know what might be leaking its juices into the carton of milk. I'd read one of his papers where the analytical technique called for "liquefying the tissue" before running the test. That meant throwing a whole fish into a food processor and blending it up like a milkshake. When he handed me the coffee I surreptitiously examined the surface of the liquid, looking for anything suspect — a fish scale, a little chunk of cartilage, a few fin rays — but decided that I needed the caffeine enough to take a side order of sushi.

The coffee was excellent: strong and very fresh. This guy couldn't be all bad. I noted that he had dumped about four tablespoons of sugar into his. I guess he wasn't planning to sleep any time in the next twelve hours either. When we were both settled with our coffee I went back to it.

"Madden," I said firmly.

"What's to talk about? My lab was supposed to get two hundred thousand dollars this year, and I haven't seen a penny."

"That doesn't prove a thing. Maybe Riesler decided that somebody else could do the work better than you. It's within his rights as project manager."

"There isn't anybody else. There are only three researchers in the world who can do these kind of tests and interpret the data. Me, my Ph.D. advisor in California, and my graduate student here on a good day. There is no other lab, not to do this work anyway."

I thought about that. The government gives a principle researcher almost total discretion in the distribution of funds, trusting that he (and it usually is a he) knows best how to get the work done. Riesler did not, however, have the right to direct the funds to research with a different purpose.

"Where do you think the money is?"

"I think Madden's ramping up another project. I think he's funnelled it into his lab budget."

"Do you have any evidence?"

"He's not exactly going to hand over his financial records to me, is he. But I hear things. It's a small community."

"Like what?"

"Like his interests have diverged. Like he has something big stewing on the back burner."

"Did you ever ask him directly where the money went?"

Edwards looked into his coffee cup and swirled the liquid around. "I tried, but he referred me to JJ."

"And what did *he* say?"

He took on JJ's nasal tones. For a guy with such a low voice he did a good imitation. I tried not to smile. "'Madden has reallocated that money to a more fruitful line of inquiry that will be more cost-effective in the long run.' What a load of crap."

"And he didn't tell you what this 'line of inquiry' was?"

He shook his head. "But I made some calls. Like I say, it's a small community, and that's a lot of money. Somebody would be talking if it had landed in their budget."

"But why finger Madden? Why not JJ? He has signing authority, and I understand the two of you are not exactly bosom buddies." Oops. An unfortunate choice of words. Edwards didn't seem to notice.

"JJ is Riesler's puppet. The guy hasn't had an original thought in fifteen years."

"Maybe he decided to branch out."

His laugh was derisive. "That'll be the day."

"Who's funding the Asia project?"

At that question Edward's foot twitch took over his whole leg and he had to put a hand on his thigh to slow it down. "The fucking Asia project. I'd like to blow the damn thing up." He took a swig of his coffee and banged the mug on the counter. "It's funded privately by a consortium. Fisheries Enterprises International. And I know what you're thinking, that maybe the Network funds are going there, but I get the impression there's lots of money."

Like maybe an extra $200,000 in this year's budget? I'd have to check out this consortium, get the exact funding figures. Then suddenly, Edwards's leg stopped moving.

"That's a good example," he said, poking the air for emphasis. "That's tilapia work, right? So why is Madden using the FEI grant to fund Elaine's research on olfaction?" Then he caught my expression and seemed to reconnect with the fact that I was a government investigator. "I shouldn't have said that. I don't want her involved in this ... she isn't involved in this. It's between Madden and me."

I was speaking almost to myself. "So Riesler's *funding* Elaine's work. Isn't that cozy." Then I looked at Edwards. "How do you know that?"

He panicked. "It's not related."

"Then there's no problem, is there. How do you know he's funding her work?"

He suddenly looked tired and defeated. "I can't answer that. You'll have to ask her yourself."

"Just for the record, I want you to know that Elaine's an old friend of mine, but that isn't going to stop me from investigating her. You're damn right I'm going to ask her myself."

Suddenly he perked up. "You're her friend?" He pushed the search results back to me. "Could you show her these? *Make* her look at them. It's relevant."

I could hardly wait for dinner.

Before I left the lab Edwards disappeared down the hall to make a copy of the search results. He'd get back to me tomorrow with any additional information he could glean from the titles. While he was gone I took the opportunity to plug in my laptop and dial into my account. I had thirty-seven e-mails waiting to be read. In the modern world, there is no escape. Most of them covered topics of vital importance, like a going-away party for Marielle and a mandatory day-long course entitled Building Positive Relationships. There was also a missive from the Office of the Director General that had been sent to Bob, who had cc'ed it to all of us. I always read Patsy's memos. I like to see how many times she can use the word "notwithstanding" on a single page of text. It's her current favourite, right up there with "linkage" in the New Age government lexicon.

Her e-mail was disappointing. She only used it once: mind you, the whole memo was less than two hundred words long. It said that, notwithstanding previous memos to the contrary, due to cost-cutting measures, no overtime would be approved unless a request was submitted in writing forty-eight hours in advance and was signed off by your supervisor, section head, and the DG. Then there was a little ramble about everyone being responsible for the budget and tightening their belts and blah, blah, blah. I whacked the message.

There was an e-mail from Bob with the subject heading "VERBAL REPORT BY END OF DAY." I whacked it without even opening it up. As I scrolled down, whacking as I went, I found what I was looking for near the bottom. It was an e-mail from Duncan with the subject heading "The Plot Thickens." I liked that. I opened it up. It said, "Greetings from the Commissionaire. Keys to Ahmed Assad, Joanne Laframboise, Robert Gregory." So Bob had been in the building the day the mystery reference search was done. I liked that even better. I decided not to worry too much about a verbal report by the end of the day.

Before shutting down the system I fired off a reply to Duncan thanking him for the good work and letting him know that the search had been charged to Patsy's code. I also reminded him to follow up on any possible connections between the Council and the Network. Edwards returned with my copy of Connell's records just as I was logging out.

"If my office calls," I said, closing the computer, "tell them you haven't seen me. Better still, tell them you're thinking of dropping the investigation." He started to protest, but I cut in. "Trust me. And I'll talk to Elaine."

That stopped him. Then he said, fumbling for words, "When you see her could you tell her that ... that ... just tell her hello, I guess. That if she needs me, I'm here."

I almost put my hand on his shoulder, but it would have been too intimate for him. I gave a nod instead. "But I think you should know, she's as stubborn as a mule."

He smiled, more to himself than to me, and said softly, "I know. That's what I like about her."

I was almost out the door when Dinah's story of the missing fish popped into my head. "You ever heard of anything like that?"

Edwards thought for a moment. "It's funny. I was talking to a Fisheries officer up the valley just about a week ago. He'd seen the same thing on a creek just outside Harrison. Never seen anything like it before. You want me to give him a call?"

"Yeah, I would. I'm sure Elaine would appreciate it."

That brightened him up. "I'll see what I can track down and call you when I've got something."

I smiled. With Elaine dangling as the carrot, I didn't need to worry about Edwards talking to any reporter, so for now, at least, the media threat was gone.

At the door I turned back to take one last look. He sat on his stool in front of the microscope looking troubled and lost. Suddenly, he looked up and caught my eye. He smiled slightly and raised his hand. "See you," he said, very gently. His forlorn looks and deep voice sent a shiver of desire up my spine.

Forbidden fruit, I thought, and walked into the hall without looking back.

chapter thirteen

Back at Elaine's lab the lights were still blazing, so I assumed that Dinah was somewhere around. I made my way to Cindy's office, switched on the light, and plunked my briefcase on the desk. The smell of formalin had been replaced by a heavy, damp chill — the cold night air spilling in through the open window — and I had to scramble up on the desk and shut it before I could start work. With a little over an hour before my date with Elaine I needed to get all my thoughts in order before grilling her for dinner. The easiest way to do this was to create a simple table with two columns. In one column I would list everything I knew, in the other column all the outstanding questions. From that I would figure out what information Elaine could supply and formulate an approach and specific questions to extract the information. I flipped open my laptop and went to work.

I began by listing all the people who seemed to be involved in the Network drama. That included Riesler,

JJ, Graham, Elaine, Edwards, Cindy, and Dinah. With all the players accounted for, I itemized, for each person, everything I knew about them and all the outstanding questions. Twenty minutes later, with the lists completed, I reached an uncomfortable conclusion. My case so far was a mess. The list of participants was unmanageably long, their relationship to the case was obscure, and the "questions" column was three times longer than the "what I know" column.

I sat back in my chair and surveyed the table from a distance, trying to get the gestalt of it. On the surface, Graham looked good. He was certainly an accomplished fraud artist, but that was the problem. The motivation for Graham's style of fraud was usually a desire for recognition, adulation, rather than the need for ready cash. Stealing funds from the Network wouldn't accomplish that. On the other hand, maybe he was diversifying, adding embezzlement to his already impressive list of criminal credentials. There was something else that didn't add up. Riesler had implied that Graham and JJ ran the Network, yet JJ seemed to despise Graham and denied his involvement, so what was the true relationship between them? Was it possible they were shielding a very lucrative partnership, with Graham providing the brains and entrepreneurial spirit, JJ the access and opportunity?

But that led me to JJ, who, without any help from Graham, had the most obvious motives for the crime. He had reason to hate Edwards, and he had a taste for high-risk stocks, but would he, could he, work alone? Everything to date indicated that JJ was a follower, either of Riesler or someone else. And how could he possibly embezzle that amount of cash right out from under Riesler? Riesler was no idiot. If $200,000 were missing from the grant surely he, as principal scientist, would be aware of it even with his supposed hands-off approach.

So, what was Riesler's involvement?

Then there was the clincher. How was Elaine tied in to all of this? What the hell was going on between her and Riesler, and her and Edwards, and was any of it related to the missing funds?

I sighed. Of all the questions, this last one, centred on Elaine's seemingly pivotal role, was my best bet for the evening. Of course I'd try for more, but if that's all I got, some insight into her relationship with Riesler and Edwards, then I'd be happy. I was pretty sure that once I understood how she fit in it would clarify a lot of other issues.

I began laying out a plan of attack for dinner that involved a quiet seafood restaurant and several bottles of champagne (Elaine has a fondness for bubbly and no head for alcohol) when the phone rang. I hesitated for a moment, wondering whether it might be for Cindy, then picked it up.

"It's me," said Elaine, with no introduction. "I can't make dinner tonight. Something's come up."

This was typical Elaine, but I wasn't in the mood to play along.

"Cancel it. You're booked with me."

There was an exasperated sigh at the other end. "I can't cancel it. It's work related."

"Elaine, you booked with me. And you know what, I'm work related too. We have a lot to discuss, and it can't wait until tomorrow."

There was a long pause. I'm not sure anyone had ever questioned Elaine's inalienable right to work at all times, under any circumstances, and regardless of the cost to others, so it took her a moment to collect herself. When she did it was with unexpected violence.

"No, *you* have things to discuss. *I* have work to do. Just because you arrive here out of the blue doesn't mean that I can just put everything down, walk away from my lab. Jesus, Morgan, what do you think — "

"One dinner together, Elaine. Is that too much for your busy schedule? Or maybe it's something else. Maybe you don't want to talk me. Maybe you're afraid, because face to face you've got a hell of a lot of explaining to do. You lied about Riesler, you lied about Edwards, you're hiding more sh— "

She cut me off, her voice low and vicious. "You never change, do you. You always want more from me than I can give."

It was like being kicked in the stomach. I was momentarily stunned into silence, and when I could finally get some words out my voice had lost its edge. "That was a long time ago, a different life, and we've resolved all that."

"*You* haven't resolved it. You never will. And quite frankly, for me there was never anything to resolve." And she banged the phone down in my ear.

For a moment I sat there immobilized. Was it true? Did I always want more from her than she could comfortably give? There was a time when ... when that might have been true. But it was long ago, in graduate school, at a time when even the simplest emotions were intensified out of proportion by lack of sleep, excessive stress, and our bizarre living conditions in isolated field camps. And I *had* resolved it, no matter what she said, a hell of a lot better than she had. At least I didn't deny the past. And bringing it up after all these years, throwing it in my face, was an inexcusable betrayal. I gnawed on that for a while, replaying in my head scenes from our shared past, reanalyzing them in the new light of Elaine's betrayal. What was said, how it was said, what it really must have meant. By the end of it I was emotionally exhausted, but the paralyzing pain I'd felt earlier had been transformed by some primitive alchemy into a much more useful emotion. Cold, analytical anger. Elaine was going to pay for this.

I heard the lab door open and close and the sound of footsteps coming down the hall to Cindy's office. I braced for Elaine, but a moment later Dinah looked in through the door.

"You still here?" she said. "I thought you were having dinner with Elaine."

I eyed her, gauged the possibilities, and reached a rapid conclusion. She'd have as much information on Riesler, JJ, and Graham as Elaine, but she was also a possible treasure-trove of material on Elaine's personal and professional life. I smiled. I was going to find out what Elaine was up to, with or without Elaine's cooperation, and when I did there would be no mercy.

I looked at Dinah and gave a helpless shrug. "I was stood up. You wouldn't be interested in dinner, would you? My treat. I really need some help sorting out all the conflicting information I'm getting about the department."

She shifted uneasily. "Well ..."

"Your choice of restaurants. Cost is no object." Then I said sincerely, "You'd really be giving me a hand."

"I've got to organize the gear and load up the truck for tomorrow before I can leave."

"That's no problem. I'll help. It'll get me in the mood for our trip."

She still looked wary but finally nodded. "Okay, but I'm not sure how much help I'll be."

"More," I reassured her, "than you can imagine."

She gave me an odd look then pushed herself off the door frame. "Okay. Whatever. I'll be in the main lab getting out the gear. When you're finished up here you can come and help."

She turned and disappeared back down the hall. I smiled, saved and closed my file, then snapped the laptop shut.

I was halfway out of my chair when I remembered something, and I gave myself a little mental kick. I couldn't let Elaine divert me from other possibilities. I picked up the phone, dialed Duncan's number, and got his machine. He was probably putting the kids to bed. I gave him several new chores, the most urgent being a complete history of Graham Connell, including his academic records and a criminal check. Given the three-hour time lag he would have most of the work done by the time we opened for business tomorrow. I had just hung up the phone when I heard a loud expletive and a crash. I came around the corner into the lab to find Dinah standing, her back to me, in a large storage closet. She swore again, then she hauled off and kicked an innocent cooler, which flew full-force against the back wall and crashed to the floor. She turned and stormed out of the closet, almost bowling me over.

"Whoa," I said, and jumped aside.

She wheeled around and glowered at me for a second before connecting that I wasn't the enemy, then she threw her arm toward the closet. "None of the gear is there. She runs off without saying a word, not a note, no message, nothing. And she can't even take the time to stow the gear? Who the hell does she think she is? Give me a fucking break." Then she crossed her arms and stared at the closet, her eyes narrowed.

I kept my own voice quiet and low, trying not to inflame her emotions. "Maybe *you* should give her a break. For all we know her mother's dying."

She gave a brief laugh and spit out a sarcastic, "Right." Then she paused, looked at me for a second, then back at the closet, obviously trying to decide if she should say more, but finally dismissed the idea. With a pout and a terse shake of her head she said, "Shit. Let's check the van. The gear must still be inside. And I swear to you, the moment she sets foot back here, I'm gonna kill her."

I followed Dinah out of the lab. Instead of turning left into the main hall we continued straight across, down another narrow corridor that led out to a double set of doors. Dinah opened one and I followed behind.

The night was sharp and cold, the sky dotted with the pinpoint light of the brightest stars. Dinah shivered and wrapped her arms around herself. We were in a dark courtyard. In front of me, just in front of the exit, was a loading dock. In the far corner was a dumpster, and around the periphery I could just make out the shadowy forms of discarded equipment pushed up against the walls. It had the feel of an abandoned warehouse.

In front of us a line of vans stood haphazardly parked under a row of feeble lights. All were an identical fading silver with *Department of Zoology, University of Southern British Columbia* stencilled in black on the side. They were dented and scratched, some even had cracked windows, and this added to the derelict feel of the enclosure.

Dinah's eyes wandered down the line of vans. "Over there," she said, and she crossed to a slightly newer van parked near the end of the line. When she got to it she cupped her hands around her eyes and peered in. "It looks like the nets are still in here. She never even cleaned the truck out."

I'd come around to the side. In the dubious light it was hard to make out what was in the cargo area, but it certainly wasn't empty. There was a big mound of something in the middle, maybe a pile of nets and a tarp.

Dinah pulled the keys from her jeans and inserted a key in the lock, turning to speak to me at the same time. "If the nets are wet we'll have to hang them in the lab overnight." I heard the key engage. She pushed the handle down, pulled open the door, and bent forward to reach inside. Then she jerked her head to the side and staggered back a few steps with her hand covering her mouth and nose. "Oh God." She stood like that for a second then took a deep breath and turned unwillingly back to the truck. "It smells like one of the coolers dumped."

I stepped forward around her. The cargo area was in chaos, nets piled in a big heap, the waders tossed on top. One cooler was on its side with the fish spewed out across the floor. Everything looked slimy and wet, and the smell was an unappetizing mixture of damp nets and rotting fish. Dinah moved in beside me and pulled out a cooler that was upright. She pulled it away from the truck and opened it up. Dry ice vapour slipped over the top and spread across the ground, covering her feet. Dinah inspected the fish inside. They were rock solid and covered with a fine white frost.

"These look okay." She snapped the cooler shut.

There were two more coolers inside. She grabbed one, I grabbed the other. Hers was full of fish, still nicely frozen, but mine was empty.

"We have to get these to the freezer fast," she said, but instead of moving she stood, momentarily lost, staring into the van. Finally she said, "It's bizarre, you know. Cindy's a total space cadet, but not with her samples. Her research is sacred. I can't believe she'd leave these sitting out, even for her mother. And look at that." She motioned to four plastic garbage cans stacked near the front of the cargo section. "She didn't even try to get

Elaine's live samples — they'd be in the garbage cans —
and you don't do that to Elaine."

We unpacked the rest of the gear in silence, first getting
the samples into the freezer then disposing of the rotting
salmon, and finally piling the nets and equipment just
inside the lab door. Since Dinah knew the equipment
and I didn't I volunteered to wash the inside of the van
while she hung the nets to dry. By the time I'd finished
it was so dark, and the light in the van so feeble, that I
couldn't see if I'd missed a pool of slime or a patch of
scales. I picked up my bucket and mop, took one last
look around, and climbed out the back door. I locked
the back doors and had turned toward the entrance
when I heard a scraping sound two vans down. I stood
still, listening. At first there was nothing, but then I
heard a quiet crunch, as if someone had stepped on a
dry leaf or stone. I felt a shot of adrenaline and started
to move nonchalantly toward the doors, away from the
line of vans. I wanted to see who or what was there, but
from a safe distance, just in case I needed to make a
dash for the building. When I was far enough to feel safe
I turned and moved up the line of vans.

The first one was clear. The second one looked fine
too, but, dark as it was, behind the third van I could see
the shadow of a human lurking between the hood and the
wall. I had to make a decision quickly. Should I let him
(or her) know that they'd been seen, or fake it. Walk a few
more steps up the line then turn around and disappear
inside. I considered my surroundings. It was dark, I was
alone, and nobody was going to hear me if this person
had a knife or a gun. I choose option two: to pretend that
I'd seen nothing. I walked on a few paces, gave a dramatic
shrug, then turned and walked in the doors. Once inside

I swung open the second inside set of doors, but instead of going through into the hallway I stepped back into the darkened vestibule and waited. Within a minute JJ stepped out of the shadows, took a furtive look around, then walked toward Dinah's van, just out of my line of sight. I swung open the door and went after him. He was peering in the back window of Elaine's van but turned quickly when he heard my footsteps.

The jolt of adrenaline had shortened my temper, and I stormed right up to him. "What the hell were you doing behind those vans, or is skulking part of your job as well?"

He took a step back. "I do check the vans every night, not that it's any of your business. I saw someone in Okada's van, you didn't look familiar, so I wanted to make sure you weren't trying to steal it."

"With a mop and bucket?"

"There wasn't much light." He motioned inside. "What happened?"

I told him about Cindy's departure and the nets and samples left behind.

He gave a snort that was meant as a laugh. "It doesn't surprise me. Cindy isn't exactly the brightest light."

Dinah came through the doors just in time to catch this last comment. She stormed right past me and stopped inches from his face, looming over him. She gave him a sharp jab with her finger. "You're an asshole." Then she gave him another jab. "You don't know what you're talking about."

JJ took a step back and brushed his shoulder where she'd touched him, as if removing a squashed bug. Then he looked back at her with a cold smile. "I told you it wouldn't last. I mean she's dumb, but she isn't that stupid."

Dinah moved forward a step, but I grabbed her arm and yanked her back. JJ looked casually at his watch, although in this light he couldn't have read the dial, and said, "Sorry to break up the party but my date is waiting." He turned and started back toward the doors.

I could hear Dinah almost hyperventilating beside me, but I kept a grip on her sleeve.

"Hey JJ," I called after him. "Did you manage to sell your GeneMed?"

He'd made it to the door and with his hand on the latch he turned to face me. "Sell it? Why would I want to sell it? It's going to go back up, and when it does I'll make a killing."

Dinah chose a tiny Mexican café on 4th Avenue. As I swung open the door I was hit with heat, noise, and the dark, luscious smells of chili and garlic. I realized I was starving. When the waitress arrived with the tortilla chips and salsa I ordered a big pitcher of sangria. I planned to limit my intake, freeing up the rest for Dinah. I was heartened to see that she emptied her first glass before the waitress even left the table. She was pouring the second when I said, "Why don't you tell me about Cindy. That is what's bugging you, isn't it?"

There was no response, and I thought maybe she didn't hear me. She poured the sangria in slow deliberate movements then lowered the pitcher to the table, took her glass, looked me in the eye, and guzzled half of it down, then set her glass carefully on the table. Finally she said, "It's no big deal," and turned to look out the window.

I waited a minute, sipped my sangria. She avoided my gaze. Finally I put my glass on the table and leaned forward. "I think it is," I said softly. "I think it's a very big deal, and I think it might help to talk."

After our evening of cleaning and hauling her short hair was in disarray — the bedhead look that some people spend hours to achieve — and I could see a tiredness pulling at her eyes and the corners of her mouth. Finally she turned back to me. "Look, you don't have to act like I'm going to burst into tears or something because I'm not. Okay? We worked together, things got intense." She shrugged. "It didn't work out. That's all."

"Things got intense. Does that mean you had a relationship or were thinking about having a relationship?"

Dinah laughed, but it was a bitter sound. "That depends on how you define relationship. We *were* sleeping together, but I'm not sure that means we were having a relationship. It was all in the closet because Cindy didn't want anyone to know ... her career and all that shit."

"JJ knew."

"Yeah, well, Cindy had a fling with him just before me. Can you believe it? That jerk? But then things started to heat up between her and me. We were out in the field a lot, one thing led to another, then it just sort of happened. She wanted out of her relationship with JJ, so she told him about me, thinking it would get him off her back, but he went ballistic. He started following her around, threatening to tell everyone what was going on between us, begging her to return. He'd show up at her apartment and bang on the door at two in morning. Sometimes he'd yell he loved her, sometimes he screamed he was gonna kill her. That's why she had to leave Madden's lab. JJ wouldn't let up."

"So what happened?"

"He finally backed off. Maybe he found somebody else to harass, I don't know."

"And what about you and Cindy?"

She gave an impatient sigh and a shrug. "With JJ off her back I thought things would get better, but to tell you the truth, nothing changed. We had this sort of thing going, but I was about fifth in line after Elaine, experiments, animals, gear, you name it. And Cindy wanted it all undercover. Since I wanted the relationship to work I didn't have a lot of options, but about two weeks ago something changed. She got really weirded out; maybe about the missing fish, could have been the stress of the field season, maybe it had something to do with our relationship. I'm not sure. Then a couple of days ago she suddenly tells me she needs some space, she needs to *think things over*. I'm not an idiot. I know what that means, and I'd kind of had it. I told her to take all the space she needed but not to expect me to sit around waiting."

"Nice, Dinah. Very caring."

She gave me a petulant shrug. "I was pissed. Then when you told me she'd left for New Zealand I was furious. I mean, that's just like Cindy. Don't deal with it, run away. But then other things started to happen. She didn't leave instructions for her work, she abandoned her samples in the truck ... " She had pulled a taco chip from the basket and was toying with the salsa, taking a minute to run over the whole thing in her mind again. Finally she shook her head and said uneasily, "I don't know. I don't doubt she'd jerk me around, but screw up her work? That doesn't make sense."

The waitress arrived with the food, chicken enchiladas for me and a bean and cheese tostada for Dinah. We were both so hungry that there was no point in even trying to talk until the plates were half empty. Before the waitress could get away I ordered another pitcher of sangria and took the next few minutes of fussing with napkins, cutting up food, and chewing the sublime concoction to consider my next move. The discussion of Cindy was a sidebar for me. Although there was always a chance it was connected to my case in some way it wasn't the main attraction, and I still had a lot of ground to cover with Dinah: JJ, Graham, Riesler, and

Elaine. On the other hand, Cindy was good currency. If Dinah trusted me I'd get a lot more out of her, and we would have a long day working together tomorrow.

Dinah poured herself another glass of sangria. It was depressing to think of that nice alcohol buzz being wasted on something irrelevant, but what can you do.

"Why don't you call her?" I asked. "Just to make sure she's all right."

Dinah looked up with a full mouth of rice and beans. She shook her head. She swallowed and dabbed her mouth with a napkin. "She wanted space. I promised I wouldn't call her, that I'd let her contact me when she was ready. Anyway, I couldn't call even if I wanted to. I don't have a number in New Zealand. Her mother's remarried and has a different name, which I don't know. You can see how far our *relationship* got."

I shook my head. "You sure she's worth all this?"

She sighed. "No ... but unfortunately, I love her. I mean, I wish I didn't, but I do."

"I'll tell you what. I'll get the number through the office —"

"They won't give it to you."

I brushed that aside, "— and *I'll* call Cindy in New Zealand. I'll use her research as an excuse, say I'm calling for Elaine and we all want to know when she's coming back. How about that? At least you'd know if she lied about her mother."

For the first time Dinah's bravado seemed to completely slip away. "I'd like that," she said quietly. "I'd like that a lot."

The rest of the meal was depressingly unproductive. I was starting to numb out with fatigue, making it difficult for me to keep all my thoughts on track. Dinah was slowing down as well, the result of way too much sangria. She was going to be sorry tomorrow morning. On the other hand, she was under twenty-five. At that age a healthy body can take a hell of a lot of abuse.

I did manage to ask her about Graham. "An arrogant little prick," were her exact words, but she seemed to have no suspicions that he might be involved in anything unsavoury or illegal. JJ, she confirmed, was constantly short of money and always on the verge of getting rich, or so he bragged to the technicians. On the topic of Edwards she was strangely positive, given her negative opinion of everyone else in the department. I waited until the end of dinner to broach the subject and tried to come at it obliquely.

"I've known Elaine forever," I said as we were getting up to leave. "I'm curious about Edwards."

"I like Jonathan," she said defensively. "I think Elaine screwed up."

I was surprised to hear her echo my thoughts completely. "So what happened?"

Dinah was ahead of me and she pushed open the door into the cold night air. "All I know is that one day Elaine came into the lab really upset. She asked if Edwards ever came in when she wasn't around. I knew they were going out together, but what a weird question. Of course he wouldn't be around if she wasn't there. Why would he be in our lab? Then she tells me to keep him out of the lab and call her if I ever see him hanging around. Next thing I hear she's split with him and he's moved to Natural Resources. I guess he didn't want to have to face her every day."

Dinah's story squared up nicely with what I knew so far. I was pretty sure that Edwards didn't move by choice, and I now knew who and what to ask to discover the truth.

By the time I got Dinah home it was almost eleven.
She lived near the restaurant on the top floor of an old
Kitsilano house. As we pulled up something caught
my eye.

"Is that van always parked there?"

She looked across the street. A silver van, with
Department of Zoology stencilled on the side, was sitting down the street just at the top of a rise.

"Never. I'm the only one who parks one of those on
this street."

I was sure I'd seen movement inside, but with no
lights it was hard to say. I thought of JJ. "Go." It was
given as an order, not a request. "I'll wait here until
you're in. Lock the door behind you, turn on all the
lights, and check your closets. When you're done, come
out on the balcony and wave goodbye."

She laughed. "Like what are you going to do?
Protect me?"

I turned and shot her a look that sent her vaulting up
the stairs and through the door before I could turn back
to the van. When I'd seen her wave from the balcony I
pulled out slowly from my spot, passed the van, and
turned right at the first cross street. Just around the corner I glanced back to see the van pull out too. Of course,
on the narrow Kitsilano streets he couldn't turn around:
obviously an amateur. Five blocks later I'd lost him.

I drove for several more blocks, keeping my eyes on
the rearview mirror and side streets, and when I was sure
he was off my tail I headed uphill toward King Edward,
a main artery that runs up the spine of the point. Once
there, I turned off into a cozy neighbourhood of perfect
wooden houses on small, manicured lawns. I moved
slowly along until I found the number I wanted.

The street was dark and the sidewalks deserted. The wind had come up and the maples lining the street shook and swayed, their restless leaves making the light from the street lamps scurry about on the pavement. I got out of my car, locked the door behind me, and crossed to the house.

The lights on the first floor were off, but the second floor was lit. A set of stairs ran up the side of the house, and I took them two at a time. They ended in a small landing and a hunter green door with a window that looked across a neat little kitchen. I banged on the door, not loud enough to wake the elderly couple who owned the place, but loud enough to get their upstairs tenant off the couch and to the door.

Except that nobody heeded the call. I frowned and tried again. Then I noticed the boxes. Elaine must have removed the important files from her office after this morning's break-in. I tried knocking one more time, then I slipped on my gloves, pulled out my lock picks, and let myself in the door.

I worked quickly, with the light out and my flashlight on. I went through the boxes, pulling out any files that related to Elaine's current olfaction work and scanning them. Mostly it was data, test solution numbers, single cell recording data, Y-maze results, not anything I could use. Then I hit the big one: a research proposal, submitted to Madden Riesler, for a joint study on salmon olfaction.

"Yes!" I said, and I stood up with the file open in my hand.

"Find something you like?"

I turned.

Elaine was standing in the doorway.

chapter fourteen

"Arm's length?" I said, pushing the file toward her. "Pretty short arms, I'd say."

She covered the space between the door and the table in two quick strides, snatched up the file, and held it to her chest. "This is trespassing, O'Brien."

"Actually, it's break and enter. Why did you lie about this?"

"I don't have to answer your questions. You're not the police." She pointed to the door. "Get out."

"You don't want to talk about Riesler?" I shrugged. "Okay, we'll let him go for now. How about Jonathan Edwards? Nice guy, by the way. Too bad it didn't work out. So why's he out of the department, Elaine? What's the big secret?"

"That's it. I'm calling the police." She aimed for the phone.

"Go ahead. I can formalize this investigation at any point. All it takes is a call to the Dean."

She whirled around. "He used me."

"Are you so sure?" I reached down and pulled out Connell's publication record from my briefcase. "Jonathan asked me to show you this. Actually, he begged me to show it to you."

At first she didn't take it. She turned stony-faced to the wall, but I knew her weak points. "What's the matter, Elaine. Afraid you might find out you were wrong?"

She gave me the evil eye and yanked the paper from my hands. "You're wasting my time."

"Just read it."

She sat down reluctantly. I got up and found myself a glass in the cupboard. There was almost nothing of interest in the fridge, typical Elaine, so I opted for a glass of water. Leaning against the sink I watched her expression change from annoyance to incomprehension to horror. By the time she pushed the paper forward to stare at the table she was pale.

I spoke gently. "Is that why Jonathan was forced to leave? Because you accused him of stealing your data?" She glanced up at me and the answer was clear in her eyes. I nodded. "That's what I thought."

"Oh God." She covered her face with her hands.

"And was Madden involved?"

"He didn't want Jonathan's career ruined. He had him moved to Natural Resources."

That was interesting. Was he hoping to get Edwards to retract his complaint? A *you scratch my back, I'll scratch yours* arrangement. If that was the case it hadn't worked. But then why should it? Edwards hadn't done anything wrong. Or maybe Madden just wanted to keep everything as quiet and orderly as possible while he waited for Ottawa to bury the investigation. I'd have to work that one out later.

I looked at Elaine sitting at the table. She was almost on the point of tears — an unthinkable state for her — and it made my job easier. "Okay," I said softly, "so let me lay out my problem. I've got Graham making a name for himself by ripping off other people's work. I've got JJ who controls the Network funds and happens to have a taste for high-risk gambling. I've got Riesler, who seems to be using a foreign aid grant to fund research on olfaction. And don't forget Jonathan Edwards, whom everyone was happy to accuse of theft, and who just happens to be missing two hundred thousand dollars from his research budget. Now you tell me, what's a girl to do?"

With a great effort Elaine lifted her head. Despite the remorse there was still a sharp edge to her voice. "What do you want from me?"

"Preferably your help."

"Madden's not doing anything wrong. It's all aboveboard."

"Then it won't hurt to take a look, will it?"

"Take a look? At what?"

"The financial records, and," I put out my hand, "I'll be needing your pass-key."

She shook her head, first slowly, then vigorously. Then, just to confirm the message (in case it wasn't coming through loud and clear), she added, "No way. Not in a million years."

I shrugged. "Then my investigation has just officially spilled over into your lab. Fisheries Enterprises International? That's the funding consortium? First thing tomorrow morning I'll contact the Dean of Research, we'll subpoena your — "

"Stop!" Then, in a voice already resigned to the future, "If you're caught I'll lose my job."

"You'll lose it anyway if I'm forced to go through official channels. If it's any consolation, *I* think Riesler's clean. My bets are on JJ or Graham, but I have to see the records to know for sure."

She pulled a key ring from her pocket, took off a key, and handed it to me. I slipped it into my pocket.

"What about Graham?" she asked, nodding to the paper on the table. "What are you going to do about that?"

"When this is over I'll report it. Best case scenario is that he's out on his ass with the job prospects of a toad but — I've got to be honest with you — it's more likely he'll walk out of here into another position, nobody will check his references, and he'll start the whole thing over again." I sighed. "It's happened before. Unless you and some of the others decide to take him to court on a civil action, but that costs money, and proving damages isn't easy."

"But the university will — "

"The university will hush it up. They don't want the bad publicity."

She hesitated for a moment. "He's been working with us, you know. On the olfaction study."

I felt a frisson travel up my spine. "Does he have access to confidential information?"

"No. At least I don't think so. I don't even have access to the test solutions."

I started to respond with some platitude but realized that she wasn't listening anyway. She had turned and was staring at the wall, running something over in her mind. I shrugged, picked up my briefcase, and started to get up. I didn't know if she'd hear me, but I felt I should say it anyway.

"I'm sorry about tonight, Elaine. Actually, I'm sorry about everything, but I *am* here if you need me."

She snapped back suddenly, and swung around. "He can't know anything, Morgan. If he does, I'm screwed."

I kept my voice neutral. "What do you mean?"

She thought for a minute, then fixed me with a level gaze. "This has to be confidential. I need your promise."

"You've got it, but only if it's legal. If it's not ... " I shook my head.

She took a deep breath and laid her palms flat on the table. "By this time next year, I will have authored the most important paper in sensory physiology to be published in this decade. I'm *this* close." She showed me an infinitesimal space between her thumb and forefinger.

Coming from a lesser person the word *delusion* would have popped into my head, but in terms of research, Elaine's feet were firmly planted on the ground. If she was saying she was on to something big, she was.

"That's fabulous. Are you publishing with Madden?"

It was like I'd hit her with a cattle prod. She leapt up and brought her palms down on the table hard enough to make me jump. "It's my research. My discovery. Madden's fronting the money, that's all." Then she seemed to see me, remember who I was, and she sat back down in her chair, but her voice was still determined. "I run the research, I get the credit. I didn't lie about Madden."

"You didn't tell the truth either." And given our relationship I was more than a little peeved. Still, maybe I owed Elaine something for breaking into her apartment. "Look, if you want me to take a peek in Graham's office tonight ..." I shrugged, "... since I'll be in the neighbourhood."

I thought she might take the high moral road and object, but she didn't. In fact, she didn't even look surprised. Instead she said, "How much do you know about what I'm doing?"

"Not much. Only what Dinah and Edwards have told me."

"And they don't know, not the details. It had to be just Madden and me." She sighed and sat back in her chair. "If you're going into Graham's office you have to know what to look for, so I better start at the beginning."

And she did. I took a chair beside her and she flipped over a piece a paper, pulled out a pencil, and began to sketch, her voice impatient and excited all at once.

"You know that all sensory organs have receptors, right? And you know that the job of the receptor is to take information from the outside world and change it into something that the brain can process. So, receptors are triggered by external stimuli, and usually very specific stimuli."

I nodded. On her paper she'd drawn an eyeball in cross section with a line connecting it to something that looked vaguely like a human brain. She tapped the eyeball with her pencil. "Your retina, here, is made up of rod and cone cells." She scribbled a dark black line at the back of the eyeball. "They're the receptors. When light hits the membrane of a rod or a cone cell, a chemical change takes place at the membrane, and this initiates a whole sequence of events that result in a nerve that's attached to the receptor being fired. The nerve impulse travels up a neural pathway," she traced the line attaching the eye to the brain, "eventually arriving at a visual centre in the brain." She drew a small circle on her schematic brain and initialled it *VC*. "The visual cortex, for example, consolidates all the information being sent from the eyes and interprets it as an image. But the thing I want you to remember is that each rod and cone cell are highly specific: each responds to only a narrow band in the spectrum of visible light. If light of other wavelengths hits the receptor, nothing happens. That's why we see colour and detail."

She drew another schematic. To me it looked like some kind of maze, but like the eye, it was attached to the brain by a line. "The ear works basically the same way." She saw my confused expression and shook her head in disgust. "That's the inner ear, remember? Those are the canals and this," she pointed to a little ball in the centre, "is the cochlea, roughly equivalent to the retina in the eye. But instead of rods and cones this thing contains hair cells, receptors that respond to the physical vibrations caused by sound."

She drew a little round ball with a hair poking out of it. "Like that." She looked up. "I'm simplifying this, okay?"

Since I hadn't taken a course in sensory physiology since my undergraduate years, I didn't mind at all. She went back to her drawing.

"The important thing again is that each hair cell — each receptor — only responds to a narrow band of frequencies. The hair is literally pushed by the right frequency of sound," she drew another little round ball with the hair bending over like a sapling in the wind, "and this mechanical stimulation triggers the sequence of chemical events that end with the nerve firing and a signal going to the brain. So what about the olfactory system?"

Above the amorphous brain — which was now attached to an eyeball and an inner ear — she drew a big schnoz with a question mark hanging off its tip. I started to laugh, but caught her expression: serious and intent. It wasn't meant as a joke. She ignored my stifled guffaw and went right on talking.

"Given what we know about these other systems, we'd expect to find receptors, here in the epithelium lining the nose, that respond to chemicals suspended in the air or, in the case of aquatic animals, in the water that surrounds them. We'd also expect the receptors to be stimulus specific: each receptor should respond only to specific odours. The receptors should then feed their information to an olfactory centre in the brain." She attached up the nose to a circle in the brain labelled OC.

"Simple, right? The trouble is, nobody can find a receptor. We've been looking for over fifty years, and we still can't figure out which cells in the lining of the nose are the receptors. And then there's the problem of the stimuli. Light and sound are easy to identify and they're simple to manipulate and measure, so we can run tests to trace the neural pathways and understand how the visual and auditory systems work. But odours? Odours are just molecules, and there are millions, billions of molecules, all different, that can become suspended in air or water. And one odour might be made up of a thousand different molecules. So what's stimulating the receptors? Are there different receptors responding to specific molecules or discrete classes of molecules? Perhaps, but we have no idea what those molecules might be, partly because we can't identify a receptor, and basically, if we can't find a receptor *and* we don't know what the stimuli are, its hard to study the system. Enter Madden Riesler."

"But he doesn't work on olfaction. I've seen his records."

She leaned back with a self-satisfied smile. "True, but Madden's lucky, and he's smart. About eight years ago he was visiting a lab in Seattle run by a researcher named Grierson. Grierson was big in orientation and homing in salmonids, and at that time was interested in the role of olfaction. We've known for some time that olfaction plays some kind of role in salmon migration, that during parts of the migration they literally smell their way home, but how much of a role and how it actually works are still unknown. Anyway, while Madden was there an honour's student in Grierson's lab stumbled upon both an olfactory pathway and its stimulus, only they didn't know it at the time. He'd been testing the olfactory response of sockeye to potential pheromones, wanting to know if they could sense them and use them as chemical cues for homing to their natal streams. The student was recording nerve activity with an electrode that he thought was sitting in the olfactory bulb. That would be roughly here." She drew a little bulb just beneath and behind the frontal lobes. "And in fish, it's the central processing area for odours." She glanced up at me. "That, at least, we do know. Anyway, he'd tested one solution and got no response, then moved on to the second, but realized that he needed to flush out the nasal cavities with distilled water. He had two beakers sitting beside him, one that he had filled with distilled water and another that some other student had left lying around. He took his syringe, filled it, and squirted the water into one of the nasal cavities. The cells went wild, firing continuously for almost a minute. He waited five minutes, to let them settle, and he did it again. Same thing. Then he got Grierson. The student had, of course, pulled his water from the unidentified sample. It sounded great at first, except for one problem. When they did the histology on the sockeye brain they found that the electrode wasn't even in the olfactory bulb. It was in some unidentified nerve bundle off to the side. The poor kid had been totally off target. Grierson assumed that it was an anomaly and chalked the whole thing up to experimenter error, but Madden wasn't so sure. He asked if he could keep the sample, Grierson gave it to him, and he's had it sitting in liquid nitrogen ever since."

"Until he found you."

She nodded. "Serendipity, the literature would call it. When I was at Berkeley I gave a seminar on some new evidence pointing to the possibility of olfactory pathways that bypass the olfactory centres of the brain. We don't know where they go or what they do, but they probably feed directly into the endocrine system. For example, this kind of olfaction probably plays a role in the synchronization of women's menstrual cycles when they live in close contact over extended periods of time. Madden saw the seminar and made the connection. He realized that maybe Grierson's student had found one of these primitive olfactory pathways. And he knew I had the expertise to design a project using his original sample, which was critical because there was less than a litre of it left and no room for error."

"So he brought you up here."

She bristled. "There was a job and I competed. My qualifications brought me up here."

"And the funding?"

"Look, Morgan, I'm a scientist, not an accountant. Somebody offers me money to fund my research and I take it, as long as there are no strings attached. And there was nothing attached to this. The only requirement was that I do good science, which I have."

"What about credit? Who gets it, you or Madden?"

"Me. I'm first author, Madden second. That was *my* condition."

"And you've found the receptor?"

"Almost. We tested purified solutions last week that made the cells crackle like a radio in lightning. Once Madden releases the codes and I know what I've been working with I'll do some radioactive tagging, run stimulus/receptor binding tests *in vivo* and *in vitro*, and when a tagged molecule binds with the receptor I have it in the bag. The stimulus and the receptor are mine."

"You have no idea what you're working with?"

"It's part of our blind control. We test the fish with both the experimental solutions and control solutions. If I knew which were which I might inadvertently influence the results. I was lucky to get Madden's help on this."

"So what about Graham. How does he fit in?"

She looked surprised. I think in her fervour she'd forgotten all about him. "He doesn't really. He's just a mule; part of our blind control. First we fractionated the original sample and determined which fraction was producing the response. That sample was then analyzed, but it still contained around sixty distinct compounds, all of which had to be synthesized and tested. Dr. Truong over in Biochemistry makes up the test solutions and the controls. When he has a batch ready he calls Madden and Madden sends Graham over to Biochemistry to pick them up. Graham brings them back to Madden, who codes them, then Graham brings them down to me. That way I never know if I'm working with a test solution or a control, I'm never in contact with Truong, and Madden, who knows the codes, isn't in contact with the research, so there's no possible source of bias. So Graham couldn't ..." She paused. Just as my brain was doing, hers leaped a few steps ahead, and we both arrived at the same conclusion at about the same time: Graham was the only person with access to every part of the process, and given his proclivities, chances were very good that he knew exactly what was going on.

"Jesus," she blurted. "Screw the experimental design. I've got to get those codes from Madden."

chapter fifteen

My watch read 3:00 A.M. I was driving along an almost deserted 12th Avenue, and for the second time in a very short period I was grateful for the three-hour time lag between Ottawa and the West Coast. My body was still jet-lagged enough to believe it was really 6:00 A.M., which made the hour uncivilized but at least manageable. I had left Elaine's only a few hours ago, just after midnight, and my night had been mercilessly short. Coffee, I already knew, would be a big component of the coming day.

When I hit 10th Avenue I decided to turn left and take the back entrance into the university through heavily wooded parkland. Driving down 16th the night was dark and unsettled, the sky a canopy of restless cloud. Around me the forest appeared as a black outline — a single entity — that swayed and undulated like a living being.

At C-lot I drove slowly, keeping an eye out for headlights. At this time of night the parking lot was almost empty, with only a few cars dotting its surface; isolated islands in a dark sea. I followed the road past the parking lot into the narrow streets that crisscrossed the medical and life sciences sectors. During the day, the promenades were alive with students walking to class or sitting on the walls and benches drinking coffee, books open, reading, studying, talking; but the only movement now came from dry leaves and litter caught up in eddies of wind.

Just before the main boulevard I turned left and arrived at the access road that ran behind the Zoology wing. I cursed the safety features of modern cars that wouldn't allow me to turn off my headlights and turned quickly into the alley that led to the courtyard. Once inside, I relaxed a little and drove to the end of the line of vans. The place I'd scouted out earlier was still there: sandwiched between the wall and the last van, a space so narrow I couldn't open the side doors. I pulled in, bringing my car right up against the front wall, well hidden in the shadows. I popped open the hatchback and clambered out the rear. A quick check of my pockets confirmed that all my equipment was in place. I listened for a second, then eased the hatchback closed.

At the entrance of my hiding place I stopped again and waited. Faint light shone through several of the windows above, but not with the brightness of a working space; probably light leaking from the halls or an experimental setup. An exhaust fan hummed steadily on my right, and dry leaves, captured by the wind, scraped along the pavement, but nothing human, or even animal, moved.

I stepped out of the darkness, crossed quickly to the doors, and pulled out Elaine's pass-key. Just as the door shut behind me I heard an engine coming down the alley. I stepped back against the wall, trying to hide in the shadows. A set of headlights swung across the courtyard. The vehicle stopped, and I heard a door open, the crunch of boots on gravel. A radio squawked, then a flashlight beam moved slowly across the windows in the door. Like a rag doll, I slid down to the floor. The beam passed across where I had been standing. I waited, hardly breathing, but no footsteps approached the door. The radio squawked again, a car door slammed, tires squealed, and the noise of the engine became faint as it left the courtyard for the access road. I stood up and let my breath out slowly. I love this part of my job, but only if I don't get caught. My methods are not exactly sanctioned by the Government of Canada.

I could see from the narrow hall ahead of me that the university, like the Council, was on a cost-cutting junket. Only one in four of the fluorescent lights was turned on, creating what could best be described as dim lighting. One of the tubes flickered wildly, creating a stroboscope effect that would have thrown an epileptic into seizures.

At the intersection with the main hall I stopped again and peeked around. It had the same dim lighting, but at least all the bulbs were working. Unfortunately, the sound of running water would block out anything but the sharpest sounds, so if somebody else was in the labs I wouldn't hear them. I decided to wait again before moving.

After five minutes of no activity I left my spot and crossed quickly to Riesler's lab, glanced suspiciously to the left and right, and let myself in with Elaine's key. The overhead lights were out and that was good news. In the darkness I could see the glow of red, orange, and yellow indicator lights and hear a steady clicking of something — an automatic counter — somewhere to my left. As I passed the tanks there was a loud splash and a spray of water. A frisky salmon, I told myself, and kept my distance.

JJ's office was dark and the door was locked, but the key worked, no problem. I left the door open so I'd have a better chance of hearing footsteps and panned my flashlight across the office. JJ was a neat little embezzler, his desk cleared for the evening. I knelt in front of the filing cabinet and gave the bottom drawer a tug. Damn. It was locked. I looked up. There was a single pop-out lock, easy as pie. I took out my lock picks and a minute later it popped open. Five minutes later I had all the files I needed under my arm. My plan was to photograph them in Elaine's lab, where I was safe from discovery, then get them back here within an hour. I closed the drawer and looked at the popped-out lock. To lock or not to lock, that was the question. I decided against it. Four-thirty to five in the morning — when I would return with the files — was too close to the arrival time of some of the more ardent students, so I would need to get in and get out fast.

I was passing the fish museum when I remembered my other mission. I reached for the doorknob, expecting the door to be locked, but it was ajar and swung open. A feeble wedge of light exposed a section of deserted bench. I could just see the glint of sample jars and the incriminating eyes of the lifeless fish on the shelves behind. Somewhere nearby I thought I heard a door close so I stepped into the darkness and eased the door shut. The only light came from the tiny square of glass in the door, but I didn't want to attract attention by turning my flashlight on, so I waited for my eyes to adapt before moving toward Graham's office.

His door, too, was standing ajar. I could smell formaldehyde, lab alcohol, and a slightly sour, fishy odour, but there was nothing moving, nothing to hear. I took a chance and swept the flashlight beam across the office. It was empty, but I noted two doors that I hadn't registered before. One was in the back right corner, and adjacent to it, on the wall directly in front of me, was another door that was wide open. I moved forward, keeping the beam high. When I got near enough, I stepped abruptly into the room. It was empty, at least of living things. Ceiling to floor metal shelving was crowded with dissecting trays, scalpels, scissors, squirt bottles: everything required to conduct the labs. One down.

The other door was locked, but again the pass-key worked. It opened to a wall of musty air and a black void: a cavernous space that seemed to drop into nowhere. Beneath my feet, an iron staircase spiralled into the darkness. Then I remembered. The preserved fish I saw in the teaching lab would be only a small part of the collection. The bulk of it was probably stored below in a sub-basement. I ran my flashlight along the wall to either side of the staircase until I found a light switch. There was no time now, but another day I'd check it out.

Secure that I was alone, I closed the sub-basement door and pulled the door to Graham's office shut. I then sat down and began to work.

Graham's desk was covered with papers and file folders haphazardly arranged into something that resembled piles. A pen lay uncapped on the desk with a block of lined paper next to it. I ran my flashlight over the desk. Tucked beneath one of the piles, the edge of a pale yellow Rite-in-the-Rain notebook caught my eye. Graham didn't seem like a fieldwork kind of guy, so I pulled it out. Just then I caught a whiff of something sweet and cloying, but just as quickly it was gone.

The cover of the notebook was blank — an indication of messy research habits — but the pages inside weren't. There were only three pages used, but each page was meticulously dated, followed by notations on the temperature, cloud cover, what I could now see was fish density, and an estimated number of redds — the nests that female salmon dig. This was followed by five columns of numbers, each column headed up by a code.

I flipped to the last completed page. The date at the top was Monday, October 21, just two days ago. The weather notations were there, as were the figures for fish density and number of redds, but the columns of measurements were incomplete. Instead of five there were only four, and the fourth ended halfway down the column. Where had I seen this before? Then it clicked.

This notebook belonged to Cindy.

Why would Graham steal current field notes? It wasn't like he could publish a paper from them. They were too raw, and I suspected that he preferred his data somewhat more refined and journal-ready. Also, these looked like field notes in progress. Wouldn't Cindy miss her notebook? Unless Graham knew that she'd taken off for New Zealand and so wouldn't be needing them.

I pondered the problem for a minute but couldn't seem to make the connections because I was suddenly overwhelmed with fatigue, a combination of jet lag and lack of sleep. All I wanted to do was lay my head on the desk and just for a minute shut my eyes, but I fought off the feeling. I didn't have time. I stuffed the field notes into an inside pocket of my jacket for later consideration.

It took a great effort, but I pulled the list Elaine had given me from another pocket. It detailed the kind of data sheets and the type of codes I should be looking for. All I had to do was find a couple, and then I could get out of here, get away from that faint but annoying smell. What the heck was that?

I checked through the files on the desk. There was nothing relating to Elaine. Then, working now in slow motion, I tried one of the file drawers beneath the desk. It opened easily but yielded nothing unusual: files of reprints mainly. From there I turned to the one nearest the door. It was locked, which made it immediately more promising. I fumbled for my lock picks but was so tired I had trouble gripping them. I bent over the drawer. The scent was heavy here, rising up from the floor. I took a big inhalation and realized, too late, what I was smelling. Sick and dizzy I reeled forward, the flashlight tumbling across the floor. I got my hand out just in time to protect my head from bouncing off the concrete, but then my hand slipped in the viscous puddle, sending me sprawling forward. I forced myself to a half-stand and reached for the door, but the knob wouldn't turn. I staggered up and flipped around, my back against the door, trying to see into the darkness. The office wasn't big. Could I make it to the sub-basement? It seemed so far away. Now the vapours were rising up off my shirt and engulfing my face. I started forward but fell to my knees, then to my hands, sliding onto my stomach, pitching forward into a great abyss. The letters $CHCl_3$ appeared on a blackboard in my brain. Dr. Dingly — Organic Chemistry 204 — materialized beside it, white lab coat, white chalk, white hair, tapping on the board. *"Chloroform,"* he was saying in a tinny voice. *"A colourless, volatile solvent with a sweet ..."*

I should have paid more attention. Everything faded to black.

I awoke face up.

There was white light and cold: cold along my back where the dampness of concrete seeped through my clothes, and bright light above. Even with my eyes closed, the brilliance bored into my head, making it pound. I heard water flowing nearby, a soothing sound, and I tried to relax into it, block out the pain. Finally I opened one eye a crack. A dagger of white light drove through the opening into my brain. My stomach heaved, and by instinct I rolled to my side. Choking on your own vomit is an ignominious way to die.

I felt immediately better, or at least able to keep my stomach contents in my stomach. I lay there trying not to move; it could have been a minute, it could have been twenty until footsteps sounded in the distance, coming closer. A key turned, and this was followed by a surprised shout and colourful language, all of which made my head ache even more. I covered my ears. Dinah pulled me to a sitting position and wrapped her arms around me.

"What happened? Are you all right?"

Given the circumstances I thought it was a silly question. However, her body created a dark cave around my face, and that was welcome. My cheek lay against soft flannel that smelled of Ivory soap and laundry hung in the sun to dry. Beneath that there was a luxurious warmth. I summoned up the courage to open my eyes. Better. I looked up slowly, squinting in case the light was too bright. I took several deep breaths and felt the systems begin to kick in.

"I'm okay," I croaked, now strong enough to push her away. "Can you get me some water?"

"Can you hold yourself up?"

I nodded, and she headed to her office. While she was gone I looked around. I was in Elaine's lab, but it looked radically different from yesterday: shelves had been pulled down, glassware broken and equipment smashed, a malicious kind of vandalism that left nothing untouched. Dinah returned with a mug and handed it to me. I sipped gingerly.

"Man, I can't believe it," she said, glancing around the room. "Did you walk in on them or what?"

The water, in small doses at least, seemed to help, but when not drinking I cradled my head against my knees. From this position I asked, "Who has access to chloroform?"

It took her a minute to connect the dots, then she said, "Everyone."

"Seriously?"

"Well, yeah. Pretty well everyone. It's the first solvent used in DNA separations. It's in practically every lab."

"Bugger," I said, more to myself than her. I heard ringing coming from somewhere. Dinah got up and disappeared into her office. I was relieved to know it was the phone and not my head.

She came back, stepping carefully over the debris. "It's for you. A guy named Duncan. I said I didn't know if you could make it."

I put my hand out and she helped me to my feet, wrapped her arm around my waist, and almost carried me toward her office.

"Cindy's office," I said. "I'll take it in her office."

"Okay," she said uneasily. "But it's even worse than mine."

She was right. The lab had been pulled apart with reckless abandon, but Cindy's office had been dismantled, systematically searched. What were they looking for? And what had they found? I picked up the phone. Dinah was leaving, but in no great hurry. I covered the mouthpiece. "Close the door, okay?"

She threw me a sullen look, but obeyed.

"You okay?" It was Duncan.

"I don't know," I said honestly. "Is chloroform a carcinogen?"

"Yeah. Toxic as hell."

Great. I rubbed my head. "What have you got?"

"Graham Connell? He doesn't exist. Or if he does, he sure as hell didn't go to Johns Hopkins. They have no record of a Graham Connell ever graduating from any faculty for the past fifteen years. You've got a ringer."

Maybe, but if I couldn't connect him to the embezzlement of Network funds or a NCST cover up it didn't do me a lot of good. Then I remembered JJ's financial records. Damn. Where the hell were those files?

"You still there?" asked Duncan.

"Got anything else?"

He laughed. "Oh good. I can see you're feeling better. I haven't gotten the results on the criminal check yet so I can't help you out there, but you were also asking about connections. I need to do some more digging but I can tell you that Riesler's been on a lot of government committees with both Patsy and the President, which we would expect, given his stature. The surprise is Jacobson. He sat on a grant review committee a couple years back with Patsy, and I wondered about that. Why Jacobson, unless as a stand-in for Riesler? So I made some calls. According to my contact, Jacobson got the job because he's the President's nephew. Or he was at the time. Which is to say, Jacobson is the blood nephew of the President's ex-wife, and since the Prez's divorce Jacobson hasn't shown up on any committees."

"Which makes it unlikely that he'd get help from the President's office in a cover-up."

"I'd say so, unless he's pulling other strings."

I sighed. Again, it was great information, but it got me exactly nowhere. I was going to have to find those files. I thanked Duncan and hung up. There was a soft knock at the door followed by Dinah with a mug in her hand. "Elaine's on her way," she said, then she handed me a mug, and said, almost aggressively, "And I brought you this. It's okay if you don't want it, but it might do you some good."

I reached out — the angel of mercy had arrived — and took a long, slow sip of the milky tea. I managed a weak smile and said, "Got any Tylenol to go with this?"

The tea gave me enough of a boost to stagger to the fish museum.

"Why don't you just call Graham?" Dinah asked. "He was here when I came in." But by the time we got to the fish museum the lights were off and the door was locked. Dinah rattled the knob. "That's bizarre. He's got an 8:30 lab." She shrugged. "I'll go see if I can find a key."

Without answering I pulled the pass-key from my pocket, pushed her aside, and opened the door. Dinah gave me a sideways glance but said nothing. I left the door open, just in case there were fumes lingering in the air. Graham's office door was locked. When I opened it I was struck first by the smell — industrial soap — then by the office itself. It looked like something from an Ikea catalogue. The surface of the desk was bare, pencils and pens were sitting upright in a cup and — I bent down and opened up a file drawer — most of the files were gone.

Graham had cleaned up, cleared out, and taken JJ's files with him.

chapter sixteen

Dinah was behind me. "What's going on?" she asked.

I felt the notebook in my pocket and pulled it out. "I found this in here last night."

She gave me an odd look. "In here? Last night? Why were you —"

"Do you recognize it?"

"Sure. It's Cindy's. But why would it be in here?"

"I was hoping you'd know."

She shook her head. For a moment I thought she wasn't going to say anything, then she blurted out, "She told me she didn't trust him. Why would she give him her field notes?"

Why indeed. There was no more to learn from Graham's office so I took one last look and closed the door behind me. It was approaching 8:30 and students were milling around the empty benches hoping, no doubt, that Connell wouldn't show. I saw

Elaine run past the door heading for her lab. Dinah saw her too.

"I'd better — " she started forward.

I put my hand on her arm. "I'll go. You find Madden. Tell him that Graham won't be in today. And Dinah, go up to the office and get them to give Cindy a call in New Zealand. See if she knows about this." I held up the notebook before slipping it back in my pocket. "And if she didn't *give* it to Connell, I want to talk to her."

Dinah had a nasty gleam in her eye. "Yeah, well, I'd sort of like to talk to her about Graham as well."

When I got to Elaine's lab the door was wide open and I caught a glimpse of her before she saw me. She was stepping delicately through the debris. With her back to me she bent down, scooped something up, turned it her hands, then threw it despondently back to the floor, looking for all the world like a victim from a war-torn country picking through the remains of her bombed-out home. I moved forward and she wheeled around. The haunted look was quickly replaced by anger.

"This is your fault. Why couldn't you have left it alone?" Then she turned her back on me.

My reaction was not polite. "I could have been killed in Graham's office last night. Who did you tell I was there?"

"What are you saying?"

"Somebody drugged me and brought me in here. I woke up to this," I said, sweeping my hand around the room. "Who would do this? Trying to get at me I understand, but your lab? Why, Elaine?"

"I have no idea." But she said it by rote. There was no meaning and no truth in it. She avoided further scrutiny by going to the salmon tank. "At least *they're* still alive." The statement had an ugly connotation.

In a second I'd covered the space between us. I grabbed her by the shoulder and swung her around. "You don't get it. This is serious. This isn't about research anymore. Look." I glanced around the room. "If you know something — "

"I don't," she yelled, wrenching free. "I don't know anything. Jesus, I wish I did." She rubbed her shoulder. The pain seemed to refuel her anger. "But if I did," she said, almost in a hiss, "I wouldn't tell you."

It was such an absurd statement, right off the playground of an elementary school, that we were both taken aback and looked at each other, shocked. Was this what we had come to? Apparently it was.

"Oh God, Elaine, I'm sorry. I didn't mean — "

"Yes, you did," she said. Then the flash of anger died and she sighed. "But I understand. And I ..."

I nodded quickly so she wouldn't have to finish. Neither Elaine nor I were good at these sorts of scenes. She glanced around her lab again, then put her hand on my arm and sighed. "I'll go call the police."

Elaine started to leave but was almost knocked over by Dinah barrelling through the door. Dinah looked wildly around the room, as if she'd forgotten what state the lab was in, then her gaze fell on me.

"She's not there."

I didn't understand.

"Cindy," she said with emphasis. "She never went to New Zealand, and her mother's fine. I talked to her on the phone."

At this news Elaine paled and crumpled into a chair. I realized that part of me, the darker side, had been expecting this all along, but there was no point in upsetting the others prematurely. I put on my best calm, authoritative cop voice and lifted my hands, palm forward, in the universal appeal to slow down.

"Let's not jump to conclusions. Cindy's been under a lot of stress." I looked at Dinah for confirmation. She nodded reluctantly.

"Maybe she needed a break. Maybe this was the only way she could get it, to take off and use her mother as an excuse. Think about it. What other excuse could you use if you were at the end of your tether and had to get away in the middle of the field season. So we don't really know that she's missing, and we do know that she was here on Monday night." Then I caught myself. We didn't know that. All we knew was that someone had sent an e-mail from her account, but we couldn't be sure it was Cindy. In fact, we had no concrete evidence that Cindy had ever arrived back from Weaver Creek. The truck was here, but had Cindy been in it? Despite these morbid thoughts I tried to keep my tone upbeat. "Dinah and I will go up to Weaver Creek today and see what we can find. You," I looked at Elaine, "call the RCMP about the break-in."

A moment after it was out of my mouth I realized that a police investigation might present me with a problem. "But leave me out of it, okay?" I continued, my voice offhand. "And make sure they run a criminal check on Graham. I'm pretty sure he's involved."

Elaine stood up slowly and nodded. She looked as if she was going into shock but then she rallied. "The police," she said firmly, then almost to herself, "and I need to get some answers from Madden too."

On my way out to the car I ran into Riesler hurrying toward the fish lab. He looked distraught, but when he saw me it was as if he had seen salvation. Today, the jeans were gone, replaced by grey flannel dress pants and a navy blazer over a pale blue dress shirt. The tie was old school, but over this natty ensemble he was wearing a less than clean lab coat, obviously a last-minute addition.

"I heard about Elaine's lab," he said coming toward me. "It's terrible. Simply awful. And Graham's disappeared? I can't believe it. He's my student, so he's my responsibility. Perhaps I didn't check his references as well as I should have ..." He looked guilty and his voice trailed off, then he rallied. "Would you, could you possibly join me for dinner tonight. I must be honest with you. I need to unburden myself, but I can't with someone from the department. I need some objectivity. I realize that it's an imposition, but perhaps you can help me sort this all out. And there are some other things, but I don't know if they're relevant. Maybe they are," he looked at me helplessly, "but maybe it's all in my imagination." He gave a self-deprecating laugh. "Sometimes I feel, well, almost paranoid I suppose. But with all this, one doesn't really know."

A willing tête-à-tête with one of the principle players? Perfect. Then I remembered Sylvia's appointment. "Could we make it late? Sometime after eight?"

His face relaxed, and he reached out and squeezed my hand. "Thank you so much. There's a little Japanese restaurant on Broadway, just near your hotel. I'll meet you there at eight-thirty sharp."

He glanced uneasily at the door to the fish museum and lifted the lapel of his lab coat. "I haven't taught a lab in fifteen years, but Graham's gone, JJ seems to have disappeared, and I'm the only one left who knows the collection." He looked at his watch. "And if I don't get in there soon, the students will leave." He turned and hurried off down the hall, but just before disappearing into the lab he turned back and said, "I look forward to our dinner, and good luck at Weaver Creek."

It took some manoeuvring to get my car out of the space where I'd hidden it early that morning. I almost scraped off the driver's side mirror in the process, but I wasn't too worried. Bob could spring for a new one, particularly since I couldn't claim any overtime.

By the time I got out to C-lot it was after nine o'clock and I was surprised to find a parking space in the second row of cars. I locked up my rental and waited for Dinah. When the van appeared on the road, I waved. She pulled into the parking lot and came up beside me. I was climbing up into the seat when she opened her door and vaulted out the other side.

"This is Cindy's car," I heard her yell from somewhere on the other side of the van.

I got out and walked around to where Dinah was standing: in front of the Volkswagen Rabbit.

"You're sure?"

"Like I don't know Cindy's car?"

I wiped off the back window with my hand. The interior certainly fit with the Cindy I knew. There were old coffee cups on the floor, and the backseat was piled with tattered reports and old magazines topped by a dirty sock.

I walked around to the driver's door. "It hasn't moved since I arrived," I said. Even now, it was covered with a heavy layer of condensation, meaning that it had been there all night. Then something clicked. I felt in my inside pockets and pulled out the keys I'd found in Cindy's office. I put one of them in the lock and opened the driver's side door.

"Where'd you get those?" asked Dinah.

I slipped into the driver's seat and opened up the glove compartment. "Under the phone book in one of her drawers. I borrowed them. It's not like she needs her extra set of keys."

Dinah pulled the key chain out of the lock and stroked the salmon in the palm of her hand. "I gave her this key ring." Then she looked at me and said, in a matter-of-fact voice, "And these aren't extras. This is her only set."

We were at 16th and Granville, a busy intersection even during off-peak hours. Now, just after nine, it was clogged with traffic. "No parking," she said, glancing around. "We'll take her spot in the back."

After finding Cindy's car I'd suggested that we visit her apartment, since we had the keys, and see if it looked like she'd gone off on a mini-vacation, perhaps with a friend. At least that might explain why her car was left in C-lot. Back in the van, heading out of the university, Dinah had been silent, obviously processing the events of the morning. Finally, at the stop light on Alma she turned to me.

"Who the hell are you?"

"I'm a visiting —"

"Cut the crap. You're no post-doc."

I met her gaze. Could I bluff my way out of this one? How much would I get out of her once she knew who I really was? I decided to take it one step at a time. "I *am* a friend of Elaine's."

"Oh yeah, I can see that. The two of you get along so well. You're a cop, aren't you."

I spoke carefully. "I was."

"And what are you now?"

"An investigator, but not with the police."

"Does this have to do with Cindy?"

"No."

She waited for me to elaborate. When I didn't she forged on impatiently. "What then?"

"I can't tell you. I'm sorry, but I can't. What I can tell you is that I'll do everything in my power to help you find Cindy. That's the best I can do."

She looked at me for a second then nodded once, reluctantly accepting my deal.

Cindy's building was a boxy old walk-up, but it looked safe and clean. Cindy, Dinah said, lived on the third floor. A woman mopping the entrance eyed us suspiciously as we let ourselves in, but she didn't ask any questions. It might have had something to do with Dinah's challenging glare. It would have stopped me.

At Cindy's door I elbowed Dinah out of the way.

"Hey," she said, trying to grab the keys. "This is my backyard, you know."

"Ever seen a dead person?" I said it to shock her, to move her out of the way, and it worked.

She recoiled but said, "I'm not afraid."

"Well you should be. I'll go in first."

I pulled a pair of latex gloves from my pocket and produced a second pair for her. She looked from the gloves to my face and gave an impatient sigh to let know that all this was silly, then she pulled on the gloves. I unlocked the door and opened it a crack.

The good news was it smelled okay, other than the musty odour of an apartment that had been closed up too long. The bad news was there was no sign of Cindy, and every indication that she should be sitting in her office at the university. Her toothbrush was in place. There was milk in the fridge, dirty dishes in the sink, and a backpack and suitcase lay in the dust beneath her bed, the sum-total of her luggage, according to Dinah. There was even a dispenser of birth control pills. The last one missing was Monday. I held it up.

"I thought so." Dinah's voice was bitter. "How could I be so stupid."

"Any idea who?"

She shook her head. "But he'd have to be a shit: she has a history of picking losers." Then she gave me a half smile. "In men, I mean."

I put the pills back in the cabinet and heard a snuffle behind me. I turned around. "You okay?" I asked gently.

She met my eyes with a level gaze, but I could see tears pooling on her bottom lids. "I just don't like being jerked around, okay?" And with that she turned and stormed out of the apartment.

I took one last look around, scanning each room, then shut Cindy's door behind me and walked slowly down the stairs, formulating my next move. When I got back to the van I was annoyed to find that Dinah was nowhere to be seen, and the damn van was locked. I'd purposely given her plenty of time to recover and right at this moment I was tired, hungry, and living off the avails of Tylenol. I was in no mood for games. I'd just found a place to sit and fume when Dinah rounded the corner carrying two brown bags. She gave me a disarming smile and held one out.

"Muffin, yogurt, juice, and a coffee. There's no use in starving, and you look like you could use a little fuel."

Dinah drove like a fiend. I'd felt safer in Graham's office the night before. It took us almost an hour to reach the Port Mann Bridge where the TransCanada crosses the Fraser River and follows its south bank. We left the highway just before the bridge, crossed underneath, and picked up the old Fraser Valley road that hugs the north bank.

Here the suburbs thinned and the vista began to change from car dealerships and strip malls to sawmills and cliffs. Across the river I could see the flood plain spreading green and lush for miles before being stopped by a grey wall of mountains. On this side, though, the Coastal Range butted against the river in a sharp bank, making a steep, dramatic shoreline that literally soared to the clouds. To my left homesteads and old farms dotted the steep rise, temporary and insignificant beneath the towering trees. To my right, the road dropped to the river, the life of the community. The Fraser has always been a working river: a massive highway, a lifeline to the gold in the north, and the source of the world's most abundant runs of salmon. I read in a history book once that Fraser River sockeye fuelled the industrial revolution, with canned sockeye being so cheap and plentiful in England that even the factory workers could afford it for lunch. How things change. With that depressing thought I bundled up my coat, put it behind my head, and dropped into sleep.

I awoke from dead slumber when the hum of the tires on pavement changed to the ping of gravel on the undercarriage. I opened my eyes to a twelve-foot Sasquatch towering over the van. I would have been concerned, except that he was hefting (and it was a he) a sign that said *Sasquatch Bar and Grill, Biggest Burgers in Town.* What town? Had I missed something? I looked around, still not fully conscious. There was nothing but roadway, river, and trees.

Dinah gave me a beatific smile. "Sleep well?"

I rubbed my eyes. "Are we almost there?"

She nodded and pointed to a dirt road beside the restaurant that disappeared up into the woods. "That's the road to the spawning channel, and this is the last toilet before we leave civilization."

I questioned her definition of civilization. From the exterior of the bar and the looks of the pickup trucks and four-by-fours parked outside, it didn't look like a place where safe sex was part of the mating ritual. "Thanks," I said. "I'll use the woods."

"Suit yourself. You want a coffee?"

I nodded, reorganized my pillow, and prepared to catch another catnap while she was inside. Sometime later a little voice intruded on my dream, which was a good thing because Bob had just appeared to tell me how badly I was screwing up this case. The voice said, "Where's Dinah? Where's Dinah?" like a trained parrot. It kept going until I opened my eyes. I couldn't really judge how long I'd been drifting, but I had the sense she should be back by now.

I pulled on my leather jacket and hopped down from the van. The sun had come out in brilliance and the air held the scent of fall, crisp and clear, but not yet ready to give up all its warmth. As I walked across the lot to the restaurant I looked up into the forest. The hardwoods were a splendour of yellows and red, set off against the dark green cedar. All those stories about the West Coast being drab in autumn were no more than Eastern propaganda.

When I opened the door to the Sasquatch Bar and Grill I was met by a middle-aged woman dressed in mustard polyester. It was a uniform designed to make all women look uniformly awful. She approached me with a perfunctory smile, menu in hand.

"Lunch?" she said, and without waiting for an answer she started toward the dining room to my right.

I was entranced by her hair, an elaborate construction of silver-blonde curls piled on top of her head. It looked like something out of the Sun King's court.

"Actually I'm looking for my friend. Tall, short auburn hair ..."

She turned and gave me the once-over. "You're with Dinah?"

I nodded.

"Well that's okay then." She pointed to a set of saloon doors across from the dining room. "Just in through there, sitting at the bar."

At this hour the bar was closed, and I pushed my way through the saloon doors into a dark, empty space. It was classic rural Canada: small, round tables with stretchy terrycloth covers, a worn red carpet pocked with cigarette burns, and the stench of second-hand smoke and stale beer. The only redeeming quality was the plate glass window along the side that let in some natural light.

Dinah was at the bar hunched over a stool. She was deep in conversation with a woman who had on the same uniform as the waitress/hostess, but on this woman the term "unflattering" took on a new dimension. She looked like a lumberjack in drag: black, wiry hair, buzz cut short; burly shoulders straining at the fabric. As I came in she raised her head and locked her eyes on mine. They were a brilliant blue, unexpected with her dark colouring. Her voice wasn't friendly.

"Lose something?"

"A cup of coffee," I said, "and her." I nodded to Dinah.

Dinah twisted around then said to the bartender, "She's cool." Then to me: "You were asleep. I figured you needed it so I left you there." She pushed a Styrofoam cup in front of the stool beside her. She gave a brief introduction, something like Eddie, Morgan, Morgan, Eddie, punctuated by a series of head twitches that managed to convey the message.

I gave a curt nod to Eddie and slid onto the stool beside Dinah. She had her feet up on the highest rung and her knees jutted out like branches on a tree. She was leaning into the counter nursing a coffee.

"I was just asking Eddie if she remembered seeing Cindy up here on Monday."

"And?" I said eyeing Eddie.

Eddie looked at Dinah, who gave her a nod, then she picked up a dishcloth and began wiping the counter directly in front of us. "She was up here on Monday real early. I wasn't on shift."

"Then how do you know?"

She stopped mid-wipe, looked up, and locked eyes with me again. "I make a point of knowing. You got a problem with that?"

"You got a problem with an honest question?"

"Back off, both of you." That was Dinah. Then she leaned over and spoke to me in a low voice. "Eddie always works the bar. During the spawning season she keeps an eye on the road, notifies Fish and Wildlife if it looks like poachers going up."

I looked at Eddie with new respect. If the beer boys knew that, her life would be on the line. Eddie gave a single nod, acknowledging the truth of Dinah's statement, then went back to wiping.

"Did you see Cindy come down?" I asked.

She nodded. "Came in for a pee. Had a burger, made a call, and was gone."

"Do you remember what time she left?"

Eddie shrugged. "Wasn't really watchin'. Eight maybe, thereabouts. All I can tell you for sure is that it was dark outside and the ball game was on."

"So we know she arrived and she left. And we know what time she left. It's a place to start." I looked at Eddie as I slid off the stool. "Thanks. That helps."

She gave a single nod and kept wiping.

When we were back out in the van and all buckled in Dinah said, "By the way, Eddie says there's a bear warning up for the channel — a momma with twins. Once we get there it's heads up and lots of noise."

chapter seventeen

The road to Weaver Creek shot up behind the restaurant at a forty-five degree angle, but after a kilometre it levelled somewhat and continued to climb steadily through northern rainforest. Somewhere high above us the sun was shining, but here on the forest floor it was dark, prehistoric: a jungle of sword ferns and skunk cabbage the height of my chest. From time to time we would pass an old stump, two to three times the size of the van, sitting stately above the ferns. It was a potent reminder of what the forest had once been.

After forty minutes of slow uphill we crossed over a fast-flowing creek, the water coursing over boulders. Several kilometres more of darkness and the forest opened into a patch of low alder brush so dense that it almost hid a gravel driveway. Dinah turned onto this, branches scraping the windshield and sides of the van as it slowly pushed through. A minute later the alder patch ended in a makeshift parking lot and wide clearing.

Dinah pulled in next to an overturned garbage barrel. I opened the door and hopped out. Above me the sky was a cloudless blue, but that did nothing to lighten the ambiance. The clearing felt unnatural, forlorn, like a neglected urban park carved out of inner city chaos. But here, instead of humans encroaching, it was the forest creeping forward to reclaim its stolen land.

Behind me I heard Dinah open her door, then she gave four sharp blasts on the horn. I almost had a heart attack. The van door slammed, and a moment later she was beside me pressing a whistle into my hands.

"Any blind corners," she said, "you blow this, and you blow it hard *before* you go around the corner."

I took the whistle, gave it a good toot, and nodded. "So? Where do we start?"

Dinah walked to the edge of the water and surveyed the creek with a practised eye. She frowned and spoke abruptly. "Let's check the gate."

The channel was constructed like a stack of S's attached end to end. Unlike a real creek, the banks were uniform, cut from the forest by a backhoe, and the gravel on the bottom was homogeneous: no boulders, no muck, just smooth granite stones about the size of hens' eggs. From the air it must have looked like some ancient pagan pictograph of a sacred snake. I hurried to keep up with Dinah.

"Who else works on the channel?"

She didn't slow. "Just Cindy. Edwards comes up a couple of times a season, but he lets us know beforehand. Fish and Wildlife check the counters every couple of days. That's about it."

There was a corner up ahead. Dinah stopped and gave three blasts on her whistle. Silence. I started forward, but she grabbed my sleeve. She blew again. There was a loud crash, then the noise of trees and branches snapping. It sounded like a semi plowing through a grove. She looked across at me, caught my expression, and laughed. "Get used to it."

At the gate Dinah walked to the water's edge and squatted over a patch of mud. She took a minute to observe it then nodded. "A black bear. A big one, but she's a regular on the creek. She's a mooch, looking for an easy meal." She stood up and walked to the pool below the gate. She stood a minute scanning the surface. "Well, she's out of luck today." Then she turned and looked at me. "The holding tanks are empty. There's nothing coming up the creek."

I walked forward and peered into the water. She was right. The water roiled and churned in the tanks, but not with the movement of fish.

I looked back at Dinah. "If Cindy were here right now what would she do?"

There was no hesitation in her voice. "Follow the river down to see if there's maybe an obstruction or some kind of fish kill."

"Then that's what we'll do." I headed for the path that dipped off the service road. When I was about a metre down I realized that Dinah wasn't behind me and I turned back to see her rooted in the same spot up by the gate.

"What's the matter?"

She looked away, uncomfortable. "What if we ..." She lifted one shoulder, letting her sentence trail off and avoiding my eyes.

I moved back up to the beginning of the trial. "What? Find something?"

She nodded uneasily.

"Like what?"

She shrugged and looked away, and I suddenly understood.

"Like Cindy, you mean. Or the remains of Cindy."

"Yeah, well ... maybe."

"But we know she left. Eddie saw her on Monday night."

"Sometimes Eddie isn't too great with dates, especially if the bar scotch is flowing."

This was not welcome news. The combination of bears plus a corpse was an unappetizing mixture, except, perhaps, for the bears. I didn't blame Dinah for hesitating. "I don't mind going alone. You stay here and do what you can do by yourself. When I get back we'll finish up together."

I turned and started down the path.

A second later I heard her yell, "Hey, blow that goddamned whistle or you'll get us both killed," and she fell in behind me.

The path disappeared about twenty metres down. From there we followed the creek, scrambling over boulders and giant logs. Dinah negotiated the obstacles with the skill of a seasoned tree planter. My progress was more laborious, and there was no room for chit chat. A slip of the foot on this terrain meant a concussion or a broken leg.

I had just pulled myself over a log when I noticed the print of a Vibram sole in the mud beneath. "Dinah!"

She came back and knelt to get a better look.

"Put your foot beside it," she ordered. I did. "You're about an eight?"

I nodded, and she stood. "Cindy," was all she said.

A movement across the creek caught my eye. I looked up to see a bald eagle perched on an overhanging tree observing us with interest. When she realized she'd been seen she tilted her head, gave us one last look, then leapt off the branch with a loud *kyrie*. There was a slow *whoosh, whoosh, whoosh* as she gained lift and disappeared down the creek.

After ten more minutes of arduous scrambling the creek narrowed and disappeared around an outcropping of rock. Dinah blasted her whistle, and we cautiously rounded the curve. The temperature suddenly dropped and we hit a wall of damp. We had entered a dark glade that surrounded a deep, swirling pool. A cascade of water spilled off a ledge to my right. Dinah was beside me.

"That's Jacks Creek," she said, tilting her head to the cascade. "It's temporary; run-off mainly."

We were starting forward when something broke the surface of the pool: a green head followed by a streak of scarlet. A male sockeye the length of my arm shot from the water, cleared the rock ledge, and with a thrust of his tail that left both Dinah and I wet with spray, disappeared up Jacks Creek.

She was staring at the cascade. "That can't be. There've never been any salmon up there. There's no breeding habitat, nowhere to spawn."

Another fish leapt from the pool, this time a female. She missed the upper ledge by a hair and fell back into the deep water. I walked forward and looked into the pool. Salmon were milling beneath the surface.

"If that's really the case then we've found your missing fish."

We climbed silently, a series of precipitous cascades. Salmon lay on their sides, exhausted and panting, at the stream's edge. I noticed several fresh sneaker prints about the same size as my foot in the loamy soil around the rocks. They disappeared and reappeared as we made our way up. My attention was focused on the water, watching the progress of the struggling animals, when I caught the scent of something that was out of place: cigarette smoke coming from above. I put out my hand and stopped Dinah.

Ahead of us the stream disappeared around a boulder the size of a house. I heard the rattle of Dinah's whistle, but before she had time to blow it I'd turned and yanked it from her hand. I touched my finger to my lips and shook my head. She gave me a curt nod and waited for me to move. I approached the boulder. The only sound was the burble of the brook and the occasional splash of a fish fighting its way upstream. I edged my way around far enough to see. A man, dressed in a light windbreaker and sneakers, sat on a rock by the shore about fifty metres ahead. He was smoking a cigarette and contemplating the water beneath him. It was writhing with salmon.

I felt Dinah come up behind me. She looked at him and let out her breath. "Jeez, it's only Graham."

At the sound of her voice he jerked his head around and an instant later he was heading full-tilt upstream.

"Hey," I yelled. "We need to talk."

He'd reached a narrowing in the creek. He stopped long enough to shoot me a contemptuous look, took a run at the bank, cleared it, and disappeared into the forest on the other side without looking back.

I looked frantically up and down the shore. If I couldn't cross at a place nearby I'd never catch up with him.

"Here," yelled Dinah, pointing to a line of unevenly spaced stones. It looked dubious, but it was my only hope. I took a run at it, flew across, and landed on my knees on the opposite bank. I was up in a second and hurtling through the woods.

To be honest, if it hadn't been for those damn files I wouldn't have bothered giving chase — I mean, the police would track him down eventually anyway — but my case depended on them. And, to be even more honest, when he gave me that supercilious sneer my blood had boiled: the chloroform, Elaine's lab, Cindy's data. Graham Connell was a shit and I was going to make him pay.

I was pretty sure he was heading for the bridge, an obvious place to hide a parked car. If I was right, he'd drop to Weaver Creek and follow it until he reached the bridge. There, he could cross over the creek, pick up his car, and disappear before I could get him, so I kept high on the slope, scrambling through brush and loose rock. My feet slipped out from under me twice, sending me sliding down the hill, but I picked myself up and kept going. I was making good time, better time than Graham could make following the creek. When I judged the distance was right I headed straight downhill. I burst through the woods to see a shocked Graham upstream.

"I've got you nailed," I panted. "There's nowhere to run."

He looked up and down the steam, then across. "Oh yeah?" he said. And he headed into the current. He was going to ford it right there. The water was only waist high, but it was flowing hard. He had to struggle to move forward.

"Bloody hell." I pulled off my jacket, and went in too. The water was frigid. When it hit my stomach it sucked the breath right out of me, but I kept moving.

I tackled him midstream. We both went down, but I managed to get purchase with my feet before him. I braced myself and yanked him up by the collar. He coughed and sputtered, but that didn't impede the rich diversity of his expletives. Then, with survival skills surprisingly well honed for a graduate student, he launched himself at me, working with the current. I went down and he flowed over me, blocking my path to the surface. With his hand on my face, pushing my head to the gravel, I was shocked into the sudden awareness that I was, quite literally, in over my head. I jabbed upward, but he'd somehow gotten astride me, and I couldn't make contact. I needed air. I thrashed with my arms and legs and got a hold of his shirt, which I yanked forward. My mouth convulsively opened for air. Suddenly Connell let go. On instinct I shot to my feet, gasping and sputtering. Through the water streaming from my face I saw him clear the other bank.

"Have fun," he yelled, and he headed for the road above.

Have fun? Then, on the bank, not five metres away, I saw a great, black thing rise on its hind legs and nose the air in my direction. My primal instincts screamed *Run like hell*. The little voice of logic fought for control. *Make yourself small*, it chirped. *Really, really small.*

I began to back away slowly, at the same time lowering myself into the freezing water. I was dismayed to note that I had red on my shirt and hoped the bear didn't mistake me for a big, juicy salmon. There was a crash from above, then Dinah barrelled into the clearing, scaring the dickens out of me and the bear. The bear grunted, dropped to all fours, and whirled around. She took one look at Dinah, spun around, and retreated upstream.

Dinah watched her disappear, then approached the water's edge. She put out a hand to help me climb from the stream. "She's a pain in the ass, that one," she said, nodding upstream.

"What took you so long?"

"This," she said holding up a small vial. "It was in the water near where Graham was sitting."

I opened it and gave it a sniff. It smelled musky and medicinal all at once. I looked at her. "You know what it is?"

"I ..." She hesitated. "I'm not sure. Maybe you should ask Elaine."

I looked at her for a minute, trying to figure out if she was being purposefully abstruse, then shrugged, picked up my leather jacket, and slipped the vial into my pocket. I'd just add it to my list for Elaine.

Dinah kept the heat on high all the way back to town. I asked her to drop me at my hotel. I could take a taxi to the university later to pick up my car, and I was desperate to get into dry clothes. A sophisticated matron dressed in pale blue silk was waiting near the hotel doors when I arrived. She avoided my eyes and moved well aside as I passed beside her, a testament to my bedraggled appearance.

I cleared the first set of glass doors and was pushing open the second when I noticed the wispy fair hair and chubby cheeks of the gnome checking in. He had his back to me. I did a quick about-face and scooted out the door. The woman, who was still there, decided to wait for her ride at the corner. I leaned against a stone pillar, waited a minute, then peeked around. Bob was heading for the elevator. When he was in, and the doors had closed, I hurried through the lobby, keeping an eye on the floor numbers flashing above his elevator. I pressed the up button. Damn. He was getting off on eighteen: my floor. My elevator arrived and I pressed seventeen. When I got off, I ran to the stairway and made it to the eighteenth floor just in time to catch the tail end of Bob through the fire door window. His shoe was just disappearing into my room. The door clicked shut.

chapter eighteen

I collapsed onto the bottom stair. I'd been out of contact since the morning, and that had been a mistake. There were probably three voice messages at my hotel and several e-mails on my account, all from Lydia, all warning me of Bob's unexpected travel plans. I shivered. My damp clothes, which had been steamy and warm in the van, had taken on a sudden chill. How long would he be in my room? Or more to the point, how long could I wait in the stairwell before hypothermia set in?

I heard a door open in the hallway and peeked out the window. Two white-haired ladies, looking exceptionally fit in denim slacks, Rockport walking shoes, and lightweight jackets, were heading for the elevator. Bob chose that moment to back out of my room. He gave them a courteous nod but waited until they had disappeared around the corner before turning and heading down the hall in my direction. I stepped back from the window. I was preparing for a surprise confrontation when I heard the multiple clicks of a door unlocking. I peeped out the window again. Bob and his bag were disappearing into the room adjacent to mine.

He was lying in wait.

I stepped back from the window and assessed my options. I could bang on his door and confront him, but in my current state I was at a serious disadvantage. What would happen if I let the situation play itself out? I pondered that for a minute. Why had Bob been sent out in pursuit of me? Who had what to hide? Letting the situation unfold might be my best chance for nailing him with something big.

I turned and ran up the stairs to the nineteenth floor. I picked up the house phone by the elevator and called the front desk.

"Cambie Hotel. Marcy speaking. How may I help you?"

"I'm late for an appointment and I need to get an urgent message to Mr. Robert Gregory in room 1823. Would you please let him know that Patricia Middlemass has arrived from Ottawa and she's waiting for him in the bar."

"I can put you right through, madam."

I feigned a look at my watch, just for the authenticity. "I'm sorry, I just don't have time. That's room 1823. Patricia Middlemass. Thanks so much." And I hung up the phone.

I arrived back on the eighteenth floor just in time to see Bob hurrying down the hall, frantically pulling on his suit jacket. I waited a minute, to give the elevator time to arrive, then was in my room, packed, and out of there before he hit the lobby. I took the elevator to the second floor, walked down the stairs to the parking garage, and exited from below. In the mall across the street I found the ladies room and changed into dry clothes. It wasn't a hot bath, but two cups of coffee and a large bowl of steaming hot and sour soup got me warm enough to focus and collect my thoughts.

First thing on the agenda was messages. I found a pay phone and called the hotel. There were four messages from Lydia, all regarding Bob's arrival. There was also an urgent call from Elaine. I dialed her office number. She picked up on the first ring.

"Okada," she said abruptly.

"It's me. What's up?"

There was silence for a moment then she said, "You ran a check on me."

Damn. Why would Sylvia tell her that? Like a rat cornered by a terrier I tried not to panic. An aggressive offense was my best chance of survival.

"Bloody right I did, all the weird stuff that's going on around your lab. And it's a *good* thing I ran it, otherwise we never would have picked up on the fact that Graham was stealing your data. Think about that."

There was silence as she juggled that idea. When she finally continued her voice was glacier cold, making it clear she was conveying information out of a sense of duty. However, I knew Elaine better than that. The fact that she was still talking was a good sign.

"There's something you should know," she said. "Madden came to see me this afternoon. I've never seen him so upset. He asked me about Cindy, where she was, what was going on, did we have news. I told him what I knew."

"That she wasn't in New Zealand?"

"But that maybe she'd taken a break."

"And what did Madden say?"

"He handed me a gold chain with a kiwi bird pendant. He was pulling samples for a fish lab and he found the necklace hidden behind some jars in the sub-basement. Cindy never took it off. He didn't know what to do. Neither do I." Then she forced the next statement out. "But I knew you would."

I suddenly realized that Elaine hadn't seen Dinah: she didn't know about Cindy's apartment or our trip to Weaver Creek. I didn't have the heart to tell her. Not over the phone. "How did it go with the Mounties?" There was a guilty silence at the other end. "You did call them, didn't you?"

She chose her wording carefully. "It was decided that the situation could best be handled internally."

"By the campus cowboys? You're kidding. Who decided that?"

"The department head and the Dean."

"So there's no APB out on Graham?"

She answered in a monotone. "There's nothing I can do. I'm sorry."

"Well guess what. I saw Graham today."

"Here?"

"At Weaver Creek. In fact, he tried to drown me."

"Why?"

I told her about Jacks Creek, the salmon, and the vial. There was a sharp intake of breath. I finished up with a question. "Elaine, what the hell is going on?"

Her voice was sharp. "Nothing is going on." Then, with less conviction, "Nothing is going on." Then, "I'll get back to you."

Why didn't I believe her. "Are you home tonight?"

"I'm going to bed early."

"I need a place to crash."

She gave an abrupt laugh. "No problem. You can just ..." and here she paused for emphasis, "... let your-self in."

My next call was to Sylvia.

"Hi babe," she said dryly. "I thought you'd be calling."

"You betrayed me. Do the words 'client confidentiality' mean anything to you?"

"I'm a librarian, not a lawyer. And you'll have to forgive me. Sometimes it's hard to figure out who is betraying whom."

"You're out of line," I said, and hung up the phone. She could go to her damn doctor's appointment alone.

I stood for a minute fuming, but it didn't take me long to figure out what to do next. Riesler had found Cindy's necklace in the fish museum. My files went missing in the same place. Maybe there was a lot more than dead fish hidden away down there.

The taxi dropped me at my car. I stored my bags inside, locked up, and headed for the Zoology wing. When I arrived, the fish museum was dark. I unlocked the door and flipped on the lights. With Graham gone the place was in chaos: half-completed dissections gaping open in trays, sample jars with lids askew, dirty instruments — scalpels, dissecting needles, forceps — scattered across the benches. It didn't smell great either: fetid and sour. I walked over to one of the dissecting trays and took a peek. I was immediately sorry I had. A jar of pickled herring would never have the same appeal.

Graham's office door was locked, but I used the pass-key to open it. Inside, the door to the sub-basement was wide open. I flicked on the lights at the top of the stairs and scanned the cavernous space. The fluorescent tubes were so encrusted with grime that they gave off little light, casting everything in dull sepia tones. Even from up here I could smell the dankness and dust.

I descended the metal staircase slowly, my steps echoing off the concrete walls. At the bottom I stopped to get my bearings. What light there was shone down a wide central aisle crowded with large plastic crates and barrels. Each was adorned with a label. I moved forward and knelt beside the nearest barrel. The label said "Fisher Scientific: *Acipenser transmontanus* (White Sturgeon)." Beside the barrel was a crate, the approximate size and shape of a coffin. "AquaTec Biological Supplies: *Squalus acanthias* (Spiny Dogfish)." I walked down the aisle a little further, scanning the other containers. All had supply house labels, meaning that these were teaching samples, ordered in bulk so students could carve them up.

I moved back to the beginning and took in the rows of shelves at right angles to the main aisle. I heard a noise behind me: a shuffle, a whisper, almost inaudible. I whipped around. It had come from behind the stairs, an impenetrable black space. I'd seen cockroaches the size of my hand in places like this, escapees from the research labs. Rats were another unappetizing possibility, but when I heard nothing more I relaxed and turned back to the shelves. They reminded me of a library, but instead of catalogued books, they were packed with jars containing preserved and catalogued fish: the reference collection and the heart of the fish lab.

I knew enough about zoology collections to know that the specimens would be shelved as they were classified. In other words, from where I was standing in the central aisle, I was looking down the evolutionary tree of *Pisces*, with each row of shelving representing a branch off that tree. Right now I was standing at the base, the most primitive end, with the lampreys, sharks, and skates. But as I moved forward down the central aisle, I would move into progressively more advanced groups, finally ending with the highly evolved species like puffer fish and flatfishes at the far end of the room. The teaching samples in the middle were probably arranged in the same rough order.

So what was I looking for? My files certainly, and anything that would link Graham to Cindy, but what? I sighed. And where? I shut off my rational brain and began a slow, methodical walk down the main aisle. I stared at the fish, and with shimmering lifeless eyes, they stared back at me.

By the time I'd done a loop, I knew what I was looking for: Cindy's purse, her wallet, and a murder weapon, because Graham *had* murdered Cindy. I was sure of it. She'd arrived at her office late Monday night to find him pilfering her data. First he'd tried to negotiate, but Cindy wouldn't listen, said she was going to turn him in. She'd even logged onto her e-mail to send a message, but Graham had killed her before she finished. Strangled her, most likely, or used chloroform on a cloth. She had probably defecated at death and that explained the formalin on her chair the next morning. Graham then shot off a message to Cindy's advisor, that seemingly came from Cindy, to buy himself some time.

My mind was racing now, piecing it all together. The night of the murder Graham had managed to get rid of everything: probably used the van to transport the body, the same van I had so meticulously cleaned the following evening. The personal effects he hid here, in his lair. But there had been one untidy detail: Cindy's car. He knew that eventually someone would notice it in C-lot, so the following night he'd ransacked Cindy's lab looking for her keys. The irony was that they had been sitting in my pocket as he dragged me unconscious from his office to the lab.

But why had he done that? To pin the vandalism on me? I gnawed at that question for a minute, feeling that something didn't add up, but got nowhere and put it aside. Even if I was missing a piece of the puzzle, it would all come together as the evidence mounted.

So Cindy's personal effects were down here, but where would he hide them? I ran my eyes down the aisles, trying to imagine how Graham would think. One thing for sure, he wasn't some two-bit operator. He'd been able to fake his way into graduate school, orchestrate an elegant piece of research fraud, and fool everyone into believing he was the next great gift to science. That took a brilliant, methodical mind.

I began another slow walk of the space. On the second loop, my brain landed on top of one of the barrels. It bothered me: *Lampetra tridentata* (Pacific Lamprey). The barrel was shut up tight, but most of those around it had been pried open and loosely closed. So? There were other sections where the barrels were all tightly closed: what was the problem? I stepped back a few paces and viewed the barrels as a pattern, then I could see the problem. Zoology lab courses, like the museum itself, are organized along the evolutionary tree. Students begin the year by dissecting the most primitive species and work their way, by the end of the year, up to the most advanced. Lamprey, I knew, were primitive: a jawless parasite that feeds off the bodily fluids of other fish. They would have been covered in September. And if I were Graham, I'd want to hide incriminating evidence in a barrel I knew would be closed for the next eleven months, and I'd make damn sure it was shut up tight. I felt a surge of excitement. It made sense. It made a lot of sense. I pulled off my leather jacket and snapped on latex gloves.

The steel tabs had been opened before, but they were still too strong for my knife. I saw a crowbar leaning against one of the barrels and used it to pry them up.

When the top was loose I flung it to the floor and peered into the barrel. The dim overhead lights reflected off a black liquid that came halfway up the barrel. I pulled out my flashlight. Flaccid, serpentine bodies of lamprey bobbed on the surface. Wonderful. There was a muffled sound behind me, mammalian, something between a squeak and a burp.

I grabbed the crowbar and swung around. It was coming from behind the stairs. The flashlight didn't penetrate far, but far enough for me to see that the creepiness of this place was playing on my nerves. Nevertheless, I lay the crowbar within easy reach.

I looked back in the barrel and touched the surface of the liquid. The formalin was oily and cold. It was also deep. With the lip of the barrel at chest height, I wouldn't get my hand anywhere near the bottom standing on the floor.

There was a stool nearby and I pulled it over. I just hoped I could touch the bottom without getting the top of my head wet. I took a deep breath and plunged in. The cold liquid embraced my arm to just below the shoulder, and the lamprey, slick and cool as rubber, nudged against my skin. By twisting, I managed to keep my face pointed up, and I was grateful for that. My hand touched bottom and I groped. Nothing. I found an edge and followed it, then I touched something out of place — a shape, a right-angle corner — but I needed air. I pulled myself out of the barrel, took a few gulps of fresh air, then jammed my torso back in the barrel. A minute later I pulled up a wallet: eel skin, with Cindy's Visa card inside.

I knew I could leave it like that, go to the police with just the wallet, but I wasn't finished. I went back and surveyed the barrels. Another one caught my eye, firmly closed within a group with loosely placed lids. *Hydrolagus colliei* (Chimaera/Pacific Ratfish): the dissection Graham was setting up the day we'd met. I grabbed the crowbar and pried open the lid. The barrel was full to the brim. The obscene little fish crowded the surface, floating head up in the oily liquid. Their bulging eyes watched my every move. I pushed them aside and plunged my hand into the barrel. It connected with something round and hard. Round and hard and with hair. I pulled once and it didn't budge. I pulled again and felt something loosen, dislodge. A bubble rose slowly from the depths, I heard the soft murmur of liquid displacing, then Cindy's pale face emerged through the fish.

"Jesus," I cried. It's one thing to expect it, it's another to see it. Then I heard a hiss from the darkness. I let go. I wanted to turn around, to see what was behind me, but I was transfixed by the macabre scene: Cindy's head disappearing with eery slowness back into the depths. The fish swirled, mingling with her hair, obscuring an eye, a cheek, the lips, the chin, until eventually she had disappeared among them. It was over. The only evidence of what had just taken place was the gentle bobbing of the ratfish gazing up at me from the surface of the barrel.

I was jarred back to reality by the sudden sound of footsteps. I grabbed the crowbar and went into the darkness after the noise. I fumbled with my flashlight, then something hit my face. I recoiled, preparing for a blow, but nothing happened. I finally got a hold of my flashlight and flicked it on. I'd been hit by a piece of paper, which now lay at my feet. Keeping my flashlight trained ahead I bent over and picked it up. A quick scan revealed it as a sheet from JJ's files. There was a sudden movement to my right, a scrabbling, and I swung the beam around. The luminescent eyes of a large rat flashed and disappeared.

Then suddenly there was real noise, the doors of a freight elevator rolling shut. The engine whirred to life, but by the time I got there the box was on its way up. I banged the door hard. The whirring stopped, and I heard the clang of doors above as someone got off. Then the engine kicked in again. Whoever had gotten out was sending the elevator back down to me.

The motor stopped as the box clunked into position in front of me. I hesitated, but I wanted to know. I pulled open the first set of doors to reveal a second set, also closed. Crowbar in hand I got a hold of one and opened it slowly. Light seeped through the crack. When I got it open enough to see that there was no one inside, I pulled the doors fully open. The elevator was empty except for a single sheet of paper carefully placed dead centre on the floor. I picked it up. It was from JJ's files, and someone had highlighted in yellow a financial transaction. According to this record, $50,000 had gone to Jonathan Edwards's lab on May 17 of the previous year.

So this was a message from Graham. He was looking to strike a deal.

chapter nineteen

Corporal LeBlanc took my identification. She scanned it, raised an eyebrow, then snapped the wallet shut.

"I thought I recognized you," she said, handing it back to me. "You still in touch?"

She meant, was I still in touch with other members of the Force. I gave her a level gaze. "Not if I can help it."

She didn't seem offended by the answer, just gave a curt nod of understanding and looked across at her partner, MacGillivray. He was the archetypical Mountie: beamingly handsome, flawless teeth, carefully trimmed moustache, and well over six feet tall. He was strolling the perimeter of the lab examining the sample jars. It looked casual, but I knew he was taking in every detail. LeBlanc, the officer in charge, was far from archetypical. Short, blonde, and with a stocky athletic build, she must have had a hell of time in training, which told me a lot about her character. Under those unassuming looks there lurked a pit bull.

"You stay up here," she ordered MacGillvary. "And no one comes through that door." Then to me, "I think we should see what you have got."

I took her down the stairs. At the bottom I waited for a moment while she surveyed the surroundings. She ran her eyes over the shelves and barrels.

"*Merde*. What is this, a fish morgue?"

"Unfortunately, more than just fish." And in the next fifteen minutes I told LeBlanc everything I knew, omitting only my midnight foray into JJ's office, the "borrowed" files, and the chloroform ambush in Graham's office.

At the end she said, "You think they are connected, this," she nodded to the barrel, "and the missing money?"

I shrugged. "I don't know. That's why I need to interview Connell."

Her smile was brief and humourless. "I think you will be lining up."

LeBlanc went up the spiral stairs ahead of me. When she was almost at the top she stopped and turned, trapping me below her. I was looking at her knees and the nice yellow stripe that ran up the side of her pants. She was eyeing me from above. I felt like a toddler, which is exactly what she intended. "What happened to your face?"

I hadn't looked at myself in the mirror for a couple of hours, but I assumed that my tussle with Graham and my evening of chloroform dreams had left some bruises. I looked up at her, and would have been intimidated if I didn't know the act.

"I fell."

She didn't move. "I don't suppose it is related."

"To what?"

"The body in the barrel."

I paused for a minute, considering my words carefully, then said, almost too softly to be heard, "We both have a job to do."

She answered, just as softly, "Just do not let yours get in the way of mine. *Compris?*" Then she turned and continued up the stairs.

A bank of fog had rolled in, creating orange halos around each of the street lamps leading up to C-lot. Ahead of me someone trudged slowly up the hill, visible only as a dark shadow, and behind me I heard voices, a couple walking to their car. Halfway to the parking lot I stopped and zipped up my coat. Would I ever shake this chill? Not until I got a hot bath, a full dinner, and a good night's sleep.

With the discovery of Cindy's body dinner with Madden was off. In fact, both Madden and Elaine had been in their offices when MacGillivray had dropped by, and with the crime scene officers now combing the site, MacGillivray and LeBlanc would be squeezing the two of them for information. I hoped MacGillivray was elected to interview Elaine. Maybe some of his manly charm could be used to extract information.

When I reached the top of the hill I crossed to the parking lot. The lamps dotting the parking area created small islands of misty light in an otherwise black sea. My car was just at the edge of an island.

The form ahead of me disappeared into the fog, and the couple behind me continued their progress up the sidewalk. When I got to my car I stood for a moment and took in the night. True, it was dark and humid and cold, but there was a beauty to it too. The air shimmered, all sharp edges gone, and the sounds — a car door slamming, voices in conversation, cars passing by

— were oddly muffled by the fog. I pulled out my keys and unlocked the car door. I had one foot inside when a gun jabbed into my neck.

"Get in," said Connell. I did as he asked. He flicked up the lock on the back door and slid into the seat behind me. The gun pressed up against my jugular. "Close the car door. You drive, I direct."

I gave a slight nod and slowly leaned out to close the door. When I finished I looked calmly into the rearview mirror.

"You're cool," he said.

"I've been wanting to chat, but this isn't quite what I had in mind. May I turn around?"

He paused for a minute, considering it. "Slowly, with your hands on the wheel."

Graham was dressed in black cords, a denim shirt, and a jean jacket. He was shaved, and it looked as though his teeth and hair were brushed: in short, he was awfully well maintained for a guy on the lam. The only sign of stress was around his eyes, a nervous squint and dark circles.

I kept my voice light. "Where to, James?"

"Spanish Banks. Take the back way along the beach. You know where the youth hostel is?" I nodded. "Go down that road. When we get there I'll tell you where to park." For emphasis he gave me a poke with the gun.

The truth is, I may not have looked frightened to Graham, but I was scared shitless. This guy had pickled a person in ratfish, for God's sake. I'd be insane not to be afraid. To make it worse, I had tangled with him twice, and both times I had come out alive due to pure, dumb luck, but how many more times would luck pull me through? My only advantage was to remain calm. If I let fear overtake my responses then I *would* slip up, and the consequences could be fatal.

I started the car and drove out of the parking lot. I kept one eye on the road and the other on the rearview mirror. Graham kept low in the backseat, his eyes darting from me to the road, keeping an eye out for oncoming cops. His left arm was slung around my neck, and the gun remained steady on the base of my skull. I tried to keep my tone conversational.

"You might get away with one murder, but not two."

His voice was flat. "You were meant to find her."

"You have a death wish?"

"Shut up and drive."

We continued on in silence down the dark tunnel, then across the flats of Spanish Banks. What lay beyond the edge of the sand was shrouded in thick fog. With Graham not more forthcoming, I needed to press, if necessary provoke him, to get him to reveal his agenda. I took a shot in the dark.

"What did Cindy find? The fish kill or you stealing her data?"

He looked at me surprised, then laughed, but the laugh ended abruptly when he tightened his grip around my neck. He leaned in close to my ear. "You know why you're in so much shit?"

Because I'm locked in a car with a nutcase, I thought, but I was pretty sure that wasn't the answer he was looking for so I kept it to myself. As it turned out, the question was hypothetical.

"Because you're smart," he went on, "but not smart enough. Turn left up here."

The road took us by the youth hostel and past the heavy wire fence of a boat club. Beyond the fence the road swung around to the right, ending in a gravel parking lot that looked out across the beach. He directed me to a parking spot almost hidden beneath a weeping willow. I pulled in and shut off the engine. The end of a pier was just visible through the fog.

"There's a boat at the end of that," he said, indicating the pier. "That's where we're going."

To get to the pier we had to cross an expanse of beach, and with this fog it was impossible to see more than three metres in either direction. We could be utterly alone, the only people for miles, or the springer spaniel kennel club could be out walking their dogs *en masse* twenty metres away. Graham was taking an incredible chance, and that didn't sound like Graham. I twisted around, keeping my hands on the wheel.

"I hate to be difficult, especially since you have the gun, but what makes you think I'm going to walk calmly across that pier to my death. I'd rather take my chances here."

"If I wanted you dead we wouldn't be having this conversation."

"What about at Weaver Creek?"

"Why the fuck did you chase me?" He sounded truly offended.

"You tried to drown me," I said.

"I was scared. I had to get you off my back before that dyke showed up."

"What about Cindy?" I said quietly.

"You think I killed her?" He shook his head in disgust. "Then you're dumber than I thought."

With the gun trained on me he fumbled in his breast pocket with the other hand. I took the opportunity to twist my head around even further, making it look like I was watching him fumble, but I used the movement to mask my left hand falling beneath his line of sight. He pulled a crumpled paper from his pocket and held it out to me.

"Both hands on the wheel," he barked, and jabbed me with the gun. Then more calmly, "Take this in both your hands, and keep them high."

I took the piece of paper. I wasn't totally focused, with most of my attention being directed to picking up noise or movement on the beach, but I had to go along with the act. There wasn't much light in the car, but the top of the paper was easy to read. It was embossed with an ornate script, *From the Desk of Madden Riesler*, but the scribble underneath was tough going. I held it higher to pick up more light. They were single disjointed words, as if someone had hastily jotted down the pertinent information from a telephone conversation. After the second line the paper had my full attention.

> ~5'10"
> *black hair/short/wavy*
> *blue*
> *O'Brien/alias?*
> <u>NCST</u>
> *JE complaint*

"Where'd you get this?"

"Duh. Figure it out."

"When?"

He smirked. "He's been playing you all along, but I bet you're fun to play."

"How do I know this isn't your writing?"

He shrugged and gave me a charming smile. "Guess you'll just have to trust me ..." He tucked the gun in his belt and climbed out of the car, "... if you don't want to end up like Cindy."

He loped across the beach, stepped up onto the pier, and disappeared into the fog. A man in a tracksuit jogged by with a black lab trotting along beside.

The trouble was, there was a ring of truth to what he said, but pathological liars are good at that. You practise enough and everything has the ring of truth. But there was something else, something that I couldn't tease out, that fit this new configuration of the puzzle.

It only took a second to decide. I scrawled a message on a piece of paper detailing the time, place, and the name of my travelling companion, which I shoved into the springs under the car seat. Then I hopped out, did a quick self-frisking, felt my pepper spray in my pocket, and jogged into the fog after Connell.

chapter twenty

The pier sat high above the water, lit by spotlights around its edge. The benches were empty, the concrete beneath them littered with dried seaweed, periwinkles, and sculpins: the combined catch of the neighbourhood children. I crunched along slowly until I reached the end. Only then, looking over the edge, did I see the boat waiting below: fifteen metres of teak and gleaming brass. Before I was halfway down the ladder the diesel engine roared to life. I hopped onto the deck. Graham emerged from a small door up front heading for the bow. He glanced back at me with a self-satisfied smile and shouted, "Cast off the stern."

A minute later the boat was heading for open water outside English Bay. I didn't go in immediately but stood for a moment in the darkness and fog, a fine salt mist on my face, listening to the rhythmic slap of water on the hull as it cut through the gentle chop. I closed my eyes — shut out all the worries and fears: Cindy's face, Elaine's behaviour, Sylvia's betrayal, even Graham — to breathe in the fresh, briny scent of the sea. For a moment I let go, abandoned myself to it. When I was ready, I slowly pulled the pieces back together, opened my eyes, took one last deep breath, and made my way to the front of the boat.

By the time I reached the wheelhouse we were clearing Point Grey and heading into the open water of the Georgia Strait. Without warning the fog ended and a stiff wind drove cold drizzle into my face and four-foot rollers into the boat. As the deck shuddered I grabbed the railing with one hand, the doorknob with the other, and lurched inside the wheelhouse.

Graham didn't divert his eyes from the window. A wiper was swishing steadily in front of his face. I reached out and pulled myself into a captain's chair just in front of the door. Fortunately it was bolted to the floor by a high, steel pedestal.

"If you're gonna be seasick," said Graham, "don't puke in my boat."

I managed to get myself securely into the chair, one of only two in the narrow space. "This is yours? It's beautiful." I had to shout to be heard.

He gave a brief nod, acknowledging the compliment. "It was built as a fishing boat in the twenties. When I got her she was a wreck. The hull was in okay shape but the fittings were shit. I replaced everything," he turned briefly and gave me his lopsided smile, "and modernized a bit."

I could see that. The wheelhouse was dark, save for the glowing instruments on the panel in front of him, an array of dials, switches, buttons and levers. It looked like the cockpit of a jet.

"Where are we going?"

Graham reached up and switched on a monitor hanging above his head. There was an expanse of blue, patches of yellow up top, and a heavy line of yellow to almost half way up the screen.

"Mayne Island," he said. He pointed to a patch of yellow on the top of the screen. "There's a cove there. You'll see it on the radar when we get in closer. Then we'll talk."

He kept both the global positioning system and the radar on, and as we crossed the strait I kept glancing from the window to the GPS screen. Outside there was nothing — grey sea, black sky, and rivulets of water streaming down the windshield — but on the monitor the simulated shoreline of Vancouver moved slowly down the screen, eventually disappearing altogether, while the patches above, the Gulf Islands, moved steadily toward us. It was unnerving to know that all that land surrounded us, tangible and solid, yet to look outside there was nothing but ocean and rain.

It took us almost an hour to reach Mayne Island. I saw it first as one or two faint dots of light sitting in a dense patch of black. As we approached, Graham reached up and rescaled the radar to give a more detailed image of the shoreline. It was now just visible outside as a dark shadow, and he veered south, moving parallel to it. After ten minutes he slowed. I checked the radar and saw what looked like a narrow opening along the shoreline. It faded into nothing behind.

"It's just a channel," I shouted. "Have you gotten in there before?"

"There's a bay in behind," he said. "It's shielded by the cliffs."

He brought the boat around and we were now almost stationary, broadside to the waves that rocked us like a cradle. He throttled forward slowly. As we moved ahead details of the shoreline began to emerge, first looming walls, then white foam breaking over jagged rock. I looked at Graham. He was completely focused on the shore. At least he was taking this seriously.

When we were perilously close to the rocks I saw a narrow opening, a dark tunnel in the midst of breaking waves. Graham flicked a switch. A powerful beam lit up the channel and the surrounding cliffs. He seemed to be waiting for something, felt it, then abruptly throttled forward. I white-knuckled the panel in front of me as we charged into the channel, so close to the shear walls of rock that I could see the lichen clinging to the fissures. Then as suddenly as we had entered it was over. The shear walls dropped away to a quiet, emerald green bay: from bedlam to paradise. Graham cut the engines and we drifted in.

"Piece of cake," he said, throwing me a grin. He hopped off his chair and headed for the bow to set the anchor.

I got out of my chair more carefully, first testing the stability of my legs, then followed Graham out. The bay was almost perfectly circular and dwarfed by massive cedars. Somewhere high above us the wind whispered in the trees, but the surface of the water was a green mirror with only the occasional drops of rain marring its surface. I heard a splash to my right and a cormorant popped out of the water. She ignored me, preened her wings, then plunged back beneath the bay.

Graham disappeared down the other side of the boat and I heard a hatch open near the stern. The row of windows by my knees lit up, causing the water around us to dance with light. It would have been a spectacular sight from the shore.

By the time I went below the stove was pumping out heat and Graham was making coffee.

"You live on board?" I asked.

"Yup," he said, not turning around. "I like being mobile."

For obvious reasons, I thought. "You got anything to eat in here?"

"Canned stuff. Beans, stew, chili. Peanut butter." He opened a cupboard beneath the tiny sink. "Sardines. And there's crackers."

Since fish products were out, probably for the rest of my life, I aimed for something spicy and filling. "Chili would be great."

He busied himself with that and I glanced around.

The boat reminded me of his office: an efficient little space where everything was within reach. There was the galley, just big enough for Graham to stand in, a navigation table across from it, and a semicircular nook for eating. Further forward there was a hallway, which I assumed led to bunks up front. I slipped into the nook.

The kettle whistled and Graham poured water into two mugs. He looked at me. "You want rum in yours?"

Why not. I was already in so far I couldn't get in much deeper. "Sure. Half a shot. With milk and sugar."

He sloshed in rum and canned milk and brought the coffee over. "The chili will take a few minutes."

He took a seat across from me. I sipped the coffee — instant had never tasted so good — and kept the cup cradled in my hands. It was the first time since our departure that I'd seen Graham in full light, and I noted that the lines around his eyes were more pronounced than they'd seemed in the car. Now that he had me as captive audience he didn't seem to know where to start so I led off.

"What's your real name?"

He laughed. "What's yours?"

"Morgan O'Brien."

"Yeah right. The post-doc from Ottawa."

"At least I really got my degree." Well, two of them anyway.

He looked surprised. "You traced that? Shit."

"And the papers. Great publication record! Both of you."

He scowled. "Who gives a fuck. It's all a game anyway. And with or without a degree I'm smarter than most of the dumbass idiots who go to Southern."

I shrugged. "Could be. Is that why you brought me here? To discuss your IQ?"

"I want the cops off my back."

I shrugged. "Not my problem."

"Yeah it is. See, I have your files, the ones you *stole* from JJ's office. I could send them to the police, or I could send them back to JJ, but I'm a nice guy. If you help me, I'll help you." He reached around, pulled the files from a cubby behind, and tossed them on the table.

I looked at them then at Graham. The rum was beginning to affect my legs. "Is that chili ready yet?"

Graham was back a minute later with a bowl for me and one for himself. He handed me a spoon. The chili was salty and good. After shovelling it in my face for a minute I took a breather and looked up at Graham. I motioned to the files on the table. "I'd say that's peanuts in comparison to your problems. You're going to have to do better than that."

"I didn't kill Cindy." He took a pack of Export A from his pocket and pulled one out. He tapped the end on the table. His voice was belligerent. "He's framing me."

"Who?"

"Madden." Then bitterly. "Madden did it."

"Why? Why would he kill Cindy, and why would he frame you?"

At this point he turned cagey. His gaze slid sideways and he shrugged. "I don't know." He lit the cigarette and took a pull.

I gave a snort of laughter. "Fine. I'll just take your word for it, seeing as you're such a reliable source. Tell you what. When I get back to shore I'll call up my pal Corporal LeBlanc and tell her the Assistant Dean of Science murdered Cindy." I pushed the bowl of chili to the centre of the table. "Can I go home now?"

His bravado faded. He sat back and took another long pull of the cigarette, then blew the smoke out slowly, watching me through the haze. Finally he said, "I was in Cindy's office Monday night."

To cover my reaction, I pulled the chili back. "That, at least, I believe. What time?"

"Around three in the morning, so I guess it was Tuesday really. I was looking around."

"You were stealing data."

That annoyed him. "Just keeping an eye on things." Then he went back to his story. "Her office was a mess; I mean more than usual. There was stuff everywhere and the place stank, like somebody took a shit in the corner. And it was weird. The lights were out and her coat was gone, like she'd gone home for the night, but her purse was in one of the desk drawers. I figured she'd forgotten it. Anyway, while I was looking around someone came in the lab. Scared the shit out of me. I switched off the light and stood in the dark. Then I heard them open up the chamber and drag something out, like a sack or something. They dragged it right out of the lab. Whatever it was it was heavy because I heard them sort of grunt and swear. I waited a few minutes then got the hell out. Problem was, when I got to the hall I could see the lights to the museum were on and I'd left them off. I didn't wait around to see who it was. The next day I heard about Cindy. It didn't take a rocket scientist to figure out what happened."

"But you didn't go to the police?"

"Yeah right."

"Why do you think it was Madden? Why not JJ? "

Graham dismissed it. "Because JJ's a soprano. Anyway, only Madden would know enough to hide her in the ratfish."

"But you did that lab the next day."

"I pull my samples the night before so I don't have to stick my face in a barrel of dead fish at seven in the morning. Madden knows that. He makes the lab schedule."

So far it was a good story but I didn't believe a word of it. For one thing, Graham was having trouble looking me in the eye. Anyone with half a brain could see he wasn't telling the truth. For another, Madden had no motive for killing Cindy. Graham did.

"So where were you on Tuesday night?" Then I looked meaningfully at the files. "Or do I need to ask."

He paused for a minute, then said, looking directly at me, "Saving your butt."

That stopped me. I looked at him and something clicked. He was telling the truth. "You pulled me out of there."

He nodded. "You were lying on the floor. Scared the shit out of me. I thought you were dead, but when I got you out of the fumes I found a pulse so I dragged you to Okada's lab. That asshole left the files in the middle of the desk, and a bunch of Cindy's data sheets too, just waiting for the police to find them. Like I'd be so stupid. So I knew for sure I was being set up. I didn't fucking wait around to see what was gonna happen. I cleaned out my office, took those," he motioned to the files, "for insurance, and made myself scarce."

"Did you flip Elaine's lab?"

He shook his head. "It was like that when I dragged you in."

"But you don't know for sure it's Riesler. You didn't actually see him."

He flicked a crumb on the table. "It's him," he said with conviction, and he butted out his cigarette.

There was something he wasn't telling me. I sipped my coffee, watching Graham toy with his mug. His chili was untouched. I waited for a minute then said, "What were you doing at Jacks Creek?"

"It doesn't apply."

I didn't react, just waited. The only sound was the water lapping gently on the hull. He clenched his jaw and began worrying a scrap of paper sitting on the table, all the while refusing to meet my eyes.

After a good period of waiting I said softly, "Don't jerk me around Graham. If you want my help I have to know."

He stood up abruptly and went to the stove, where he employed diversionary tactics, clanging the kettle, banging cups, arranging cutlery. As he got up I noted that the gun was no longer in his belt.

Up close and under pressure Graham's rough edges were beginning to show. That, and the fact that he had a myriad of skills he didn't learn at school, brought me to the next question. It was a stab in the dark.

"What were you in for?"

He shrugged, his back to me. "The usual." Then he swung around. "Nothing violent. I'm not into that."

"B&E?" An affirmative twitch. "Fraud?" A slight shrug. "Blackmail?"

His face went blank for a second, then his facade returned. He shrugged and turned back to the sink. I kept my eyes pinned on him. How would blackmail fit in?

Finally I said, "I'm still waiting for an answer. What were you doing at Jacks Creek."

He swung around with a sneer on his face. "Why don't you ask your buddy Okada? She knows all about Jacks Creek. Me? I'm just a dumb graduate student. I couldn't possibly understand what's going on."

chapter twenty-one

It was after midnight when Graham dropped me off at my car. I'd been dozing below, caught between dreaming and wakefulness. The hatch opened and he said gruffly, "Hurry up. I don't want to hang around."

I shook off my dream, something about pursuing and being pursued in a dark house that magically rearranged itself every time I thought I had my quarry trapped. Passages morphed into walls, walls became windows, doors became stairs, and when it happened, my quarry would disappear behind a wall, and the dark shadow of my pursuer would emerge from an unexpected opening. To paraphrase Graham, it didn't take a psychiatrist to figure out the connection.

I sat up and rubbed my eyes. Graham was silhouetted in the light above, fidgeting impatiently. Partway up the ladder he reached down and grabbed my arm, yanking me to the deck.

"Here." He pushed a scrap of paper into my hand. "My cell phone number. Call around four. Let it ring twice, hang up, and call again. I'll pick up on the second call."

"And if you're off the hook for the murder you'll come in with my files?" He nodded. "If not?"

He looked away, out to open water. "It's too soon to say."

I watched the boat pull away from the dock and kept my eyes on it until the red and green running lights faded into the fog. When he was gone I pulled out an evidence bag and dropped the scrap of paper in. Graham hadn't been wearing gloves, and since he had a record his prints would be on file. If it came to that.

When I finally arrived at Elaine's there were, miraculously, several parking spaces open on her block; nothing right in front of her house, but a brief walk in the chill air would set me up nicely for bed. I pulled my bag and briefcase from the back of the car and walked briskly to her house. Coming up the side stairs I was surprised to see a light on in the kitchen. I was even more surprised to find the door unlocked and the kitchen empty.

"Elaine?" I called. There was no answer. "Elaine, it's me, Morgan."

There was a rustling, then a voice from the living room. "More ... Gan."

I frowned, dropped my bag, and went to investigate. It was a pathetic sight: Elaine slumped on the chesterfield, a highball glass balanced on her pelvis, a half-empty mickey of cheap scotch sitting on the coffee table next to her feet. Did I mention I have no tolerance for drunks? I looked coldly from Elaine to the bottle and back again.

"So? Did it make you feel better?"

She looked at my face, squinting to meld the two images into one. I could see the comprehension seep in.

"Sorry," she mumbled. "Forgot," and she took another swig of scotch.

Suddenly, I wanted to be anywhere but here. I had an overwhelming compulsion to run away, to put as much distance as I could between her and me, but I fought the panic down. "I'll lock up." My voice was hard. "You should go to bed."

I was locking the kitchen door when I heard her speak, whether to me or herself, I couldn't be sure. I stood still and listened.

"S'not my fault ..." she mumbled. "S'not my fault."

I stood frozen in place. I'd learned from living with my mother that there's no point in talking to a drunk. Still, sometimes there *is* a nugget of truth floating in the jetsam. I felt a little tingle of guilt at the direction my thoughts were taking. Would I be taking advantage of Elaine if I chose now to pump her for information? It didn't take me long to find an answer. Elaine was a big girl. She got herself drunk. It was her responsibility. I filled two glasses with water and returned to the living room. Elaine was still sprawled on the couch, but now her eyes were closed and her breathing steady. I walked around the coffee table and sat down beside her. I knew it would be more effective if I took her hand and played the role of father confessor, but there are limits.

"Elaine," I said sharply.

She jerked and opened her eyes a crack.

I took the glass of scotch from her hand and put it on the coffee table, sliding it and the bottle out of reach.

"Sit up," I ordered. She shut her eyes firmly and shook her head. I poked her hard in the ribs. "Sit up, damn you, or I'll pull you up myself."

She rolled her head in my direction and opened her eyes. "Go away. S'not my fault."

"Maybe it is."

I'd said it just to goad her, but tears welled in her eyes.

"For Christ's sake, sit up." I took her arm and yanked her to a half sitting position. "Drink this." I handed her the glass of water.

She took it and slouched forward. I had to move quickly before I lost her again. I pulled the vial from my pocket.

"What's this?"

She turned and squinted. After a second she said, "It-sa vial." Then she lost interest and went back to staring at the glass of water.

"Graham says you know all about Jacks Creek." She looked at me, confused, then her eyes narrowed. She reached out and made a grab for the vial. I pulled it away. "Tell me about Jacks Creek."

"S'not true. Graham ..." she said, shaking her head, "... lies."

That was an understatement. I unscrewed the top of the vial and pushed it under her nose. She pulled back and shook her head, as if to rid herself of the odour.

"Where'd'you get that?"

I screwed the top back on. "Why?"

She made another grab for it, spilling water on her jeans. "S'mine," she slurred. "Top secret." Then she fell back into the couch. "Never mind. We'll make more." And her eyelids shut.

I caught the glass as it slid from her hand. Elaine was out cold. I debated trying to get her to bed, but it just seemed like too much trouble, so I lifted her feet onto the couch, loosened her clothes, then rolled her onto her side, just in case she barfed. In her room I pulled a couple of blankets off the bed and went back to the couch and covered her. It was an oddly reassuring routine, a remnant of my childhood years, and although I was angry with her I was happy to be near. At least if she vomited in her sleep I was here to make sure she survived, an effort she wouldn't thank me for first thing in the morning.

Elaine's home office doubled as the guest room. I found sheets and pillows in the linen cupboard, made up the futon, and fell exhausted into bed. I had expected to be asleep in an instant but just as I was about to free fall into the great abyss, the scenes of the day caught up with me. My painful awakening in Elaine's lab, my panic beneath the waters of Weaver Creek, Cindy's face rising ghostly from the fish, the cold metal of Graham's gun against my neck.

I shook myself awake and turned on the reading light. Sleep would be impossible now. My only hope was a diversion, to get my mind working on a less dramatic track that would take me down the road to slumber. I got up and wandered over to Elaine's desk. The bookshelves above it were laden, but with tomes on sensory neurobiology, fish physiology, and vertebrate form and function. There were no bedtime novels, but I did notice some photo albums on the top shelf. I pulled one down, hoping to find happy memories of Elaine and me preparing for a day in the field, but this album had recent photos taken sometime within the last four years.

I flipped idly through. It looked like Berkeley: Elaine standing in front of a single-cell recording apparatus in a large lab, first alone, then proudly with an older, bearded guy in a T-shirt and jeans, probably her advisor. There were some outdoor shots of the campus, some touristy photos of San Francisco, then a series of Elaine teaching, pointing earnestly at charts and overheads. I peered at the data behind her. It looked like experimental results, so it was probably a research colloquium.

Must be, because the next photos were group shots, probably the technicians and students from the lab. Elaine was dressed in the same clothes as the presentation but was standing in the middle of a crowd — the guest of honour — flanked by the bearded guy and a bunch of youngish academic types. So these were probably photos of her final research presentation, the culmination of her post-doc at Berkeley. That was confirmed by the next page, pictures of some sort of post-presentation garden party. It was a crowded affair. The food table was packed with trays of catered hors d'oeuvres and a healthy selection of quality California wines. With the exception of the bearded guy, who appeared in several photographs, the crowd was well dressed for a university do. People were clumped in tight groups, laughing, talking, and drinking.

I was about to turn the page when I saw something that stopped me dead. Hidden in the crowd was the handsome face of Madden Riesler, caught in profile, laughing with a woman standing beside him. She was partially obscured by the man in front. Partially, because it's hard to hide a woman who is five-eleven and wearing three-inch heels.

I flipped to the next page. This shot must have been taken several seconds later. The couple in front had moved, revealing Madden and his companion in full. She was a good head taller than him, blonde, elegant, refined, and, as always, in control. They were standing face to face, holding hands, looking into one another's eyes: a man and a woman in love.

I closed the book slowly and stared unseeing at the cover for a good minute before I turned, picked up the phone, and dialed Lydia's business number. My voice mail message was short and to the point. I needed the complete travel records of Patricia Middlemass over the past five years: not just a listing, but copies of the forms — where she was going, the stated reason, and how much she billed for the trip. Mixing business with pleasure at the Crown's expense could get a person fired.

When I finished the call I hung up the phone, checked to make sure Elaine was still alive, then went back to bed and slept like a babe.

By seven o'clock I was up and showered. Elaine's body was still in the same position as the night before, but she was breathing softly and was definitely alive. I stood in the darkened room for a moment, looking down at her, the flushed face, the sheen of sweat on her brow, and I wondered what she had told Dinah of Cindy's death. I was working on the assumption that she *had* told her, probably by phone yesterday evening, but had omitted the details. And I was pretty sure that Dinah would have been told to report to work. Elaine didn't know about their relationship and the science must go on.

Back in the kitchen I wrote a note to Elaine suggesting Tylenol and Perrier, did a quick mental inventory, picked up my briefcase and bag, and locked the door behind me. A pale, heavy fog hung over the street, sputtering with rain. When I got to the car I wiped the condensation off the windows with my sleeve. I made a detour to a 10th Avenue bakery and twenty minutes later I was in front of Dinah's apartment, a bag of croissants at my side. The fog had darkened into rain and the street lamps flickered uncertainly, trying to decide if it was night or day. I sat for a moment collecting myself. I could see a light on in one of the windows above. What state would Dinah be in? Distraught?

Overcome with guilt? Or cool with denial? I hated walking into the unknown.

Rain plunked on the windshield, falling in drops the size of golf balls. Reluctantly, I stuffed the bag of croissants into my jacket, picked up my briefcase, and headed across the sidewalk full-tilt. The front door was open, and a row of mailboxes inside gave me Dinah's apartment number. It looked like she had one of only two apartments on the top floor. There was no buzzer, and the door into the foyer was ajar.

At one time, before being chopped up into separate apartments, this house must have been the mansion of some West Coast robber baron, but now the grand foyer was carpeted in astroturf and all that remained of the chandelier was the ornate plaster work above and a bare bulb dangling from a single wire. The staircase was still impressive, though, an arc of dark wood that swept up to the second floor. It could easily accommodate four abreast. Beyond that, between the second and third floor, the stairs narrowed to a tight, dark corridor designed, I presumed, for the servants.

Dinah's door was off a small landing at the top. I knocked once and a minute later it swung open. Dinah didn't seem surprised to see me. She gazed at me for a minute then turned away.

"We have to talk," I said gently.

She gave a little shrug. "Whatever," she said, then she turned away and moved off down the hall, leaving me to let myself in and shut the door behind me.

I wandered down the hall after her, checking out the rooms as I went. The apartment was like a dollhouse built under the roof, everything in miniature. There was a bedroom, barely larger than the double bed, a tiny kitchen where Dinah, with her back to me, was preparing coffee, and a living room that managed a couch and coffee table, but nothing more. A door from the living room opened onto a small balcony sitting under the peak of the roof. I waited for Dinah at this door, leaning against the wall. The balcony itself sat high in the branches of a maple, and through the leaves I could see the pavement glistening below, the tops of multi-coloured umbrellas bobbing down the sidewalk toward the 4th Avenue buses. Behind me, I heard Dinah come into the room. She hesitated, then crossed to stand beside me. Neither of us spoke. The soft gurgle of brewing coffee floated in from the kitchen.

After a minute I turned my head toward her. "I'm so sorry — "

Before any more words could escape she shook her head, willing me to stop. She stood there for a moment, half turned toward me biting her lip, then she turned away and folded in on herself. After several convulsive shudders she brought herself under control and straightened, but avoided looking at me by gazing out the balcony door.

When she finally started talking it was as much to herself as to me.

"It was over between us. I knew that, and I was still so pissed off with her that when I heard the news ..." then she had to stop for a moment before she could continue. "... when I heard the news my first reaction was ... almost happy. Like, you know, serves her right." She turned and looked into my eyes searching for judgment, but there was none. "Then it sunk in, that she's gone: I'll never see her again. How can that be?" Then she turned back to the tree outside. "It can't be."

I said nothing.

She stood quietly watching the water fall in droplets from the reddening leaves. Finally she sighed again. "I'll get the coffee."

When she came back I was sitting on the couch. The bag of croissants was on the coffee table and so was the vial, placed dead centre. She walked in, a coffee cup in each hand, and stopped abruptly when she saw it. She paused for a moment, then continued forward. When she had settled in beside me she turned and looked me in the eye, asking the question without words.

I answered. "Elaine told me."

Relief crossed her face. She leaned over and picked it up, rolling it in her hand. "I'm sorry about yesterday, but I couldn't say anything. I work for Elaine and I signed a non-disclosure agreement."

"You work for Madden."

She looked surprised. "Only on paper. I report to Elaine. I take my instructions from her." She held the vial up to the light, balanced between her thumb and index finger.

I reached out and took it from her. "I think *this* may be connected to Cindy's death." I dropped it back in my jacket pocket.

"But Elaine said Graham killed Cindy."

"That's one possibility."

She cocked her head. "What's the other?"

I thought about that for a minute. "I'm not sure, but all roads lead to Jacks Creek, so I need to know everything you know about this vial."

"But Elaine told you already."

I didn't actually lie, just evaded the truth. "I need your corroboration to make sure all the facts line up. Anything you can tell me would help. And as for your non-disclosure agreement, this is a murder investigation now, and in a court of law it's worth shit."

She shrugged. "It's the stimulus solution. The one that worked. Of course, I'm not supposed to know that because of the blind control, but you'd have to be an idiot not to know."

"Why?"

"The colour. The smell. It was different from almost everything else we tested, and the response was so wild. After months of hearing either nothing, or just this faintest static, you send this thing into the nasal cavity and the cells fire like machine guns. Its hard to forget something like that."

"Would Graham have known?"

"Not unless he saw the data. He'd have no way of connecting this solution to a positive run."

That answered one question. Chances are Graham knew exactly what was in the vial. "If it's from Elaine's research why would he have it up at Jacks Creek?"

She looked confused. "I wondered that too. Even if he stole it, why would he bring it up there?"

I pulled over my briefcase and rooted around until I found Cindy's field notes. Through Graham there had to be a connection between Jacks Creek and the vial; I didn't know what it was, but I knew it was there. And I was pretty sure that there was a connection between Jacks Creek and Cindy; there had to be. So if J=V and J=C, then V must also equal C. There had to be a connection between the vial and Cindy, the question was how to find it. For once, Patsy helped out. I laid Cindy's Rite-in-the-Rain field books on the table.

"Can you figure out the dates that the fish disappeared on Weaver Creek from these?"

She pulled them toward her. "Yeah. Cindy would have written them all down, but why?"

"Can you do it right now?"

She sounded unsure. "I guess so."

I pushed a pad of paper and a pencil over to her. "Just write them down here. I'll be back in a minute."

I picked up the phone in the kitchen and tried Edwards at his lab. He answered before the second ring. I skipped the pleasantries. "Did you get a hold of that guy in Fisheries?"

"I did. I was going to call you about that today. It was the first they'd heard of Weaver, but they've had three other reports of similar incidents, two in the upper Fraser, and another in the valley near Hope. By the time they could get there to check things out everything was back to normal, so they'd sort of discounted the whole thing."

"You didn't get the dates, by chance?"

"Of course I did. Just doing my best to be helpful."

"The Government of Canada appreciates your effort."

"Then the Government of Canada can take me to lunch at Tojo's." He read me the dates and I jotted them down on a piece of paper.

"Are you in later?" I asked.

"I think so." I heard him shuffle paper on his desk. "I've got a class at 9:30, but other than that I should be in my lab until noon."

"Good. I'll pop by. We need to talk. And the Treasury Board would be delighted to buy you lunch. By the way, Jonathan, don't give up on Elaine. I think she's coming around."

There was silence at the other end, then an uncomfortable, "Yeah, well ... see you later."

Back in the living room I pulled out a croissant and handed another to Dinah. She chewed on it absently, finishing up her list, then she lay down the pencil. "Okay, done. Who were you talking to?"

I ignored the question. "When you travel for work do you fill out travel claims for mileage, meals, that sort of thing?"

"There's a mileage log in every van, and we submit receipts for meals, hotels, whatever."

"There've been three other fish kills further up the Fraser," I said, adding the dates and the locations to the list she had prepared. "When you submit a claim, where does it go?"

She regarded me with a quizzical expression. "To the grant holder first for sign off, then to the finance clerk in Zoology. She issues the cheque."

"So who keeps the records?"

"Well, there are ..." Then she stopped and her expression changed. "You can't be serious. This," she said, poking the paper with the dates, "has nothing to do with any of us." I didn't answer. She sighed. "The finance clerk keeps central records, the grant holder has copies."

"So in your case — "

Her eyes flashed. "Hey!"

"It's hypothetical, but I need to understand. Would Madden have the records?"

She hesitated. "I guess. Or JJ. He handles all the financial stuff."

"For the FEI grant too?"

She shrugged. "Madden signs for it, but I bet JJ does the paperwork."

I slipped the notebooks back into my briefcase and stood up. Dinah did too.

I put my hand on her shoulder. "Take the day off. The department will be in chaos. You won't get anything done."

"Yes I will." She collected up the dishes on the table and started for the kitchen. At the door she stopped, turned. "I'm going to be helping you."

"I don't think so."

"Look, I owe it to Cindy. I don't owe her much, don't get me wrong, but if I can help to clear this up —"

"I don't need an assistant."

"I know the travel clerk. She'll let me have the files. Without me you'll have to come clean to get them."

And that definitely presented problems. I was pretty sure that Bob would be onsite that day making every effort to impede my work, so the truth was I could use a little undercover help.

"You're hired," I said. Then I added, "Just try to stay out of trouble."

chapter twenty-two

When we arrived at the Zoology building Dinah dumped her backpack and coat in the lab and went upstairs to schmooze with the finance clerk. She had the rest of the croissants tucked under her arm. I went into her office and made a phone call. A technician answered and put me on hold. After a series of clicks another voice came on, gentle and warm.

"Yes? Dr. Truong here."

In my head I'd gone over various options for approaching Truong. I knew he was the biochemist who purified the solutions for Elaine's olfaction work, but beyond that I knew nothing of his status or involvement in the research. Also, I knew that the post-doc story wasn't going to hold up much longer, especially with Bobbins onsite, but the truth wasn't an option either. I might be asked to get a warrant, or worse, my Ottawa office might be notified. I made a quick decision to stick as close to the truth as possible but keep the details vague. I explained that I was working temporarily with Elaine and we were trying to determine the contents of an unmarked vial that we thought might be from the samples he'd sent over for the olfaction study. There was a pause at the other end of the line.

"Olfaction study? You mean maybe Fisheries Enterprises' project? I know Dr. Okada is working on that."

"That would be the one. It was funded by FEI."

"And you say you have a vial — "

"Unmarked. The coding came off. So we have the results of the runs, but we need to know what's in the vial."

"The work for FEI, strictly proprietary. I can't release — "

"But Dr. Okada is on the team."

"True, but the experimental design clearly stipulates no contact to maintain blind control. You tell me olfaction, but I don't know this. I know we work on receptor binding, but not olfaction. You need to speak to the project head."

"Madden Riesler?" He confirmed it. "But I thought this was an aid project. Why aren't the results in the public domain?"

"Aid project?" He laughed. "Who told you that? This is one hundred percent proprietary. I can't even publish results. Maybe the work is aid related, I don't know, but this is definitely an industrial contract. Listen, we all meet today anyway, special meeting. First time, last time. Dr. Riesler says FEI is happy with results and is shutting down project ahead of schedule. I'll ask him for you."

An alarm bell went off in my head. I lowered my voice. "The truth is, Dr. Truong, the technician mixed up some samples and I'm trying to bail her out. You don't need to tell me what's in the vial, I just need to know if it's part of the FEI study. You might be able to do that just by smelling it. It's very distinctive. If you know it's one of yours we'll just give it a temporary code so we don't lose the data from those runs and you can analyze it and match it later. You'd really be helping us out."

I was hoping Truong's personality matched his voice. He paused for a minute then clicked his tongue. "Easy to do. I've made the same mistake myself. Sure. You bring it around this morning I'll take a look." Then he chuckled. "And I won't mention it at the meeting."

When I hung up the phone I leaned back in my chair and contemplated this new information. There were two things that didn't make sense. FEI was an international aid organization funding tilapia work. Why would they want to own Alistair Truong's research on olfaction? Also, what was there to own? Elaine had told me that Truong was purifying solutions, so what could you patent? Clearly, someone wasn't telling the truth, but was it Madden, Elaine, or Alistair Truong? What I needed was some reliable information on FEI.

I stood up, unsure of what to do next. Normally I would have called Sylvia. She could have traced the organization and been back to me by lunch, but I suddenly wondered if I could trust her. Where did her loyalties lie? Duncan was another possibility. He could make some calls and, if FEI was legitimate, get back to me, but that might take a day or two. My other option was perusing Riesler's files. He would have the original contract with its terms, conditions, and signatories, but getting into the office might be a problem. It was just past nine in the morning, the beginning of a busy workday. Madden was probably already at his desk. I fingered the vial. Maybe Dr. Truong knew more than he was saying and a personal visit would kill two birds with one stone.

I closed up my briefcase, buried it under some papers in one of Dinah's desk drawers, and started out of the office. I was just beyond the door when I stopped — a premonition — and went back. I pulled my briefcase out of hiding, found my lock picks and dropped them into my pocket.

As I walked by the fish museum I caught a glimpse of Madden in a lab coat setting out trays. A technician trailed behind him, doling out fish. I was halfway up the stairs when I realized that opportunity had just opened up a door that moments ago had been closed. Madden was taking Graham's 9:30 lab, which meant he would be tied up for at least the next hour. I thought about that for a second. I would still have to break into an office in the middle of the day, and maybe Truong could tell me everything I needed to know without my having to compromise any laws.

I walked slowly up the stairs. With each step I changed my mind: Truong, B&E, Truong, B&E. I reached the main floor on Truong. That seemed as good a process as any for arriving at a decision, so I pushed open the doors leading outside. Just then, Bob rounded the corner, coming up the walk. He was surrounded by students so he didn't see me. I turned and shot up the stairs to the second floor. On the landing I stood near the banister and watched Bob enter the foyer, hesitate, then walk off in the direction of the main office.

So Bob was here to see Madden. It all fell into place. Madden and Patsy were lovers. Patsy had tried to derail the investigation from Ottawa, and when that hadn't worked she'd sent out Bob to interfere with me. I felt a spurt of anger in my gut and my plans suddenly changed.

At this time of the morning classes were in session and the fourth floor was almost deserted. Only one or two doors were ajar, showing diligent professors working at their desks. They didn't even bother to look up as I passed. I was just another student interrupting precious research time.

When I reached Madden's office I pulled out the pass-key and slipped it in the lock. It jammed. Madden's office was keyed on a different system. I switched to the lock picks. In the silence the clinking of the metal picks, one against the other, sounded like the peeling of church bells. I probed with one hand, and tried to still the extra picks with the other. I'd been at it about a minute when the doors to the stairway behind me opened, then swooshed shut. I stopped moving and gripped the picks. Footsteps passed in front of Madden's hallway and receded down the corridor. There was the rattle of keys, a door clicked open, then it shut with a bang: silence again. I went back to work. My pick caught, the knob turned, and I was inside.

I didn't waste any time. I crossed to the curtains and pulled them shut. Madden had a corner office. One entire wall was glass, and the rest was taken up by a huge oak desk, a credenza, and matching bookcases. Filing cabinets took up the entire wall at the end of the office. As I went over to them I glanced through the window of the door that connected to his private lab. It looked neater than the day I arrived, the surfaces clean, the equipment sparkling and neatly arranged, as if he were expecting a VIP tour.

At the cabinets I did a quick reconnaissance. Like any well organized person he had all the drawers labelled. Four of the cabinets were devoted to research: experimental data and reprints. The two nearest the lab were for administration. Contracts took up the two bottom drawers of the cabinet against the wall. I squatted down and pulled open the first drawer. It was jammed with hanging files arranged alphabetically. I thumbed through, searching for F, but the C section took up over one-third of the drawer: Canadian Fish Foods Limited, The Canadian Institute for Fisheries Management, Canadian Sea Products, The Canadian Salmon Marketing Council etc. etc. etc. I had just reached the end of the drawer, the E section, when I heard a key in the door.

I turned and froze, but the knob didn't move. Then I heard a door open and the fluorescent lights in the lab went on. There was the tinkling of glass as someone carried a tray of glassware across to one of the benches then put it down. A drawer slid open. It sounded like it was just on the other side of the connecting door. I eased the cabinet closed. From where I was squatting someone in the lab would have to actually walk into the office to see me, but I needed to know who was in there. Madden might come into the office. A technician would stay in the lab.

I stood up, back against the wall, and edged over to the door. Through the window I caught the unappetizing sight of JJ rummaging around in one of the drawers. In front of him was a tray of vials, all of them exactly like the one I had in my pocket. And whatever he was looking for he couldn't find. He banged the drawer shut and opened the one below.

I figured I had a few minutes. It was a risk, but I'd come this far. I slid back down the wall and slowly opened the bottom drawer — not too far, because F should be right at the beginning. Not surprisingly, the *Fisheries* section was packed as well, and my heart gave a little surge as I caught sight of a file labelled Fisheries Enterprises International. I snatched it out of the drawer and it fell open in my hands, empty as the prairie in the middle of a drought. What the hell was going on?

The drawer in the next room banged shut. I heard JJ pick up his vials, and his footsteps approached the connecting door. He stopped for a moment, then walked past. It was definitely time to go. I eased the drawer shut and stood up, my back still against the wall. I approached the window and snuck a glance through it. JJ was kneeling, his back to me, fiddling with the lock on a half-sized refrigerator tucked into a corner. He was having trouble getting it open, which meant that I was home free. But just as I was passing across the window a face appeared in the tiny square of glass in the lab door. Bob cupped his hands around his eyes and peered in, but with JJ kneeling, the lab looked empty. Bob's head then disappeared and I heard his footsteps round the corner as he approached Madden's office door.

In the next half second three unpleasant scenarios played themselves out in my brain. *The knock, JJ coming into the office to let Bob in, and both of them finding me there.* Nope. I erased that as a possibility. *My leaving via the lab, making some excuse to JJ as I scooted through the door.* That wasn't an appealing option either. How about: *I open the door and ask Bob how his evening with Patsy went?*

His footsteps stopped. I could almost hear the displacement of air as he lifted his hand to knock, but the second before it touched I jerked open the door and threw myself at him, pinning him to the wall. Before he could utter a word I'd clamped my hand over his mouth. We were so close I could feel the pounding of his heart through my chest. It took him a moment to recognize me, but I knew he had when the fear in his eyes transformed to fury. I had to work fast. With my free hand I groped in my pocket. I pulled out the photograph of

Patsy and Riesler, the one I'd borrowed from Elaine's photo album. His pale eyes glanced at it then back at me. My voice came out between a rasp and a whisper.

"Ever heard the word *accessory*, Bob? And we're not talking matching shoes and gloves." I gave him a hard shove, just to emphasize my point. "If you say a word to anyone about me being here then you're implicated. And you know I'd squeal."

With that, I pulled the door shut behind me and banged on it, then took off down the hall. Hopefully Bob would have changed from purple back to pasty white by the time JJ arrived at the door.

In the biochemistry building I checked the directory posted in the foyer for Truong's office and lab number. They were one and the same. I took the stairs up to the fifth floor and reached the top panting, but it felt good, a release of tension. I stopped for a moment and closed my eyes, breathing deeply. The truth is that my run-ins with Bob and JJ had left me rattled, so I took a moment to dampen my reflexes and clear my mind before I headed down the hall.

Dr. Truong's door opened into a large, airy lab with a central bench and another bench running beneath a wall of windows. A woman, perched on a stool and working at a computer, looked up from the screen as I entered. She smiled a greeting.

"You looking for Alistair?"

I nodded.

She motioned to the corner with her head. "Back there. I think he's in."

She returned to her computer. As I walked by I glanced at the screen. She was playing with an elaborate molecule, spheres attached by thick yellow, red, and blue lines. She grabbed an outer sphere with the mouse and pushed it toward the middle. As she did so, the whole molecule flexed, snapped into a new position. She moved it again. It snapped into another configuration. It was like watching a contortionist develop a new routine.

As I crossed to Truong's office door I noted three other people working in the lab. One was pipetting, a second was hunched over another computer, and the third was watching something in what looked like a drying oven, while periodically making notations on a piece of paper. They all ignored me.

A hotel sign hanging around Truong's doorknob was flipped to *Maid, Please Make Up the Room*, so I knocked lightly.

"Come in." The voice was almost too soft to be heard.

I entered a small office overflowing with papers and books and stiflingly hot. Truong looked up from his desk, and I introduced myself. He came around and shook my hand, smiling. I would have placed him at between forty-five and fifty-five, with gray just beginning to show in his hair. His movements were staccato and he had the air of a man with many things to accomplish before the end of the day. He pointed to the coat rack near the door.

"Sorry about the heat. Lab is freezing, my office is the tropics." He shook his head. "Can't do anything about it. Windows are sealed shut to save energy." He shrugged. "What can you do."

I took the seat across from him and kept my coat on my lap. We went through the usual pleasantries and when they were over I handed him the vial.

"That's the one we need help with," I explained.

He swivelled around and held the vial up to the window, examining it against the light. He tilted it back and forth, watching the liquid flow and pool. Finally, he unscrewed the top and took a sniff, then he smiled and gave a nod.

"I have to run tests, you understand, to know for sure. But it's probably one of the last set. Best thing to do, you label those runs 132X. I'll give this to my technician, we take a look, and tomorrow — " He reached for the phone. I shot my hand out and stopped him, then pulled my ID from my pocket.

He looked at me, confused. "What's going on?"

I didn't have time to say anything beyond the word *investigator* before he was out of his chair, heading for his files.

"I've followed all regulations," he said, "all protocols. My documentation is — "

I motioned him back to his chair. "Your work isn't under scrutiny, but there have been ... irregularities in the FEI contract. We're trying to sort them out."

He smiled an apology. "But I'm just a little cog in a big wheel."

"Anything would help."

His dark eyes searched my face. "You put me in a difficult position. I have a confidentiality agreement with FEI. Word gets out that I leak information, no more clients," he looked slowly around his office then back at me, "No more job."

There was a photograph on his desk: the wife and two beautiful daughters, both nearing university age. He was a man who needed to keep his job, but then, so did I.

"There's been a murder," I said flatly. "There's a chance it's related."

"That graduate student in zoology? But she has nothing to do with us."

As always, the university grapevine worked at the speed of light.

"Not directly, but she was Elaine Okada's student. And the person under suspicion is Graham Connell, again not direct, but — "

"Graham? Blond, sharp, always asking questions? He picked up the solutions for Dr. Riesler."

I nodded. He turned his head and drifted away momentarily, trying to make sense of what I had just told him. On Truong's desk were three large models, linear molecules with bright side chains that jutted out around them like a piece of modern sculpture. I picked one up and turned it over in my hands. "What is this?"

"Carbohydrate structure. Critical in cell-to-cell communication. I designed that for a pharmaceutical company. Lots of interest in using carbohydrate structures to develop new drugs."

"You designed it?"

"Sure. I use a naturally occurring carbohydrate as the basis, but sometimes we can improve on nature. Change an amino acid here, add a different side chain there, and in the end it works better than the original."

"Is that what you were doing for FEI?"

He nodded his head. "Similar, yes. Madden came to me with purified solutions. He already had a good idea of what is in the solutions, but not the structure, the conformation." He picked up another molecule from his desk, entirely different from the one in my hands. "This," he held up his model, "and that," he pointed at mine, "are the same."

He smiled, satisfied with my look of confusion. "Of course not. Not the same at all. But they have same number of carbon atoms, same number of oxygen, hydrogen, and so on. So the composition is the same, but the arrangement is different. It's very important in living systems how the atoms are arranged. Even one little change," he yanked a red side chain off his molecule and attached it one site up the linear stem, "and the molecule," he shrugged, "... doesn't work. Doesn't do what it's supposed to do. So I take Madden's purified samples, all have similar molecules, complex bioactive molecules — " He saw the look on my face. "Molecules that have some biological function — proteins, enzymes, special carbohydrates — so first we look at structure of each molecule." He wagged his finger at me. "This isn't easy to do. Sounds easy, but very complicated." He waved his hand, brushing the details aside. "So. We find the similarities and differences, but not so many differences, many similarities. We know we're looking for a molecule involved in receptor binding, that means lock and key situation. And we know that all these molecules we're working on act as weak keys. They do the job, but not great. We can do better."

"So we look at the molecules, try to figure out which piece of this whole thing," he ran his finger down the stem of the molecule, "is the key. We design several molecules that look good, and Madden takes them and tests them. First, we get nowhere. Very depressing. Lots of work, no results. Then we take a different approach. We stop looking for similarities between molecules, we look for differences, but subtle differences. Something almost the same in each molecule, but just slightly different. Then we find peculiar side chain, peculiar for two reasons. Number one," he held up his index finger, "contains unusual element. Boron. This element, it's rare in bioactive molecules. And side chain itself, it's the same composition in every molecule, but conformation slightly different: it bends a different way in each molecule, and we know from proteins and enzymes that how a molecule bends, how it folds itself, can affect its ability to function. Best example, if you take a key and twist the end it's still the same key, but doesn't fit in the lock. It won't open the door. We know that Madden's solutions have been frozen, reheated, subjected to tests for purification. All these things can make a big molecule twist, fold, maybe pop into a different conformation, so we start to look at this. We ask how many different conformations of the side chain can we produce. Twenty-three." His voice was triumphant, but he quickly sobered when he remembered the bigger context. "This vial ..." he held it up high in front of him, "... I believe that it came from the last batch. It would be the side chain in one of its conformations, but I'd have to do analysis to know which one."

"So you didn't take the samples that Madden brought in and purify them?"

"No, no. Not my job. I'm a molecular engineer. I design molecules. He brings me samples that approximate what he needs and I design a molecule to do the job."

But Elaine had said he was purifying samples from Madden's original solution. I was sure of it.

"And you heard nothing back after the last samples went over."

He shrugged. "We don't expect to. It's part of a blind control."

"Have you ever met anyone from Fisheries Enterprises?"

He smiled slyly. "Officially?"

I laughed. "Unofficially will do."

"Guy came in one day, Taiwanese, said he was interested in working in my lab. Had a doctorate from somewhere in England. Asked me many questions but he was wearing a silk suit, probably made by Hong Kong tailor. Very expensive. He didn't need a job, he was checking my credentials." He shrugged. "I know he's with FEI because I see him later, at the Faculty Club, eating lunch with Madden. A group of them, international convention, only guys in the restaurant with white shirts and expensive suits."

"Why an international convention?"

"There was Pak Li, Taiwanese guy. Another guy was dark-skinned, maybe Italian or Greek. And the other guy, I heard him speak with an accent that was German? Dutch? Maybe Scandinavian? That's the only time I see them, but two days later my participation in project is confirmed."

He stopped talking and the only sound was the hiss of the radiator. I was trying to fit what he had told me into what I already knew, but the oppressive heat was slowing down my thought process. I sighed and stood up. Truong had given me as much as I needed for now.

He held up the vial. "You still want me to analyze this?"

I thought about that for a second. I was reluctant to let my only hard evidence go, but I needed a firm link to the olfaction study. "How much do you need for the tests?"

He held it up to the lights and squinted. "Half of this should do it."

"How soon can I get the results?"

"Call around three-thirty. The meeting starts at four."

He followed me out to the lab and got the technician to pipette half of the remaining liquid into a separate vial, then he shook my hand.

"Good luck with the investigation. I hope FEI comes out okay." He laughed. "They spend lots of money."

I kicked myself. I should have told him to keep quiet about the investigation. My fault, not his. At the mention of FEI one of the graduate students looked up from his work. As I left I saw him get up and approach Truong and the technician. Just paranoia, I told myself.

He probably worked on the FEI study and was worried about his funding.

I headed back across the road. It was time to take Edwards out to lunch.

chapter twenty-three

"The salmon's good," he said.

I looked up over my menu. Was Edwards making a joke?

"I thought you were trying to save the salmon."

He dropped his menu to the table. "Might as well enjoy them while you can. Another five years ..." He shrugged.

I had nixed the idea of sushi when we met, opting for the golf club restaurant instead, one of those places where the menus are the size of billboards but so ornate that they're impossible to read. We had a window seat at the back of the restaurant overlooking the greens. The rain had let up when I was in with Truong, and now a delicate white mist hung over the fairways, collecting in dense pools between the knolls. In the distance a lone golfer, clothed head to toe in rain gear, rose slowly out of a patch of fog, dragging his golf cart behind him. At the top of the rise he hesitated, scanned the area, then descended into the mists on the other side.

Chad, our waiter, came over to recite the daily specials. He ended with the "starch of the day": a Saffron Flavoured Cous-Cous Steamed in the Traditional Way over a Six-Vegetable Broth. I was going to give him a quiz, ask him the precise names of the six vegetables that had gone into the broth, but the manager was looking over and I thought the kid might lose his job if he didn't get it right. As it was, I opted for something mammalian: a small filet mignon. Its "starch complement" was a bed of Hand Harvested Loon Lake Wild Rice Sautéed with Wild Mushrooms and Garlic and Simmered in a Chanterelle-Cognac Broth. It sounded yummy and I didn't think I'd be whipping up this dish at home.

Chad disappeared with our order. Edwards sipped a glass of white wine, the pale liquid and delicate glass at odds with his brooding features. On the way down from the university we'd made small talk, partly because I was still trying to organize my thoughts. I felt I knew so much that I knew absolutely nothing. I was afloat in detail and had no idea where to begin to find meaning and unity in all the fragments. That was assuming there was some meaning and unity. I was hoping that Edwards, with his deeper understanding of the subject matter, might help me pull it all altogether, but I didn't even know where to start. I decided on the beginning, at the lab in Seattle where the student had stumbled across the active solution.

"Ever hear of Grierson?" I began.

Edwards had been gazing serenely out the window, but at the sound of Grierson's name he choked. He grabbed a napkin from the table and pitched forward, coughing and sputtering into it. Chad glanced over nervously, preparing for the Heimlich manoeuvre. I waited until Edwards had reached the gasping stage then said, "I take it that means yes."

He glared at me for a good half-second, then reached for his wine glass and drained it. Before the base hit the table Chad was beside him.

"More wine, sir?"

Edwards looked at me, then Chad. "A carafe. The big one."

Chad hurried off.

Edwards said nothing, just turned and looked out the window, pointedly refusing to make eye contact with me. When Chad returned with the wine he poured himself another glass and emptied that one too. Then he banged the glass down and turned on me.

"How'd you find out?"

"About your ..." I searched for a word that was vague, yet evocative of great knowledge, "connection with Grierson?"

He snorted. "My connection. That's a good way to put it."

I said nothing. Just waited and let the silence draw itself out. Edwards poured himself another glass of wine, drained it, then he said, "I don't know what you heard but I didn't steal it." What the hell was he talking about? I didn't answer, hoping he'd continue. He did. "That's why you asked me here, isn't it. I mean if I could steal from Grierson, why not from Elaine, why not falsely accuse Madden, why not — "

Finally I couldn't hold myself back. "What are you talking about?"

"That damned solution." He shook his head. "I thought all that was behind me."

I looked at Edwards and did a rapid calculation, counting eight years back. He would have just been finishing up his undergraduate work. The light clicked on.

"Jesus. You were the student that — "

He cut me off. "Fucked up? Is that what you were going to say? That couldn't get an electrode in the olfactory bulb."

"That's not how I heard the story."

He knocked back another glass of wine. "Yeah? What did you hear?"

"That Grierson didn't want the solution. He didn't want to follow it up, so he gave it to another professor."

"Well, whoever told you that is wrong. It did disappear," he said belligerently, "but I didn't take it."

Chad arrived with the plates and slid them in front of us. I hoped Edwards would eat something before all that wine flooded his brain. I'd never get a man his size back into the car if he was reeling drunk, and I needed him sober enough to give me logical, coherent answers. I tucked into my meal, hoping he'd follow my good example. Unfortunately, he didn't. He stared out the window and toyed absently with the stem of his glass. I figured if he wasn't going to eat he might as well talk.

"So tell me what happened."

After a minute he turned to look at me, his face unreadable. When he spoke his voice was flat.

"It wasn't an anomaly. I'm as sure of that today as I was back then. It was olfactory. For Christ's sake, you pump it into the nasal cavity and the neurons fire. If that's not the definition of olfactory, what is? The problem was the nerve bundle. I mean, Grierson was right. I screwed up. I was aiming for the olfactory bulb and I missed it, but some of the greatest discoveries in science have been made by errors just like that. The problem was that we had no idea what that bundle might do, where it might go, and as far as Grierson was concerned, if it wasn't in the known olfactory pathways, it wasn't olfactory; and if it wasn't olfactory it wasn't related to migration and homing; and if it wasn't related to migration and homing it had no place in his lab.

"I wanted to continue, but I was only an undergraduate, an honours student, and without my advisor's support ..." he shook his head. "So Grierson took the solution. A couple days later it disappeared." He was silent for a moment. He refilled his glass, but drank at a more civilized pace. The alcohol didn't seem to affect him at all. He continued then, more quietly. "Then the shit hit the fan. He accused me of stealing it. There was never any proof, but I was an easy target."

"What do you think happened?"

"I always figured Grierson kept it, waiting for me to disappear into obscurity so he could run the study himself." At this point he grinned. "But I didn't disappear into obscurity, did I? Even though he blacklisted me I managed to stay in the field. And you know what? I keep an eye on those publications. If Grierson ever publishes anything that's even vaguely related I'll nail him to the wall."

An unpleasant thought entered my head. Unfortunately, it arrived at my mouth before I had time to stop it. "That's Elaine's specialty. Is that why you dated her? To get a personalized literature search every time you hit the sack?"

His eyes narrowed and he leaned back in his chair. "Fuck you."

"Sorry, but it would be a logical conclusion."

"Logical, maybe, but wrong."

Then another thought struck me. "You started dating Elaine, then you were accused of stealing again. I wonder, is that a coincidence?"

He threw his napkin down on the table. "That's it." He was halfway out of his seat, whether to make an exit or punch out my lights wasn't clear.

"Keep your shirt on. That's not what I meant. I'm wondering if you were set up, an easy target, as you said yourself."

He sat back down, looking a little more civil and interested. I continued.

"Do you remember seeing Madden around Grierson's lab?"

He thought for a minute. "Not really. But he was around the department then, that's for sure. He gave a seminar that impressed the hell out of me."

"Were he and Grierson friends?"

He raised an eyebrow. "Grierson wouldn't know the meaning of the word. Riesler was competition."

So somebody was lying. Was it Edwards? I didn't think so. Madden? Maybe. Or was it Elaine, who simply chose to ignore the provenance of the solution because for her the end, her research, overrode the means. She couldn't care less how the solution fell into her hands. But it still didn't make sense. Why all the fuss? I put down my knife and fork, sat back in my chair, and sighed.

"Okay, Jonathan, enlighten me. We're talking about a bunch of fish here. They can't be worth all this: lying, stealing," I hesitated, "maybe even committing murder."

"What are you talking about?"

"Riesler ..." I paused, then figured I might as well get it out in open, "... and Elaine have that solution."

He sat for a minute in dazed silence, then shot back, "She's not involved. I know her. She's honest."

His loyalty was touching. I hoped it wasn't misplaced.

He took a deep breath and leaned toward me. "And we're not just talking about a bunch of fish. We're talking about one of nature's greatest mysteries. How do millions of salmon find their way from the northern seas back to the exact streams they were born in. If

Grierson's solution holds the key it's probably worth a Nobel Prize."

"And you think it might?"

"That's the question, isn't it. How much do you know about salmon migration?"

"Not much."

"Then you're not alone. And yet it's been studied to death. How do these fish, which are not exactly the brightest beings on earth, get back to their birth streams to spawn. That's a trip of thousands of miles, and once they get into the freshwater rivers some of them travel hundreds of miles inland to tiny tributaries several times removed from the main river. That represents literally thousands of decisions the fish has to make as it travels upstream. Do I turn here? No. Here? No. Here? Yes. And so on, over hundreds of miles. It's almost unimaginable. And in Pacific salmon we know it's not learning because they only do it once. Make the trip, spawn, and die. What a life."

He reached for his wine but thought better of it and took a sip of water instead. "So how do they do it? You know what? We don't really know. We can send a robot to Mars, but we can't figure out how nature organized this dumb fish so it could accomplish that task. We know some things. We know, for example, that on the high seas celestial navigation may play a role: they navigate by the stars. But we also know that if it's overcast during the period of migration they still make it home, so there has to be more to it than that. The magnetic fields of the earth may be involved, thermoclines in the ocean, but it's all pretty fuzzy.

"What we do know, though, is once they reach freshwater, they use smell. If you blind them they still get home, but plug up their nostrils with petroleum jelly and that's it. They get lost. But what exactly are they smelling? And how does this olfactory mechanism work? They have to know what smell to follow, and that smell has to attract them, pull them toward it. And to make it more complicated, as far as we can figure out, it only works when the fish are in their final reproductive state." He sat back in his chair and crossed his arms. "Try sorting that one out."

"So if someone stumbled upon the answer — "

"Their reputation would be made."

"And what if it involved more than just stumbling? If it required a concerted research effort?"

"*If* you could get funding, and that's a big *if* ..." He noted my surprise. "There's no industrial tie-in, no jobs created, no profit to be made. Welcome to science in the twenty-first century."

"But let's just say you managed to pull together funding ..." or, I thought suddenly, siphon it off of other projects like the Network and foreign aid grants. That had potential.

He continued. "Then you'd pull together a team — it would take big talent from several disciplines — and you'd get on with it."

"Would you keep it quiet?"

"Damn right. People are scooped all the time."

"And if the team succeeded — "

He held up his wine glass in a toast. "They'd all have it made."

"If they were all acknowledged."

Edwards gave me an odd look. "Of course they'd all be acknowledged."

This guy was a minnow. Suddenly he looked uneasy. "This is all fantasy, right?"

I pulled the vial out of my pocket, placed it on the table, and told Edwards what I'd seen at Jacks Creek: the fish pooling in the wrong place and this vial on the site.

"So?" I asked. "How does that fit in?"

He rubbed his beard. Then he shook his head. "I don't believe it."

"I was there."

"You're implying that the solution in this vial was drawing them in, but you don't know that. You haven't linked what's in here to what you saw at Jacks Creek. There are researchers around those creeks all the time. Maybe this vial got dropped by one of them and has nothing to do with the fish. It's all supposition. You have no causal relationship."

"Jesus, Jonathan, put two and two together."

"Yeah, and you're coming up with five. What about the other fish kills, or are you telling me that Riesler's developed individual molecules for each population of sockeye. Why would he do that?"

"Maybe one size fits all?"

"Can't. The system doesn't work like that. Each stream population has to home to a unique smell, otherwise they'd all end up in the same place." Then a note of uneasiness crept into his voice. "Unless ..." Then he shook his head and said definitively, "It can't be that simple."

When Chad came over with the bill I paid on my credit card. During all the fussing with wallets, little trays and pens, Edwards processed. I put the signed receipt back on the tray and slid the customer copy into my wallet. I asked a question that I knew would get his attention.

"Would you consider Elaine 'big talent'?"

He nodded reluctantly.

"And what about Alistair Truong. Ever heard of him?"

"He's involved?"

I nodded. "Is he 'big talent'?"

"He won the Life Sciences award last year."

"Last question. If I can tie Riesler to all the fish kills up and down the valley, what would you say then?"

He didn't respond right away, took a minute to think it through. When his answer came it was delivered in that sonorous, low bass. "I'd say we have a problem."

Edwards didn't speak on the way back to the labs. I stopped the car in front of his building. As he was climbing out he said, almost absently, "I'll make a few calls, some neuro guys I know. I'll get in touch later."

"What for?"

He looked down the road for a moment, squinted as if trying to see something that wasn't really there, then looked back at me. "Just to make sure I'm right."

Then he slammed the door and strode off down the pathway. I suppressed a jab of lust as I watched him disappear around the corner. If Elaine wasn't interested then sign me up.

I parked in C-lot and walked down slowly to the Zoology wing, letting my mind wander over all the information I'd collected. Between Elaine, Truong, and Edwards, I now had enough to develop some plausible theories about what might be going on. The most likely explanation was that Riesler had made his bid for immortality and he didn't intend to share the prize with anybody else. That would certainly be consistent with what I knew of his publishing record. The exact nature of that bid remained a little fuzzy, but I was sure I could pry it out of Riesler himself once everything was exposed.

So why was I still uneasy? Why didn't things feel right?

Graham for one. I couldn't fit him into the picture. Was it Graham who put the vial in Jacks Creek, or did he find it there? Did he know what was in the vial? And if he did, what did it matter? This was one paper he could never publish: it was too big, too public, and he'd never get away with it. I tried another track. If Graham did know what was in the vial, what would he do with the information? Sell it? He'd have to have a buyer, and as Edwards pointed out, the work had no industrial relevance. Maybe he could sell it to another researcher. Or maybe he could *threaten* to sell it, or leak it, to manipulate — to extort money from — Riesler. That seemed the most likely possibility. Maybe Graham gave it a shot and for some reason the extortion scam blew up in his face. That's why he needed me.

But that still left Cindy. How did she fit in? Had she found Jacks Creek just as we had? And who was there when she found it? Riesler or Connell? Who killed her, and to hide what?

And finally there was the damn Network. Riesler must be skimming money off several grants — both the Network and FEI — to pay for his opus, but that didn't square up with Truong's story that he had been vetted by someone from FEI.

By the time I reached the Zoology wing my head was spinning. There were still too many details that didn't fit, and that made me uneasy. If I had the right theory, that Madden had made his bid for fame, then all the facts should fall neatly into place. If they didn't then the theory was probably wrong.

What I needed was to sit down, type out my meeting notes from Truong and Edwards, and review my notes from the last couple days. Maybe something would come up that would finally crack this thing open.

I hopped down the stairs and came around the corner to Elaine's lab. The door was open, the lights on. I could hear the muffle of voices pitched just above the sound of the flowing water. As I came in one of the voices broke into laughter. That, at least, was a welcome change. I headed for Dinah's office to retrieve my laptop and nearly stumbled over Sylvia, who was draped across Dinah's chair like Cleopatra on her throne. Dinah was sitting on a table, just across from her. Her legs were swinging, elbows on her knees, her wolf eyes glinting. They both turned to me in surprise. The conversation died.

chapter twenty-four

"**W**hat the hell are you doing here?"

Sylvia raised her eyebrows in mock surprise. "Are you speaking to *moi*?"

Dinah snickered, but I shot her a look that wiped the levity off her face. Sylvia rolled her eyes.

"Give it a break, Morgan. Personally, I don't have time for this shit."

"Neither do I."

"Honey, you got a lot more time than I do."

"You always fight dirty."

She smiled. "Whatever works, babe. So, why did you never mention your lovely assistant?"

I glanced at Dinah. "I didn't know I had one."

"Well, despite you we've met, and it's been delightful." Then she turned to me, serious. "As a peace offering I *have* compromised my professional ethics for you. Not that you weren't a jerk on the phone yesterday, but I love you just the way you are."

"Why did you tell her?"

Sylvia looked at Dinah. "Could you give us a minute?"

Dinah slid off the table and sauntered out of the room.

"Cute," said Sylvia, watching her exit, then she turned back to me. "Because she called and asked, and I knew Elaine had to be desperate to come to me for help. She said she needed to know the names of all the people you'd investigated, so I told her." She paused for a minute before continuing, watching me for a reaction. "You know, sometimes the end doesn't justify the means, Morgan. Believe me, I know, especially since the end is so much closer for me."

I cringed. This was not a discussion I could handle right now. "Okay, but can we talk about this some other time?"

Sylvia shrugged. "She also asked for this." She pushed a large brown envelope across the desk. "I thought you should see it."

The envelope was addressed to Elaine, but Sylvia hadn't sealed it. I pulled out the contents. It was a computer search, but instead of science papers the search had covered the business and general press databases, pulling from publications around the world. All the articles were related to fishing.

"What the hell is this?"

"She asked me to run a search on an organization called Fisheries Enterprises International, anything I could find. She also gave me a name, a guy named Dr. Pak Li. The search on FEI picked up nothing, and believe me, I scoured every database I know. Dr. Pak Li was more forthcoming, but I didn't like what I found."

I'd spread the information out on the desk. "Can you leave these with me?"

She shook her head. "You're not my client."

"Okay, so why are you letting me see this?"

"Because FEI doesn't exist, or if it does it's never been mentioned in any publication that covers charitable and aid organizations, and, you have to admit, that is highly unlikely. Dr. Lo does exist, but he's not associated with anything called Fisheries Enterprises International. His name shows up in print from time to time as a key defence witness for a company called Pisces International, international because the company has branch offices in Asia, Europe, and South America. He's their chief conservation scientist. I got curious about why he was showing up in the international courts so I ran a check on Pisces itself, and that's when things got interesting. As far as I can figure out from the articles the head office of the company is on a boat. And they do own boats, big freezer processors that cruise the high seas, always within international waters. Their fish come from smaller boats that more or less follow the processors and deliver their catch. Pisces is the target of several international lawsuits — drift net fishing, infringement of territorial waters, net and gear infractions, you name it — but they have no head office on dry land so they're incredibly hard to pin down. And they claim that how and where the fishermen fish is none of their business. They've contracted for the catch but how it's pulled in isn't their responsibility, and the freezer boats are careful to stay beyond the two-hundred-mile limit. But there's even seamier stuff. Key witnesses for the prosecution, mainly crew on the smaller boats, never seem to make it to court. There are a lot of accidents at sea. The whole thing put me on edge."

I picked up an article from a French newspaper and scanned it. Phrases like *missing witnesses* and *case could not proceed* jumped off the page. "Don't deliver this. Give me a day."

She shook her head and gathered up the papers. "I tried that. She needs it for a meeting this afternoon."

The FEI wrap-up: the same meeting Truong had mentioned.

"Can I take copies?"

She put her hand up to her face. "I do have a sudden urge to powder my nose. Would there be a bathroom nearby?"

I grinned. "Please. Let me escort you."

It was right across from the copy room.

When Sylvia left to deliver Elaine's search results I returned to the lab with my copies. Dinah was nowhere in sight so I unearthed my laptop and flipped it open. I needed to consolidate my information, review my notes, and see if I could make any sense out of what I knew so far. I began with Truong, typing up the conversation as the scene replayed itself in my mind. When I came across his comments on FEI, I stopped. So Pak Li, the guy who had "interviewed" Truong, was attached to Pisces, a company that no reputable fisheries scientist would work for. I wondered if Truong might remember some of their conversation, something that would help me tie things together. I picked up the phone and dialed his number. The phone rang through, but I got his voice mail, which suggested that I leave a message. I didn't bother. I figured I'd just keep calling until I got him.

When I finished typing up my notes on Truong, I moved to Edwards. That interview, as I recalled it, ended with his emphatic belief that the vial in my pocket had nothing to do with Jacks Creek. I chewed on that for a minute. I was sure it did, but he was right; I needed to run some tests to confirm it. Maybe Graham had stolen the vial from Elaine's lab, but it had nothing to do with Jacks Creek. Maybe it was in his pocket and fell out as he vaulted over the stream.

I got up and walked out into the main lab. One vat still had sockeye in the swirling water near the bottom. I touched the surface. This time the school didn't move, just undulated slightly, shifted position. I watched them for a minute more, considering, then went back into Dinah's office. I tried Truong again. Still the voice mail. I hung up. I looked at my coat lying on the chair then reached down and pulled out the vial. What did I have to lose?

I went back to the tank and stood over it, watching the fish move below the surface. I stood there for a good ten minutes, trying to get some idea of the baseline behaviours. The sockeye didn't do much. There was a slight shifting within the school now and then, but for the most part they remained clumped and unmoving near the bottom.

After ten minutes I took the vial, unscrewed it, and placed a drop of liquid on the tip of my finger. I rubbed this on the side of the tank just above the waterline. Wavelets splashed and rolled against the side, brushing past the spot where I had rubbed with the solution. It took less than five seconds. The fish began to mill. A large one broke from the school and darted back and forth across the tank. Another one shot to the surface, cleared it, and in a graceful arc, dove back to the bottom. I heard Dinah come in behind me. Without taking my eyes off my subjects I asked, "Where have you been?"

She came up beside me. She had a bucket on one arm and I could smell the slightly rancid odour of fish pellets.

"Feeding the others. Just 'cause everyone else has gone berserk doesn't mean my job ends. What's with them?"

The fish were now moving, circling the tank. After several tours around the surface they converged, snouts up, on the spot where I had smudged the liquid.

"Cause and effect," I said, then looked at the bucket of food. "I thought salmon stopped eating when they entered the river. That their stomachs disintegrated or something."

"They do. I'm feeding the others."

My heart gave a little thump and I remembered the silver sockeye that Madden had shown me that first day in his lab. "What others?"

"The ones in the aquatic room. You haven't been in there?"

I looked back at the sockeye still milling around the spot. I hoped they'd get over it. I slipped the vial in my pocket. "No, but I think you'd better show me."

Dinah took me to a steel door, cobalt blue, no window, directly across the hall from Madden's lab. Since my arrival at Southern I had never seen anyone either leave or enter that door. I'd assumed it was a storage room. Dinah pulled out a separate key, not attached to her regular ring, and unlocked it.

"What's with the special key?"

"Extra security. We were hit by an animal rights group last year."

She pushed the door open and held it for me. The room was huge, the size of half a soccer field and brightly lit with full spectrum fluorescent lights. It smelled briny, with an overlay of rotting seaweed and a touch of dead fish. I stood in front of columns of tanks, aquamarine blue, that decreased in size as my eye travelled from right to left. I had to force my voice to be heard over the noise of the water. "It looks like a hatchery."

"It is," said Dinah.

She pulled at my sleeve and I followed her across the room. As the vats got smaller the fish in them decreased in size, going from large adult salmon to fingerlings. She pointed to a series of troughs arranged against the left hand wall. Inside, trays of milky orange salmon eggs lay on screens, the black eyes of the embryos visible through the surface.

"We bring in wild-caught," she said, "but we also rear some here. That way we can control the genetics and the environment."

"Where are Elaine's fish?"

"Over here." Dinah headed toward the back of the room and crossed to the big vats. She pointed to the last three tanks the third row in. I walked down the aisle slowly, looking in each of the tanks. Bright red sockeye, ready for spawning. I turned back to Dinah.

"So who were you feeding?"

"Those guys." She pointed to a tank two rows back. "We just got them from Madden."

I walked over and looked inside. Six large, healthy, silver sockeye.

"But they're ocean run. They're not spawning."

She came over before answering and stood beside me, watching the beautiful creatures shimmer in the current. "Spawning or not, it doesn't make any difference to us. Why should it?"

Because Madden was cracking the mystery of migrating salmon. How could ocean-phase salmon be involved?

"So Elaine uses ocean-phase sockeye in her tests?"

Dinah nodded. "And spawners. Whatever we can get our hands on."

I took the vial out of my pocket. I put a bit of the liquid on my finger and then rubbed my finger on the edge of the tank. A second later the fish became restless, darting back and forth. Within five minutes the agitated milling became more pronounced, then the fish started to move *en masse*. They circled slowly, rose and fell in the water column as if searching until, just as the others had, they mobbed the spot I'd touched, swimming forward, but with nowhere to go.

Dinah's voice was uneasy: "What's going on?"

"How old are these fish?"

"I don't know, but they're immature."

"So they wouldn't be heading up the Fraser looking like that?" I was referring to their silver colouration, so different from the crimson of spawners.

She shook her head. "If these guys were in the wild they'd be in the Gulf of Alaska fattening themselves up for the trip home."

I stood and watched them for a minute, then shook my head. How could this fit in? I needed to talk to Edwards and Truong, and I needed to do it fast. With Dinah in tow, I hurried back to the lab. Even with her stilt legs she had to move to keep up with me.

We were coming around the corridor to Elaine's lab when she said, "Oh yeah, I did that travel thing. Remember? The results are in the lab."

"I can live without the detail. Just give me the big picture."

"Madden's and JJ's receipts match with the dates and locations of the fish kills, but they weren't necessarily there together."

"Connell?"

"He never left town."

I nodded. The fog was beginning to lift.

Back in the lab I tried Edwards first. I got his voice mail and slammed down the phone. Next I tried Truong but got his voice mail too. That was strange. I checked my watch. Truong had an important meeting in half an hour and he was expecting a call from me before that meeting. Where the hell was he?

Who could I call that would know more about what was going on than me? Then I thought of Connell. He probably knew more than anyone. I pulled his cell phone number, still in the baggy, out of my pocket and dialed it, following his instructions. On the second call there was a hum and a buzz, and the phone connected.

"Graham?"

There was a moment's hesitation. "Oh, it's you."

"Who were you expecting?"

"What do you want?"

"What do *I* want? I'm calling to tell you you're off the hook. You can come in with my files, the sooner the better."

There was another pause. "The deal's off. I got a better offer."

I was taken aback, and it took me a minute to formulate an answer. "It must have been some offer to beat getting you off a murder charge."

Then he laughed. "Yeah, well, my ship came in."

I took a stab in the dark. "When did you figure it out?" It was so quiet and the line so clear that I could hear the sound of water lapping on the hull. He didn't answer, so I turned up the heat. "You didn't work it out yourself, did you. Cindy had to tell you."

That got him. "I knew something was going down. She just confirmed it."

I heard a mental *click* as something fell into place. "When she called you from the bar."

"Stupid cow. I tried to convince her it was just some weird thing, but she wouldn't believe me. She was going to blow the whistle."

"And you saw a chance for big money. You wanted a cut."

"Why not?"

"So you killed her."

"I already told you." Then his voice became suspicious. "You said I was in the clear."

"Maybe that deal's off too."

"Okay, I'll keep my end of the bargain. JJ's stealing from the Network. Who the hell do you think? And if you want to try and pin the murder on me go ahead. They can arrest me when they find me, if they can find me. Anyway, I gotta go. I'm waiting for a call."

"Jesus, Graham, I hope you know — "

"Yeah, yeah. Adios, O'Brien." He hung up. I finished my sentence anyway.

"— who the hell you're dealing with here."

When I tried the number again I was informed by a mechanical voice that the cellular customer I was trying to reach was not available to take my call.

Nor was Edwards. The guy was pissing me off. I left a pointed message telling him to get in touch with me as soon as he could, that it was urgent and I needed his input. I checked my watch again. Fifteen minutes before the meeting. It was time to track down Dr. Truong. If worst came to worst, I'd just hang around until all the players arrived and crash their little party.

Despite the early hour it looked like Truong's laboratory neighbours had either geared down for the night or all gone off to a research colloquium. The floor was almost deserted, with only two doors ajar and lights shining within. At the end of the hall Truong's lab door was shut, and I could see through the knobbly glass that the lights were off. My stomach did a little flip-flop as I tried the door. It was locked. Maybe they'd decided to meet in a conference room rather than his office. I poked my head into the lab next door.

"Dr. Truong. You have any idea where he would be?"

A woman looked from a cluttered lab bench and gave me a peevish look. "No idea," she said curtly.

Gee, thanks. But the voyage had been a success. The mechanism on these doors was even more basic than in Zoology. Back at Truong's door I pulled out a special credit card I keep for such occasions and used it to let myself in.

The computers glowed in the dull light. One had beautiful molecular forms dancing across the screen, mutating with every collision. Another had a banner message that scrolled "We're all living in a chemical soup" in an intricate magenta script.

I could see light beneath Truong's office door, but the hotel sign was turned to *Do Not Disturb*, so I stood quietly by the door and listened, straining to hear voices, anything, even the whisper of a turning page. Finally I knocked, and when I got no answer, I tried the knob.

The door swung open.

chapter twenty-five

Alistair Truong was seated at his desk, but he didn't look up to greet me. He couldn't. Half his face was blown across the surface, fouling the books and reprints with blood and wads of pale grey tissue. It was an execution-style killing: quick, efficient, and completely devoid of emotion. A professional death.

I took a deep breath and fought to control my reactions. What I wanted to do was collapse on the floor and wail great, heaving sobs for Truong, his wife, his two daughters. Instead I closed my eyes, blocking out the horror, and turned my face away. It took all of my concentration to shut down the emotions and get on with the business at hand. When I opened my eyes again I avoided looking directly at the desk and took in the room around me.

Someone had pulled the office apart, scattered the books and emptied the files on the floor, and with every second I stood in the room, my presence contaminated the scene. I needed to leave as quickly as possible, but not before I got some answers. I moved carefully toward the filing cabinets, picking my way across the papers scattered on the floor. I passed the open door, keeping my eyes low, trying not to disturb the mess. As I moved forward an image, like an afterthought, caught up with me. There was someone standing behind the door. In a lab coat. Slouched against the wall.

I whirled around, sending a flurry of papers across the floor. As if on cue, the body slumped, crumpled, and slid down the wall. Truong's technician lay sprawled, face up, at my feet.

Somebody was cleaning house.

At the filing cabinets the E/F file drawer hung open. I moved the folders apart with my pen. The F section, from Fa through to Fr, had been removed. I knelt down and, still using my pen, sorted through the sheets scattered on the floor. A quick search revealed what I already knew. The file I wanted hadn't been scattered. It had walked out of the office with the person who murdered Truong.

There was nothing else I could do here. I picked my way across the floor, trying not to brush anything, and at the door did one last survey, hoping to see something I missed. Beneath the chair, the one I had sat in earlier that day, I saw a piece of brilliant turquoise sitting amongst the papers. I knew I shouldn't, but I went over and picked it up. It was a dangling earring, darkened silver with turquoise stones. I'd given the pair to Elaine after her dissertation. I stuffed the earring in my pocket and quietly closed the door behind me. Outside in Truong's lab I picked up the phone and dialed 911. As I shut the lab door I could hear the voice of the dispatcher saying, "Ambulance, fire, or police. Hello?"

I hurried back across to Zoology. It was nearing five, and students were streaming up to C-lot, hurrying to arrive at their cars before the dark skies opened up with rain. I was concerned with only one thing: finding Elaine, or finding Madden and killing him if I found out he'd hurt her.

On the upper floors the hallways were quiet. The professors had packed up and gone home for the night. The few students who were left, finishing up labs or completing runs, were somewhere on the teaching floors below. I went to Elaine's office first, opened the door, and looked in. I had hoped, prayed, that I would find her in her chair calculating frequencies, latencies of response, but the office was empty, and like Truong's, the files had been removed.

The fluorescent lights in Riesler's private lab were off, but I could see incandescent light through the window of the connecting door. I had a moment of hope, a brief second of thinking that maybe this was all some paranoid nightmare, but when I knocked on the door there was no answer. I knocked again, waited, then pulled out my lock picks and let myself in.

Whoever had been cleaning up hadn't missed Riesler's office. There were no bodies on the floor, but several half-filled cardboard boxes lay beneath the bookcase, and files had been pulled and scattered. But unlike Truong's office, and for that matter Elaine's, the important knick-knacks were also gone: the trophies, prize plaques, and framed diplomas had disappeared from the shelves and walls. So Madden had done his own packing, taking what was important with him.

I went over to the desk and pulled open the central drawer. I don't know what I expected to find. Maybe a note saying, "Gone to the Cayman Islands. Wish you were here," but there was nothing except an old eraser, some pencil leads, and a few stray paper clips. I yanked out the drawer and hurled it against the wall. It gave a satisfying crash, and the contents scattered. I yanked out the next drawer, rifled through it, hurled it against the wall. In fact, I did the same thing with all the drawers: emptying them, then pitching them against the cabinets or the wall. It felt good, but there was nothing in them to help me.

From there I scanned the shelves, but they didn't look promising either. Then I noticed the blinking red light on his desk: he had messages waiting on his Meridian phone. I was aiming for it when I heard footsteps in the hallway outside. I froze, turned around, and there was Bob gaping like a cod. With the drawers pitched and their contents spewed across the carpet it looked like an earthquake had destroyed the office. A second later he recovered and turned to glare at me.

"This is —"

"The way things are done in the field, Bob." I left the phone alone, moved over to the files, and pulled open a drawer, hoping to distract Bob. "You're too late. Madden's gone."

He looked taken aback. "But we'd scheduled a meeting to discuss the Network. And shut that file drawer," he snapped. "You don't have authorization."

I ignored him and continued what I was doing, speaking almost absently. "Patsy won't be happy that Madden's gone."

"We're working on a containment basis at this point." He edged forward. "I told you to get your hands off those files."

I turned around to face him and spoke calmly. "We have three murders and my best friend has disappeared. Fuck containment."

His lips stiffened. "You're off the case, O'Brien. I'll take over."

"Whatever." I shut the file drawer and moved back over to Madden's desk, where I hit the redial button on his phone. Connell's cellular number came up on the display. I knew it. Connell and Madden had struck a deal. I started for the door, but Bob stepped in front of me, blocking my path. His face was inches from mine.

"I said you're off the case."

"What are you going to do. Arrest me?"

He put out his hand. "Give me your ID. You're suspended."

I looked Bob square in the face. I didn't have time to negotiate and I couldn't give up my identity card. If I was in contact with the RCMP or the Vancouver police I would need it to establish my credibility without long explanations and background checks. We locked eyes. My voice was deadly quiet. "Don't make me do this, Bob. We'll both regret it."

His face inched closer. "You so much as touch me, I charge you with assault."

"If that's the way you want it," I said. I took a deep breath and kept my eyes locked on his, then with slow, deliberate gestures moved into a fighting stance. I shifted my right leg out and back, centred my weight over it, and brought my hands up in front of me, all the time willing Bob to back off. I could see sweat beading on his upper lip, but I have to give him credit. He held his ground, which left me with no other options. I grimaced, pulled back for a roundhouse kick, and started my leg's trajectory forward. At this point he cringed, brought his hands up in front of his face, and in this moment of inattention I tucked my leg, executed a graceful pirouette, and pulled open the door that connected Madden's office to the little lab next door. I was on the stairs and halfway down to the basement before Bob realized what had happened, and if I hadn't been so upset about Elaine I would have been laughing all the way down. As it was, I was on the first landing, hurrying downward, when I heard his voice from above. "I'm calling security," he shouted. "Or the police. Your career is over."

I stopped just long enough to yell back. "Try the RCMP. They have jurisdiction. And ask for Corporal LeBlanc."

I heard him kick the railing and swear.

In the basement, Riesler's lab door was open. One of his technicians was doing a final temperature check of all the tanks and she looked up as I came in. "Can I help you?"

There was a student near the back running electrophoresis gels, but other than him the place was empty.

"JJ around?"

"He went to the pub for dinner." She checked her watch. "He should be back soon."

"Thanks. I'll wait." I crossed to JJ's office and tried the door. It was locked, so I pulled out the pass-key and let myself in. The technician scurried over and grabbed my arm.

"Hey, you can't do that. You can't go in there if it's locked."

I removed her hand, pulled out my ID, and gave her a grim *don't-mess-with-me* look.

"I suggest you ..." I raised my voice and directed it to the student in the back, "... and you, finish up your work and go home."

She stammered something about notifying Madden and disappeared out the door of the lab. I left the door open and began a methodical search of JJ's files. I wanted him to see me when he came in. I found some travel authorization files. I threw them on the desk. Next I pulled out some Network files, budgets, and expenditures, and added them to the pile. I heard a flurry of activity in the hall and JJ rushed in, the technician just behind him. His eyes were wild, and I could see the sheen of oil around his mouth, a remnant of his pub dinner. He headed for me, intent on doing damage, but instead of cowering, I stepped forward and gave him a controlled wallop in the solar plexus. I got a whiff of Molsons and second-hand smoke. A direct hit to a belly full of beer can cause some tummy upset so I stepped back, out of vomit range, just in case. I hadn't hit him hard, but he'd been totally unprepared. He doubled over, gasping.

The technician and student stood wide-eyed and silent. JJ heaved, desperately trying to pull in air. Finally the technician came to her senses.

"Should I call the police?" Her voice was a hoarse whisper directed at JJ.

I moved back and perched myself on the corner of his desk.

"Excellent question. What do you think, JJ? Should she call the police?" His eyes flicked up at me. I continued. "I have no objection. In fact," I rooted around in my pocket, and pulled out a crumpled paper. The yellow marks highlighting specific financial transactions glowed on the paper. "Corporal LeBlanc would be very interested in seeing this."

"You stole that," he gasped.

I looked up at the technician. "That's LeBlanc. L-E-B-"

By this time he'd begun to catch his breath and he turned to the others. "It's no problem. I can handle it."

"Maybe we should stay around." The graduate student's voice was tentative. "Just to make sure — "

"Get the fuck out of here," JJ said, then he tried to push his way around me to get behind his desk. He obviously wasn't picking up the nuance. I was pissed off, unafraid, and totally primed to get physical. I hopped off the desk and gave him a shove backward. He teetered into the guest chair. I sat back on the desk.

"How's the market?"

"What do you want?"

"Information."

"Like what."

"Like, where's Madden."

His eyes narrowed, and he shrugged. "In his office. How should I know?"

"What do you know about FEI?"

His eyes shifted away from mine. "I manage the Network."

I turned and picked up the travel files. "But you help out with FEI." He didn't answer. "And I like the way you manage the Network. How much have you embezzled so far?"

"I don't know what you're talking about."

I reached for the phone. "But Corporal LeBlanc will know exactly what I'm talking about, especially after the forensic audit." Then, in my best Captain Highliner voice, "Ya ever bin ta jail, JJ?"

He darted forward, aiming for the phone, but I caught him with my foot and shoved him back into the chair.

"Give me back my files first."

I hung up the phone. "I don't have them." I smiled innocently. "Graham does."

"Graham? That little fuck?"

"That big blackmailer." Then I paused for effect. "I hope your investments paid off big, because Graham's a guy who likes to live well."

He paled as the implications slowly sunk in. Greedy people hate to share, especially with other greedy people. I continued, "Of course, I could probably get those files back when Madden and Graham get together this evening, but the problem is, I don't know where they're meeting."

I could see him trying to gauge how much he should tell me.

"A little cooperation would go a long way, JJ. Especially in front of a judge."

Then he shrugged and said, "He took the boat." He reached up on the wall behind him and pulled down a black notebook that was dangling from a hook next to the door and flipped it open. "The manifest says Howe Sound."

There was something about the way he said it that I didn't like.

"But that's not where he's going?"

He eyed me suspiciously. "Why should I tell you? What's in it for me?"

I shrugged. "We'll cut a deal on FEI. That only leaves the embezzlement." Then I slid off the desk and moved forward, putting my hands on the arms of his chair. "And perhaps you should ask the more pertinent question. What you will get if you don't help me out."

He pushed himself back in his chair, trying to get some space between him and me. "I don't know for sure, but he didn't take the Howe Sound charts. He left with the southern Gulf Islands."

That make more sense. "When?"

"Just before I went for dinner."

"Last question. Was he alone?"

"You have to have two people sign out the keys, but Madden said Okada was waiting in the van. I took his word for it and signed for her."

Then I did something I regret. I stood up, loomed over him, then backhanded him so hard that his head flew against the wall. I'm not proud of that kind of violence — gratuitous and unnecessary — and seconds later I was sickened by it, watching his head loll back and tears rise to his eyes. A dribble of blood seeped from his mouth, and I knew it was me I wanted to punish, not him, because if something happened to Elaine her blood was on my hands, and I'd never be able to live with that.

"You should see a doctor," I said gently. "Your jaw could be broken."

Then I laid the paper on his desk and left.

chapter twenty-six

When I got back to the lab there was a message from Dinah. Jonathan Edwards had finally called. I dialed his number and didn't even bother to say hello.

"You have a boat?"

It took him a moment to respond. When he did his answer was hesitant. "Not personally, but the department has one. What's going on?"

"Can you run it?"

"Sure. I use it for my research."

"Then I need you, and the boat, now."

"It's not that — "

"I don't have time to discuss it. Elaine's in trouble. If you can't get me a boat I'll hang up now and find someone who can."

It only took him a second to decide. "I need to know where we're going. For the charts," he added hastily.

"The southern Gulf Islands, but bring everything in

the vicinity. I'm not sure where we'll end up. I'll explain when you get here."

"Give me ten minutes," and he hung up the phone.

Dinah was standing at the door watching. When I put down the receiver she said, "I'm going with you."

"Nope." I pulled over an extra chair. "You're going to lead the posse."

Then I sat Dinah down and in the next ten minutes sketched out the broad details of what I knew, reminding her that Sylvia could piece it together if anything happened to me. I was hoping that LeBlanc would believe Dinah, but I knew that even if she did it would still take the RCMP at least an hour to get someone out on the water looking for Riesler. I hoped that by getting out there fast I could intercept him at his rendezvous with Graham.

Edwards arrived as I was finishing up.

"Do you have the charts?" He nodded. "Give me Mayne Island."

We spread it on the desk, and I hoped to hell that the cove I showed Dinah was the one that Connell was waiting in. We were rolling up the charts when Dinah said, "Hold it. Wait here."

"We don't have — " I started, but she was already gone.

By the time I'd finished rolling up the charts and packing up our gear Dinah still hadn't appeared. I pulled on my jacket. "We can't wait," I said to Edwards, and we left the lab. We were on the stairs when Dinah caught up. In her hand she had two small silver cylinders, each about seven centimetres long with a wire dangling from one end. She gave one to Edwards and one to me.

"What's this?"

Edwards laughed and shook his head. "Telemetry markers. You know, transmitters for radio tagging fish so you can follow them in open water."

I looked at Dinah. "Brilliant. What's the range?"

"These ones? A couple of kilometres at the most."

"It's better than nothing. And Dinah, don't let up on LeBlanc. I need her out there."

Dinah gave me a wry smile. "I like a woman in uniform. Can't stay away." And she took off up the stairs.

We were out the door, climbing into Jonathan's van when I remembered the vials in Madden's lab. Had he taken them too?

"I need a minute," I said, and hopped out.

Upstairs, Madden's lab looked as pristine and clean as it had in the afternoon. I headed for the drawers, pulled out the top one, and emptied it on the lab bench. I sorted through detritus. No key. I swept everything onto the floor and started on the next drawer. No key there either. Shit. It was going to be faster to pick it. I pulled out my tools and crossed to the refrigerator. The key was poking out of the lock.

Inside there were several bottles of photographic developing fluid, some reagents, and six rolls of film, but the tray of vials was gone.

On the way to Granville Island Edwards focused on the road, negotiating the heavy traffic to make the best time possible. He swore under his breath, shook his fist more than once, and banged the steering wheel with an open palm. I stared out the window and tried to block it out. There was nothing we could do beyond what we were already doing.

When we finally pulled into the marina parking lot, we grabbed the charts and almost ran down the ramp to the floating docks. Edwards was ahead of me, and he turned abruptly and climbed onto a sleek, white yacht. This was no research vessel. It was the prize toy of someone with a lot of money and a big passion for deep-sea fishing.

"Nice boat," I said.

He put out his hand to pull me up. "It belongs to the department head. He keeps an extra set of keys in the office." He smiled. "So this better be good since I'm going to lose my job for it."

We cast off and Jonathan took the helm, expertly backing the boat out and bringing it around to creep out of the marina. I scrambled up on deck with a grapple hook, just in case. The engine purred as we inched our way out into the channel. Once there, Jonathan increased the speed a notch, and I lay down on my stomach, arms slung over the bow. The night was sublime; the brilliant lights of the downtown, softened by a pale mist, danced on the surface of False Creek. I was soon lulled into an altered state by the gentle movement, the rhythmic caress of the waves on the hull. I surrendered to it, let my body relax and my mind clear to nothingness except movement and sound.

I was rudely awakened by a face full of cold spray as we cleared Point Grey. Jonathan opened the throttle and the boat surged forward, the bow rising high above the water's surface and slamming into the swells that rolled inexorably down the strait. I pulled myself up with the help of the railing and, holding on tight, made my way up to the wheelhouse.

Being a pleasure craft, the bridge was high above midships with a panoramic view of the grey sea. To get up there I went astern and crossed what was more like a patio than a deck. I peeked into the cabin. There was a palatial living room, a kitchen, and a well-stocked bar.

It was all very tempting, but in the end I took the ladder to the pilot's deck above.

Edwards was sitting at the helm; I sat in the navigator's seat. It was a hell of a lot more comfortable than the seats in Graham's boat — generously padded and upholstered in white leather — but the pilot's area was open, the deck only half covered by a retractable canopy, making it cold and noisy. The boat was also faster than Graham's, and at the speed we were going I figured we could reach Mayne Island in a half hour or less. Edwards seemed to read my mind.

"She's built for speed, not stability. We're fine as long as the wind doesn't pick up."

"I did trace Riesler to the fish kills," I said. I had to yell to be heard over the engine and the wind.

Edwards gave a nod, indicating that he had understood, then he spoke. "And I was wrong. There is a possibility — a very remote possibility — that some kind of key molecule might be involved in homing, but it would have to be restricted to populations of salmon that are all divergent from the same stock, like all Skeena River system sockeye or all — "

"Fraser River sockeye?"

"If they're all from the same stock, and that's debatable."

"Maybe it's not the stock. Maybe it's the river system, the water they're exposed to."

"It's possible, but I still don't buy it."

"I tested the solution."

"And?"

"It worked." I paused here for effect, to make sure he clearly understood what I was saying. "Jonathan, it worked on ocean-phase sockeye too."

"Impossible. They don't use olfaction at sea." Then he thought for a moment, and shook his head vehemently. "You screwed up. Did you run a control?"

My voice was sharper than I intended. "Some male moths can detect one molecule of the female pheromone from over ten miles away. You said yourself, open ocean migration is a mystery. Maybe olfaction is one of several factors. Maybe that's why they're searching the thermoclines. Anyway, if you don't believe it you can tell the buyer yourself. I'm sure they'll value your opinion."

"A buyer? For what?"

"How much is the sockeye catch worth? Just the Fraser run."

"I don't have an exact figure." He shrugged. "Millions."

"And who has access to it?"

"The bulk? Canada and the U.S. Some stray off the two-hundred-mile limit, but — "

"It's not profitable, is it. In fact, the only time it's really profitable to catch them is when they're migrating, because they clump in schools and appear in predictable places, so you can get huge catches with little effort. But what if you could convince them to clump together while they're out in the ocean feeding. That would change the profitability of open ocean fishing, wouldn't it? But you'd still have the problem of fishing licences, catch restrictions, closures, unless you can pull them off the two-hundred-mile limit. If you can pull them into international waters you can fish as you like. How much would that be worth?"

He added speculatively, "And if you used drift nets, you don't even have to get them to clump that much." He rubbed his beard then shook his head again. "*If* you could do it, it would be worth millions. But you couldn't do it."

"I think Madden has, and I think he's leaving town with the buyer. Graham too. And I think Elaine is being used as a hostage." My voice trailed off. "At least, that's what I'm hoping."

He turned to me. "You're *hoping* Elaine is a hostage?"

I gave a curt nod and turned away. I could feel him watching me, trying to decide if the implied meaning was the real meaning. When he realized it was he sobered. "It would only work for four years."

"Why?"

"That's the dominant population cycle. If there was an unrestricted catch for four years, the fifth year the population would crash." He looked across at me, the light shining up from the panel giving him a ghoulish look. "So if you're serious, say goodbye to the sockeye."

We continued in silence until pale halos of orange light appeared up ahead, faint through a bank of fog that almost hid the island behind it. As we entered the bank, the visibility dropped and Edwards throttled back. There was a bright light off to my right.

"What's that?" I asked, pointing to it.

"The opening to Active Pass. Galiano Island is on the other side. Mayne is dead ahead."

"Then we need to turn left, follow the shoreline down. Do you have radar?"

He leaned over and flicked a switch on the instrument panel. A screen lit up. We were a little blip in the centre, the shoreline was to our right.

"Can we rescale? See more?"

He twirled a knob and the blip became smaller, the shoreline longer. Ahead, almost off the top of the screen, I saw what I was looking for: a small channel with a blind end. I couldn't be sure, but the topography looked like what I remembered seeing on Graham's radar.

"Here," I said, pointing to the screen. "Try here."

Edwards headed the boat away from the shore, out of the thickest fog, and opened the throttle. I glanced from the screen to Edwards, who was intent on navigation. I'd dragged an innocent into this with me and if anything happened to him it would be more blood on my hands. I spoke over the engines.

"If Connell's there you'll leave me on his boat. You'll go out to open water and wait for the RCMP."

He kept his eyes on the water, a big bear of a man. "I don't think so," he said quietly, his eyes moving between the instrument panel and the sea ahead.

"Don't be a hero, Jonathan. We have three people dead and I don't want Elaine added to the list. You're out of your element here, so when I tell you to do something you do it; no questions, no hesitation. And if you screw up, I hold you responsible."

He gave a nod, acknowledging only that he had heard me, not that he agreed. He kept his eyes on the water with a stubborn set to his face. The tension was broken by a point of land looming out of the mist.

"We're close," he said. "There's a spotlight on deck. Take the grapple and go up. I'll go into shore as close as I can and hopefully you'll recognize something."

I hopped down onto the deck and, once on the bow, trained the spotlight on the shore. Through the fog the light reflected back at all angles, making the shoreline look like the set from a 1950s horror flick, complete with cliffs, rocky beaches, and ragged points of land. We inched along for a good ten minutes, Edwards with his eyes on the shore and the depth gauge, me squinting through the fog, aware that every minute was time lost. Then a ghostly hand appeared, reaching through the fog to pluck me from the deck. It was an arbutus, and I'd seen this tree before, hanging on the cliff just north of the channel. I trained the spotlight just beyond it.

"There," I yelled. It was at that moment that I thought I heard the roar of an engine, but the noise was quickly swamped by the wind. I climbed back to the wheelhouse. Edwards brought the boat around, idling in front of the entrance. The seas were rougher tonight than the evening I'd gone through with Connell. I hoped Edwards knew what he was doing.

"Go in slowly," I said, "and cut the engines the minute we're through."

The boat rocked in the waves, and, like Connell, Edwards waited for a second, then between peaks gave a surge of power. We shot through the narrow opening. He cut the engines, and we drifted into a silent void.

Here in the enclosed bay the fog seemed to ooze directly from the green water. It hung so thick that, within two feet of the boat, fog and water merged into one.

At first I heard nothing, the sound of the engines still ringing in my ears, but as we drifted forward my ears began to adapt, to pick up bits of sound. There was a *plop* off the bow as a seabird rose and dove again, or maybe it was a fish attracted to the light. I leaned forward, trying to peer through the fog, straining to hear the sound of voices or the presence of another boat. I gradually became aware of a thin, tinny sound, almost like a whine, coming from ... it was impossible to get a fix on the direction. It stopped, then started again, vaguely familiar, but out of place. I turned my head left and right, trying to localize the sound. To my right, off the bow, I thought I saw a lighter, hazy patch in the dense fog. I pointed for Edwards and he steered us toward it.

As we approached, the hazy patch of light resolved into discrete halos and the tinny sound became more distinct. Suddenly, the stern of Graham's boat condensed out of the fog. Light shone from the portals at the side, but there were no voices, only the odd whining that I could now define: a top-forty radio station being played on a cheap transistor somewhere below deck. I silently thanked Graham for that. It had masked the noise of our arrival.

I leaned over and grabbed the railing, pulling us up along side. A second later I was on Graham's boat. Edwards was behind me in an instant, but I turned and pushed the boats apart, making it difficult for him to leap across.

"Set your marine radio to the emergency channel." My voice was low, but firm. "Keep the volume down. If you hear anything coming from this boat that doesn't sound right, get out of the bay as fast as you can and start broadcasting. Otherwise I'll call you when I'm ready to be picked up." Then I gave his boat a firm shove and watched it dissolve back into the fog.

I had boarded on the forward, port side, just a bit behind the wheelhouse. It was dark, but the portals over the galley were blazing with light. I felt something bump the front of the boat and looked up quickly, in case Edwards had ignored my instructions, but there was nothing there.

At the first bright portal I stooped down and looked in. A radio on the map table played merrily along, but the galley was empty. I watched and listened for several minutes, expecting to hear some movement, see some sign of life, but there was nothing, and the emptiness sent a frisson up my spine. I heard a shuffling out on the water, Edwards somewhere close by, and I felt comforted by that.

At the back hatch I tapped and called out softly. "Graham? Are you in there?" But there was no reply. It seemed like sacrilege in the silence, but I banged more loudly. When there was still no answer I pulled the hatch open and hopped down into the cabin.

The first thing I did was reach over and switch off the radio. I did a quick scan of the space then held my hand to the stove. It was off, but still warm. There were two closed doors at the end of the dining area. One, I knew, was the head. The other, down a small corridor, would lead to the forward bunks. I checked the head first. It was surprisingly neat for a guy, but empty. I closed the door and moved down the narrow hallway. There was a door ahead of me, and it was ajar. I heard something nudge the boat again and tried not to let myself get spooked. Edwards was near. I braced myself, pushed the door open, and stepped back. The room was dark, but someone was asleep on the right-hand bunk. "Graham?" I said quietly.

There was no movement, no answer. I tried again, and still there was no response. Then I noticed a lamp on the wall above me. With my heart pounding I flicked it on, throwing the tiny space into brilliant white light.

I gave something between a strangled laugh and a cough and caught my breath. The person on the bunk was no more than a tangle of clothes and a sleeping bag. I was alone on the boat.

When my heart had stopped pounding I returned to the galley. I couldn't imagine Graham leaving the boat like this, unlocked, fully lit, and the batteries running down. It didn't make sense.

I scanned the space again. My files lay where Graham had put them the evening before, in a cubby behind the table. I grabbed them and stuffed them into my jacket. At least I'd accomplished something. Then I noticed two mugs in the tiny sink. One was half full and, when I touched it, still warm. The spicy, sweet smell of dark Jamaican rum floated up from the coffee. So if Madden had come and gone, it wasn't long ago.

I crossed to the head and yanked the door open. Graham's razor, toothbrush, and comb were all neatly arranged in the medicine cabinet. Back in the bunk room I switched the light back on and pulled open a drawer. There were stacks of Jockey shorts, t-shirts, and jeans. So there were two possibilities. Either Graham was nearby, negotiating with Madden, or Graham was now a victim of his own greed. I kicked the drawer hard. Now how the hell would I find Madden?

I scrambled back to the deck. The boat was creepy, like some modern-day Flying Dutchman: everything in order but the crew mysteriously gone. The fog didn't help.

"Jonathan!" I called.

There was a scuffling, then a rattle, Jonathan pulling anchor. I heard something nudge the boat again up near the front. A log? A sea lion? I moved forward to see what it was, leaning out over the railing. Below me, a dingy sat beneath the bow, bumping up against it. And there was something else, white, beside it in the water, attached by a rope. At first I thought it was a mooring buoy, a pale plastic bubble rising just above the surface, but as I watched, a ghostly hand swept up from below pointing into the bay. The current then caught the head and lifted it from where it hung below the body, spreading the thick blonde hair around it like the arms of an anemone.

"Jesus. Jonathan! Get me the hell out of here." There was more scuffling, a distinctive grunt, then the diesel engine shattered the silence of the bay.

The yacht bumped Graham's boat. I looked up at Jonathan. He was staring down at Connell, his face so pale that it appeared green in the lights shining up from the instrument panel. I hopped onto Jonathan's boat and pushed us off, watching Graham as the two boats pulled apart. When I turned back to the wheelhouse there were two faces in the window: Jonathan, and Madden, who was smiling down at me.

chapter twenty-seven

"Come up," said Madden firmly.

I didn't move.

"He has a gun, for Christ's sake. Get up here or he'll kill Elaine." That was Edwards, his voice pitched half an octave up by fear.

I raised my hands shoulder-high so Madden could see that I had nothing to hide and made my way around to the patio deck, moving deliberately. On the ladder, I made sure that both my hands were flat on the top deck before my head appeared over the edge. When my eyes were level with the floor I saw Elaine, her hands bound behind her back, her mouth taped shut. She was lying against the instrument panel at Madden's feet. He had a handgun trained on her head. I must have hesitated, because Madden glanced down at her and then back at me.

"She's quite all right. Just dopey." Then he looked down at her again and shook his head. "She shouldn't have talked to Truong. She wasn't supposed to. It was stipulated in the design. Of course," he looked back at me, "that's your fault, isn't it."

As I came up onto the deck I kept my eyes on Madden and my voice conversational. Edwards was backed against the left-hand wall.

"I'm your best hostage, Madden. Leave Elaine and Jonathan here."

"Hostage?" he laughed. "You're not hostages, you're loose ends, and my colleagues have been very clear about loose ends."

Elaine moaned and shifted. I heard the clink of glassware behind her and registered the location of the vials. Madden was watching me. At first sight he had looked calm, in control, but now I could see that he was distracted: thinking and calculating. There were too many people on board. Things were getting out of hand. I waited. Finally he barked at Edwards.

"You'll take the helm." He threw him a roll of duct tape from his pocket. "But first tape her hands. And if anyone even blinks the wrong way, Elaine gets a bullet through the head."

Edwards caught the tape in midair and hesitated.

"It's okay," I said.

He crossed over to me. "He said he'd kill Elaine. I couldn't — "

I tried to smile reassuringly. "Keep cool. Just remember what I told you."

Instead of turning to give him access to my hands, I moved forward a step. This forced him to come around behind me, and it blocked Madden's view of what Edwards was doing. I was banking on the fact that Madden wasn't a professional thug. He handled the gun inexpertly, and Elaine was probably still alive because he couldn't stomach a gory, cold-blooded killing involving someone he knew so well. He was saving that task for the clean-up crew at Pisces.

With Edwards behind me I moved my right wrist up my back, making it easy for him to tape just one wrist. Madden watched but was preoccupied. I planned to keep him that way.

"Why don't you kill us now? It would be easier that way."

"I'm not a killer. That's not part of the agreement."

"Really? Cindy might disagree ... if she could."

He sighed heavily and the gun drooped a bit. "That was unexpected and most regrettable, but there was nothing I could do. She saw me at a test site and we were so close wrapping up. If she had managed to talk to Elaine ..." He shrugged and looked away.

"But framing Graham for it was brilliant."

Despite the tension Madden smiled slightly. "He was hired to do a job and he did it, rather well actually."

I was shocked. "You knew about his past? You set him up from the beginning?"

"Quite. Like a good game of chess. Put everyone in position before you make your move."

"Except he got out of hand. He knew too much and wanted a cut."

He shrugged. "There are always unforeseen variables. JJ, for example ..." He shook his head in disgust. "Getting greedy the minute I turned my back. Then Jonathan starting an investigation, you arriving on the scene." He sighed. "No matter. We just had to wrap things up a bit earlier than planned, but even given the uncertainties the whole thing has gone off rather well."

"Not for Dr. Truong and his technician, or did they tell you about the technician?"

Riesler looked up at me sharply. "I had nothing to do with that." Then abruptly to Edwards. "Finish up."

Jonathan ripped the tape. I made a struggling movement, then seemingly gave up. It was time to go in for the kill.

"Nice gun. Yours?" Madden didn't answer. I continued. "It looks a lot like the one Graham put to my head. What a funny coincidence."

"Graham was a resourceful young man."

I paused for a minute and said, "You sure the safety is off?"

Madden looked startled and lifted the gun to look. Now I was sure he'd never even fired a handgun. If he had he would have known that on the Glock, the safety was part of the trigger. In Riesler's moment of inattention I launched myself forward, but I hadn't been watching Jonathan and he lunged first, ineptly and too soon.

"No," I yelled, but it was too late. Madden jerked the pistol at Jonathan. I lashed out with a side kick, but my position was off, too far back. My foot connected with Madden's shoulder just as the gun went off, throwing the shot wide but without enough force to disarm him. Jonathan was hit in mid-lunge. He screamed and grabbed his arm, blood oozing between his fingers. Unable to stop his forward momentum he careened into the railing on the other side, stumbling as he hit. I stepped over and gave him a good shove, sending him into the water below. Graham's boat wasn't far, and his chances down there were better than up here.

Madden had fallen back against the instrument panel and he was scrambling to regain his balance. He still had the gun in his hand. I pounced, but not soon enough. I found myself looking down a pistol bore inches from my face. We stood for a moment in a frozen tableau until he spoke, very softly.

"I think we can assume the safety is off. Would you care to test the number of bullets in the magazine?"

I backed away. He rose to his feet with the gun trained on me. Then we heard a boat, a diesel engine close by. Madden was startled and looked toward the noise. Elaine lashed out with her legs. It threw him off balance again and he fired wildly. I took a run for the railing and launched myself over the side, pushing hard with my legs to get as much distance as I could. By the time I hit the water I had my jacket half off. I struggled out of it, and threw it in closer to the boat, then I swam, not straight out from the boat, but angling out and back, looping around for the stern.

Madden appeared above, a dark silhouette leaning over the deck. He shot into the bay. There was a *plouffe, plouffe, plouffe*, as three bullets connected with my leather jacket. Given the darkness and the heavy fog, it would be hard for him to know that it wasn't me, and he'd want to believe it was. He shot twice more for good measure, aiming out beyond the boat where I would have been if I had swum away in a straight line, then he disappeared. I heard him say something to Elaine.

I swam as silently as I could toward the stern. Within minutes I had a splitting headache and my extremities ached. At least I could still feel them. How many minutes can one survive in the North Pacific in winter? Ten? Twelve? It was all for the best that I couldn't recall the exact figure.

There was a platform at the stern of the boat and I concentrated all of my energy on getting there. I could hear Madden banging around up top. Suddenly the engines roared to life. I lunged forward and managed to grab the stern ladder just as the transmission engaged. The boat pulled away and I hauled myself up onto the swimming platform. As we came around a ghost boat, drifting free, materialized out of the fog. It had *Department of Zoology* stencilled on the stern. A second later it was mist. I linked one arm around the swimming ladder and, with the other, pulled my knees up to my chest, hoping to preserve some body heat. Then I waited to see what would happen next.

Out in the Strait of Georgia the wind was up, which made the visibility better but the seas rough. The swells had become two-metre breakers capped in white. Once in open water Madden slowed, and, true to Jonathan's prediction, the boat pitched and heaved dangerously. I heard the squawk of a marine radio but couldn't make out any words. I uncurled myself and went up the ladder just far enough to peep over the stern. It was like riding a bucking horse, and I had to hold on tight not to be thrown.

Madden was standing, facing forward, his feet splayed for balance. He had the microphone to his mouth. As I watched he nodded, said something else, then hung the microphone back in its cradle. He threw the throttle forward and headed north into the waves and wind. I crouched back down and held on tight.

After ten to fifteen minutes of the boat slamming through the waves I saw the light at Active Pass come into view on my right. Madden turned toward it. Now that we were broadside to the wind, the waves buffeted the hull and the boat rolled precariously. In these conditions, Madden would be totally intent on navigation, on getting safely into the Pass, but once inside we would be in the lee of the islands and the waters would calm. He would be less preoccupied with survival. It was time to move.

By now I was shivering. I squeezed my fingers several times just to make sure everything was still working, then started up the ladder. At the top I waited a second. Madden was braced against the chair, but standing, one hand holding onto the panel for balance, the other on the wheel, trying to keep the vessel on course.

Just as I got ready to move Elaine let out a loud moan. With Madden further distracted I vaulted over the stern and flattened myself against the deck. Elaine continued to make a commotion, drawing Madden's attention, and I scuttled forward on my stomach. Once I was under the overhang I quietly let myself into the living space below. A minute later the wind and waves died, the fog thickened, and we entered Active Pass.

I kept one eye on the windows, monitoring our progress, but at the same time made my way quietly forward. Just beyond the living room was a corridor, and at the side of the corridor, in a little recess, was a ladder going up to the pilot's deck. I'd seen the trap door above, and if I played it right I could scare the daylights out of Madden when I rose unexpectedly from the floor. It was all a question of timing.

When we cleared Galiano Island Madden turned north again, into the wind. We were more sheltered here than in the strait, with Saltspring Island on one side and Galiano on the other, but the boat still shuddered and pitched. I had my head up against the trap door, listening for a sign that the time was right. I heard Riesler move, then the crackle of the radio.

"I can see the point," he said. There was a muffled reply. "Ten minutes," he answered, "but I have Dr. Okada with me. We'll have to decide — " More static. It sounded like someone giving Madden instructions.

I opened the trap door, just enough to see Elaine at eye level. She saw the movement, looked surprised, but a moment later her face was impassive. I closed the door and waited until I heard Madden sign off and the microphone land in its cradle. The second it hit I sprang through the floor, screaming like a banshee. Madden spun around and at that moment Elaine rolled, throwing him off balance. The gun was on the instrument panel and I threw myself at it. He grabbed for it too and he got there first, but before he could lift it I came down full-force on his wrist. He screamed, but kept a firm hold. I locked his wrist in my hands and twisted, bringing his hand and the gun in front of me. Then I rammed him against the wall with my back. Elaine had pushed herself into a corner as far back as she could get. Without a navigator the boat veered wildly, coming broadside to the waves. The vials slid out from under the panel.

Madden struggled behind me. He was wily for an academic, but I had the advantage of weight. I lifted his hand again and banged it hard against the panel. He tried to knee me from behind, but was too close. Then suddenly we were engulfed by noise and a tornado of wind. The boat rocked and the water around us began to froth as its surface was lifted into a fine spray. The canvas canopy luffed and snapped like the mainsail in a gale as cacophony and blinding light descended from the sky.

The Coast Guard helicopter had finally arrived, and the timing couldn't have been better.

Madden slouched behind me and let go of the gun. I relaxed my grip. It was over. I kicked the gun across the deck. Then a blow landed on my kidney with enough force to throw me forward and off my feet. I crumpled onto my knees, nauseous with pain, then fell to my side, moaning. Madden scooped up the vials from the floor and disappeared down to the deck below. A rope ladder dropped from the vortex of light.

With some dim awareness I suddenly grasped the reality. This wasn't the posse, it was Riesler's ride out of here. I pulled myself up and scrambled after him.

I tackled Madden when his free hand and one foot were already on the ladder, but somehow he managed to hold on. He writhed and struggled, but I held tight. We had been locked like that for a minute, neither of us giving way, when the tone of the propellor changed and the helicopter began to rise. I could feel Madden being lifted off the deck, and I was being pulled with him. I had a brief vision of the two of us dangling in the wind over the channel before we plummeted with the vials into the water. What the hell would that solution do if released into the sea? I let go, rolled to the deck, and grabbed the slack on the ladder. There was a large cleat at the stern and I took several wraps, hoped to hell it would hold, then went up again after Madden. By this time he was two metres off the deck. The ladder flailed in the wind, and Madden was having trouble keeping his balance with only one free hand. I grabbed at his foot and caught it. He kicked back at my face, trying to loosen my grip.

"It's over, Madden," I yelled. "Look down the channel."

A bar of flashing red lights was just visible coming around Galiano Island.

From above, a dark form appeared on the ladder and descended toward us. Madden kicked at me again.

"They'll kill you," he shouted.

The form above Madden yelled, "Hand me the vials." Madden turned and reached up, stretching his arm. A hand reached down through the light.

I didn't have time to think. My only concern was stopping the transfer of the vials from Riesler to Pisces, so the moment before contact I sprang, grabbing for Madden's belt or pockets, anything to throw him off balance, but when I was mid-lunge he kicked backward like a horse. His heel caught me in the chest and I lost my hold on him. I started to fall, but as I let go I reached out and grabbed the rung under his foot, the one holding all his weight, and I yanked it out from under him. The last thing I heard was Madden scream.

I hit the deck on my back, and my head bounced off the boards like a squash ball. The world went black. A second later the case of vials hit the deck, narrowly missing my face. The sound of glass shattering so close to my eyes forced me awake, and I looked up to see Madden dangling by one hand, trying desperately to regain his footing as the ladder bucked in the wind.

The form above him disappeared into the light, and suddenly both Madden and the ladder were dropping toward me. They had cut the ladder from above.

I rolled aside and scrambled to my feet. Madden hit the deck with a sickening crack. The helicopter lights went out and the thing began to rise. It wheeled around and something flew out of the cockpit. On instinct I ran, heading for Elaine above. It hit the deck beside Madden and exploded into flame.

The RCMP boat was closing in, but not fast enough. Elaine had gotten herself standing and was heading for the rail. I was a second behind her. I reached around and ripped the tape off her mouth.

"I can't undo your hands, but I'll grab you down there."

"You better."

"Trust me," I said, and I pitched her over the side.

I heard her yell "Never," just before she hit the surface.

I went in after her and nearly blacked out when I hit the icy water. As I came up I groped in the darkness for Elaine. She was gasping beside me, her head bobbing up and down in the waves. I grabbed her by the hair, pulled her face up, and hoped I could stay conscious long enough for us both to be saved. Then I started swimming forward, trying to get some distance between us and the boat before it exploded. It took less than a minute for the world to begin to close in around me. My legs were so heavy, and it was an effort to keep my grip on Elaine. I just needed to rest. My eyes were almost closed when a spotlight lit the water around us and I heard someone dive from a boat. I was sliding under, could feel Elaine slipping from me, when a face appeared over the waves, and I remember thinking that I must have already died and this must be hell.

Bob was going to save my life.

He would be a hero.

chapter twenty-eight

"**I**s she awake yet?" The voice was LeBlanc's, and she was peeved. I made a point of being still and kept my eyes shut. Medical equipment bleeped and chirped nearby. There was a rustle beside me, then a hand, soothing and cool, covered my forehead. It stayed there a minute, as if taking my temperature, then pulled away.

"Give her time, Corporal. But even when she comes around you have five minutes, no more." It was a man's voice, unfamiliar.

"And her head, will she be okay?"

I heard a shrug and a noncommittal, "We'll see."

"Then I'll be back in an hour," continued LeBlanc, "and no one sees her before me."

When I was sure LeBlanc had left I opened one eye a crack. It didn't hurt nearly as much as I thought it would, the result of high-quality pharmaceuticals. There was a man sitting beside my bed reviewing a chart: lab coat, stethoscope, black moustache and hair. Without looking up he said, "I know you're awake. I just didn't think you were ready for an interrogation."

My eyes popped open. That hurt, like an ax going through the centre of my skull. I squinted to reduce the light. "Where am I?"

He looked up and smiled. "Shaughnessy Hospital Neurology Unit." He pulled a pen light out of his pocket and leaned over me. He shined it first in one eye then in the other then clicked it off and slipped it back in his pocket. "Do you remember anything?"

I closed my eyes and tried to think back. The last thing I could recall was the horror of Bob's face appearing over a wave and Elaine beside me, slipping beneath the water. With that memory my eyes shot open and I struggled to sit up, but there was a jab of pain in my arm, and I looked down to see an intravenous tube snaking out of the bed. Dr. Corbett (according to his name tag) seemed to understand and he helped me up, first bracing me and then adjusting the bed and the pillows behind me. It took a monumental effort and I had to rest before continuing. When I was finally able to reopen my eyes I asked, "Elaine Okada. Is she all right?"

Corbett was now observing me, one leg crossed over the other, a clinical expression on his face. He looked every inch the neurologist, and he was obviously trying to decide how much I should, or could, know. I decided for him.

"The truth," I said.

He spoke carefully. "She's physically okay. Mild hypothermia, the aftereffects of chloroform, but nothing serious. Mentally? We'll have to wait and see. I'd say she's a good candidate for post-traumatic stress syndrome. You, on the other hand, took quite a beating. You'll be staying with us a couple of days."

As he was speaking the memories began to materialize, but in fragments, disjointed in time. A fire, Cindy's face, eating chili with Graham. I suddenly had a thousand questions but the energy to ask only one. "The vials. What happened to — "

He put his hands up, stopping me. "I'm sure that Corporal LeBlanc will be happy to answer all your questions when she comes back later. In the meantime get some rest," he stood, "and just so we're clear, you don't leave until I sign you out."

At that point the nurse arrived with drugs. Like a good girl I took the Demerol and went right back to sleep.

The next time I woke up LeBlanc was sitting by my bed. She was reading a novel, a detective thriller of all things, but as I opened my eyes she glanced up and closed the book.

"You look like hell," she said. "And you deserve it."

"You don't look so great yourself. When are the Mounties going to make a pair of uniform pants that actually fits a woman?"

Corbett popped his head in the door and tapped on his watch. LeBlanc dismissed him with a wave. "*Oui, oui. Cinq minutes. Franchement*! What is he, your guardian angel?"

"A quality medical practitioner. So I assume you found the fingerprints. That's why you're here."

"On the telephone in the lab and on the outside knob of the office door, but you were inside Troung's office too, weren't you?"

I nodded. "I didn't know he'd been shot. I was supposed to be meeting him, and I didn't figure it out until I was already inside."

She kept her eyes steadily on mine, her expression blank. "I don't suppose you removed anything from the scene?"

I thought of Elaine's earring and glanced around the room for my leather jacket. It was lying on a chair in the corner, tattered and looking damp. I evaded the question. "Have you found Truong's files, or Riesler's?"

"Then you don't have them."

It was halfway between a statement and a question, and I shook my head.

"Shit. We were hoping ... but no, eh? Of course, if the company has the files," she raised her hands in an expression of helplessness, "there's nothing we can do. The research itself was perfectly legal, and from what I was told the company owns all products of the research, including the files. You don't have a sample of this solution, do you? The one Dr. Truong was developing? Everyone is going crazy looking for this."

"Was there anything left from the fire?"

"Nothing. Everything was destroyed. You know, I find it very strange. Five people are dead, but these scientists are more concerned about finding one of these vials than they are about those murdered people. I will never understand that."

"It's a career founded on obsession, LeBlanc. Just like being a cop."

Corbett reappeared at the door. "Time's up, Corporal. She can give you a statement tomorrow."

LeBlanc stood up, tucking the thriller under her arm. "Don't leave Vancouver without letting me know."

I wasn't even sure I could make it to the bathroom, so promising to stay in town wasn't a problem. LeBlanc was halfway out the door when I thought of something.

"Hey LeBlanc, how'd you find us?"

She stopped and turned. "The radio tag, and it was a good thing. By the time we got to the cove you'd left."

"But it was in my jacket, and that went overboard."

"You need to thank Dr. Edwards. When Riesler brought Dr. Okada on board she was still drugged, and Edwards had to help. He managed to plant his marker on her." She shrugged. "He thought that Riesler might try to take her with him." She turned to leave, then on second thought turned back. "And O'Brien, that redhead of yours, keep her away from me."

When LeBlanc had left I managed to get out of bed, wheeling my intravenous stand along with me. I made it to the chair, picked up my leather jacket, and brought it back to the bed. It was ruined, with three big tears through the back. I did a quick inventory of the pockets and smiled — the important things were still there — then I stuffed the coat in a large drawer in the cabinet by my bed.

I must have dozed again because when I opened my eyes Elaine was beside my bed and Edwards sat in the corner chair. They looked like they had been waiting a while. The pain had returned, but it was less intense than before. I groaned and Elaine took my hand. Edwards stood up to leave.

"I'll just ..." he stammered.

I managed to shake my head. "It's okay. Pull up a chair."

I was surprised to see how close he pulled his seat to Elaine's, and even more surprised when he slid a protective arm around the back of her chair. Things had progressed while I lay unconscious.

"Should I call a nurse?" Elaine asked.

I answered with my own question. "How are you?"

She smiled. "Better than you." Then in a softer voice. "Thanks to you." Then she glanced at Edwards and smiled. "And thanks to Jonathan. I feel so stupid —"

I cut her off, looking at Edwards. His left arm was in a sling. "You can swim. Boy, am I ever glad."

"It was a dumb thing to do. You'd warned me and I didn't listen. I'm sorry."

I nodded, accepting his apology. Elaine looked at the door then moved closer to me and leaned toward the bed. "Morgan," she said in a hushed voice. "We need that solution. We have to know what was in it. Dinah said —"

My response was not hushed. "Jesus, Elaine, the thing should be buried in a salt mine in an undisclosed location."

She sat straight up. "You've got no right —" then she stopped herself by clamping her mouth shut, glaring at me, and taking a deep breath. When she was back in control she said carefully, "You can't turn back progress, Mo. What's done is done, and I can't isolate the receptor without it. I'm so close." I could feel the heat of her scientist's passion reaching out. "It would be an incredible leap forward."

I looked from Elaine to Edwards. "You must have some idea —"

He shook his head. "Truong was as much an artist as a scientist. Even if we had the files it would probably take us years to figure out what he did. With a sample, we could —"

"We?" I said, again looking from one to the other.

Edwards nodded and Elaine answered, already the fused couple. "We'll be working together now. We have compatible interests, and now that I know about Jonathan studying with Grierson ..." She turned and gazed at him with a look as close to tenderness as I'd ever seen on her face. He shifted a bit uncomfortably under the surveillance and cleared his throat before speaking.

"I'll be getting the Network money, again thanks to you. Fortunately JJ managed to make about as much as he lost, so the full amount will be coming into my account. But with the permission of the Network I'll be redirecting it, using it to set up a program to monitor the Fraser sockeye migration ... just in case."

"But you said it would take years to reconstruct the compound from the files."

"Maybe they have some of the solution. Maybe they'll get lucky with the files. I mean, who would have thought they'd get this far? I just wish you had a sample. Then at least we'd know what to look for."

I regarded Edwards and he probed me with those hazel-green eyes. After what felt like a long moment, I shrugged. "It was in my jacket. Sorry."

"You saw I fished it out for you," he said.

I nodded.

Elaine sighed and bent her head. "I was so damn close."

"I'm sorry, Elaine," I said softly. "I'm really sorry."

I was getting tired, and it must have shown because Edwards stood up.

"We'll leave you alone now," he said. "But you'll stay with us when you're out."

Us? Wow. I looked at Elaine getting up from her chair, but she glanced away uncomfortably. I felt a quick jab of something, but as quickly as it came it was gone, released. I reached out and put my hand on her arm. "Why'd he do it, Elaine. Do you know?"

She turned and put her hand over mine, holding it there for a second before speaking, gazing down at me. Finally she said, "Money. That's what he said anyway, but you know what? I think it was the challenge. So much of his life had become administration, teaching, chasing after grants, and then this incredible research

challenge came along. An intellectual puzzle that someone was willing to give him a lot of money to solve.
Could he do it? And if he could, why not? He said that
with overfishing and habitat destruction the Fraser
River fishery would be dead in ten years anyway. He
might as well get something out of it."

The last person to visit me that day was Bob. I was just
finishing dessert, orange Jello with one hundred percent
synthetic whipped topping, when he arrived with flowers, chocolates, and a cappuccino.

"I won't stay long," he said, as if reading lines from
a script. "I know you need your rest."

"So were you on the evening news? Big hero and
all that?"

He puffed up even more. "Just part of being a good
supervisor. You think I just push paper, but my job
involves more than deskwork, you know."

"A lot more than deskwork with this case."

It took him a moment to catch my meaning, and
when he did he winced and turned to unwrap and
arrange the flowers. He was avoiding my gaze. When
the flowers were organized he turned back to me, his
authority recovered.

"These are from everyone, by the way. Of course,
we're all concerned, looking forward to your return,"
then he added, "not that there's any rush. Take as much
time as you need. Perhaps a week or two off ... you
could take it as vacation, sick leave if you —"

If he didn't stop babbling I'd be physically ill. "Sit
down, for God's sake, and have a chocolate."

"Oh," he pushed them toward me. "These come
directly from Ms. Middlemass, who, as I'm sure you
must know, is most concerned about your health."

"I'll bet."

"Oh yes, definitely. And when you get back — "

I raised my hand and stopped him, then spoke in a soft, but firm, voice. "When I get back, I pick and choose my projects."

"Well now, I'm not sure we can — "

"Did you know they were having an affair?"

He sat bolt upright. "That's not true."

"I have proof. What did she tell you, Bob? That you were obstructing an investigation for the greater good of Canada?"

He shifted uncomfortably.

"She was protecting Riesler, and the only greater good she had in mind was her own. Riesler didn't want anyone snooping around his lab, she did what she could to help. It's as simple as that. And if I spill this do you know who's going to be nailed? You. You'll go down, maybe with Patsy or maybe on your own, depending on how convincing she can be when cornered. Personally, I suspect she's got her ass covered on this one. Any material evidence will point to you. So, let's start the discussion again."

Bob's face had gone through several hues, from cherry red to ashen. He now sat quietly in his chair, his hands clasped and dangling between his legs. He must have known all along that he was being manipulated, but with Patsy one didn't have the option of saying no. Reluctantly, he nodded.

"When I get back I pick and choose my projects. That's number one."

He sighed. "Certainly that can be ... well, after all, you're a senior ... actually, you're *the* senior investigations officer now. So —"

"Number two: no one interferes with my projects."

"But I'm still the supervisor. I'm legally responsible for — "

"Do you want to be a hero, or do you want to get fired? Make your choice."

I saw an almost imperceptible nod.

"Good. Number two, no interference. Number three: Lydia takes paid leave from now until early retirement, whereupon she leaves with a golden handshake."

That was too much for him. He squirmed in his chair, wiped his hands on his pants. "But that involves the Human Resources Branch, and as you know they have regulations to follow. Procedures and such. I don't have the authority to — "

"I have the travel records for all of Patsy's trips that coincided with Riesler's. That means that she not only obstructed an investigation but she also defrauded the Crown for travel expenses. Let her know that I have them. And let her know that Lydia needs her confirmation letter by the end of next week."

Bob nodded grimly. He looked like he really wanted to leave.

"Just one last thing. Did you tell anyone in the office that you saved my life?"

He didn't move, but the look of chagrin answered my question.

"God damn it." I kicked the guard rail on my bed and a nurse came scurrying in. Bob had hopped out of his chair and positioned it between the bed and himself. What did he think I was going to do? Hurl a bed pan at him? I sighed heavily. "Number four, and I hope you're listening carefully, Bob."

He nodded uneasily.

"When I get back I want a corner office, a decent chair, and an office suite *with* credenza."

By now he was doing what the clerks and secretaries call Bobbing. Usually it's done in deference to Patsy, so I considered this a good sign. His head was moving rapidly up and down as if dissociated from the rest of his body. At the same time he was edging his way to the door.

"A new office suite? No problem. I'm sure I have the budget for that. We'll order a package, matching. Of course the ordering process can take some time but maybe we can expedite ..."

When he reached the doorway his monologue ended abruptly. He raised a hand. "Have a good day," and he turned and fled.

"Teak," I bellowed from my bed. "Solid. Not veneer."

Dr. Corbett released me on Monday, and it was Sylvia who came to collect me and drive me to the airport.

"You sure you don't want to stay longer? A little R&R?" She scooped up my bags, refusing to let me carry anything.

I shook my head. "I've got stuff to clean up in Ottawa."

As she started the car, she said casually, "I asked Dinah if she wanted to come, to see you off, but ..."

"You think she'll be okay?"

"I'll make sure she is."

There was something in her voice, a layer of unspoken meaning, that made me turn and look at her in surprise. She glanced at me, gave me a shrug and an enigmatic smile, then put the car into gear. We turned first onto Oak Street, then from there on to 41st since I had asked her to cross to Granville and take the more commercial route out to the airport. Once on Granville I kept my eyes peeled on the shops at the side of the road, and when I saw what I wanted I told Sylvia to pull over. I grabbed my leather jacket from the seat behind.

"I'll just be a minute," I said, slamming the door.

Inside the bank I went directly to the back counter. The teller, looking well turned out in a bland tie and white permapress shirt, was happy to serve me. I signed three times and paid in cash, then he led me into the vault. He found my new box, inserted his key, took one of mine, and a second later pulled it out.

"You can take it into a private room," he said, motioning to the doors outside the vault.

"Don't need to," I said. I pulled the vial from its hiding place in my leather jacket. I held it up to the light. There were maybe ten millilitres of the solution left. I twisted the top, making sure it was tight, then dropped it into the safety deposit box along with one of the two keys I'd been issued. If the teller found this odd he said nothing. He replaced the box, returned my remaining key to me, and three minutes later I was in the car, next to Sylvia, heading for the airport.

We were just coming up the rise on the Arthur Laing Bridge when I said, "Pull off at the top."

She looked at me. "Are you nuts? Look at the traffic."

I looked behind me. It was pretty wimpy for Vancouver. "There," I pointed. "I'll just be a minute."

She rolled her eyes and directed the question "Why?" to the heavens.

As soon as she was on the shoulder I hopped out. At the railing I stood up on the base, leaning forward to get a full view of the Fraser below. The sun was brilliant, reflecting off the muddy surface in a sheet of dazzling light. Tug boats, tankers, and fishing boats solemnly chugged along the thoroughfare. Hidden beneath the surface would be thousands of salmon moving upstream to spawn. I heard furious honking behind me.

"Okay, okay," I yelled.

I reached into my pocket and pulled out the key, flat and shining silver. I leaned out, held it for a moment between my thumb and forefinger, then let it go, watching as the metal caught the light, flashing and sparkling on its journey to the river. Finally it hit the surface, and with a splash and a shimmer disappeared forever.